W9-DDO-285

THE HUMOR OF THE FABLIAUX

THE HUMOR OF THE FABLIAUX

A COLLECTION OF CRITICAL ESSAYS

EDITED BY

Thomas D. Cooke

Benjamin L. Honeycutt

University of Missouri Press

1974

ISBN 0–8262–0168–7

Library of Congress Catalog Card Number 74–82563
Printed and bound in the United States of America
University of Missouri Press, Columbia, Missouri 65201

CONTENTS

ACKNOWLEDGMENTS

We wish to express our gratitude to the Research Council of the University of Missouri—Columbia for its generous support toward the realization of this collection. We also thank Diane Sullivan for her assistance in many technical matters, and John Peterson, who typed the manuscript with great care, perseverance, and good cheer, and especially Mrs. Ann Todd Rubey and her staff at the University Library, whose generous assistance and considerable knowledge made many of our tasks much easier and more pleasant.

ABBREVIATIONS

CFMA Classiques français du moyen âge. Paris, Champion.

MR Montaiglon, Anatole de, and Gaston Raynaud, eds. *Recueil général et complet des fabliaux des XIIIe et XIVe siècles.* 6 vols. Paris: Librarie des Bibliophiles, 1872–1890.

SATF Société des anciens textes français. Paris, Picard.

All quotations from these works are cited by volume and page number.

The spelling and form of all titles of fabliaux referred to in this collection have been regularized according to the canon established by Per Nykrog in *Les Fabliaux* (Copenhagen: Ejnar Munksgaard, 1957), pp. 311–24. Reprinted with Postscript, Geneva: Droz, 1973.

INTRODUCTION

The Old French fabliaux, most frequently described as *contes à rire en vers* after the definition of Joseph Bédier, are representative of a type of comic tale common to extremely diverse cultures at practically any given point in time. This polygenesis renders quite difficult the task of establishing with real authority definite relationships between, on the one hand, certain older tales treating similar motifs and, on the other, the French fabliaux of the thirteenth century or to determine precisely the indebtedness of the master raconteurs of the Middle Ages, Chaucer and Boccaccio, to the French tales. It should suffice here to emphasize that any such tale, whether Indian, Latin, French, German, Italian, or English, reflects to some degree the society for which it was written and also the author's lack or mastery of literary artistry.

The comic tale in thirteenth-century France adopted the standard meter of courtly romance—the octosyllabic couplet—and its popularity with audiences from all levels of society is demonstrated by the survival of a corpus of some 160 fabliaux. These verse tales, especially popular in the Norman and Picard regions of France, are, as one would expect, uneven in quality, but they are, as the preparation of this volume of essays would indicate, completely worthy of the close attention of the student of literature. Among them are, indeed, as the title of Howard Helsinger's article in this collection suggests, pearls in the swill. Those who dismiss the fabliaux as merely scatological or as rather elaborate jokes and thus of little literary value seem to see in the genre a preponderance of swill. To the contrary, we have found a large number of pearls, and it is our position that the literary artistry and comic technique of the fabliaux become obvious upon any careful examination of the nature of humor in the genre. This conviction and the lack of any serious attempt to develop many of the valuable observations on style and technique in Per Nykrog's excellent study of the genre led to the organization of a symposium on the fabliaux. This session, held during the Seventh Annual Conference on Medieval Studies at Western Michigan University in 1972, suggested the formulation of this volume of essays. It is our hope that these studies will confirm our belief that many authors of fabliaux were consummate literary artists and that the fabliau as a genre deserves a more elevated position than it has previously enjoyed in the hierarchy of literature.

Thematically, the fabliaux present a delightful potpourri: the typical *ménage à trois* motif, the comically moral tale, the apparent courtly tale, stories based partially or exclusively on word play, the deceits of the scheming wife, among others—all of them served up with the sauce of ribaldry and with a cast of characters distinctly evocative of the flavor of thirteenth-century French society: the peasant, the priest (usually either avaricious or lecherous), the knight, the cleric, and the smug or socially ambitious bourgeois. By no means are all of the fabliaux obscene or bawdy, and if, in these essays, we seem to choose many of our examples from the more obscene tales, we plead our conviction that the fabliau is a genre in which art and obscenity serve each other well.

* * *

The first three essays in this collection of previously unpublished articles examine the cultural background of the fabliaux in order to arrive at a fuller and more perfect understanding of their humor. Knud Togeby considers the thirteenth century's concern with different levels of style, from which he derives a new definition of the fabliau: *nouvelle de niveau bas du XIIIe siècle*. Further examination of the milieu of the fabliaux throws light on other features of their humor, such as the structure of parody, which can be seen as a reflection of the courtly genres of the period. Jürgen Beyer finds that the informing spirit behind the fabliaux is "reductive," bringing the ideal and the saintly down to the level of the real and the human. Although that spirit found partial expression in other genres such as the fables of Marie de France, the *comœdia elegiaca,* and the tales of the *Disciplina clericalis,* it received its first full expression in the fabliaux. Stephen L. Wailes compares the Latin literature of the *vagantes* with the French and German fabliaux on several aspects of humor and finds close agreement between the first two traditions but general disagreement between these and the German stories. In German fabliaux, clerical lovers are stylized in a complimentary manner, as in the "debates" on clerks and knights as lovers. The evidence suggests that the audiences in France and Germany were socially different and that the Germans were unfamiliar with the *vagantes* of France.

The next three essays develop in some detail the nature of parody and irony in the fabliaux. Per Nykrog states, here for the first time in English, his belief that the audience for the fabliaux could be courtly as well as bourgeois. Indeed, he finds that many elements in these tales could be understood only by a cultivated audience who in fact were laughing at stories that depicted the bourgeoisie trying to imitate the refinements of the upper classes. Hence he regards the fabliau as a courtly burlesque. Benjamin Honeycutt points to ironic contrast and opposition as the essential tool for the comic treatment of the knight in the fabliaux. The difference between the knight's own words and his actions or between the author's description of the knight and his subject's subsequent behavior illustrate this technique. Howard Helsinger finds that the medieval love of allegory achieves a comic expression in the fabliaux. Frequently the *fableor* parodies the religious intention of medieval allegory by dramatizing the various instances when the letter of the law actually quickens.

The following two essays consider ways in which the authors of the fabliaux used various devices to control and determine the audience's reactions to their humor. Norris Lacy directs his attention to the use of esthetic distance. Several basic techniques produce this distancing: generic identification—the audience is more receptive because the poet has prepared them to expect a humorous story; narrative economy—the author avoids drawing the reader into the story; and finally, he applies certain more subtle techniques, such as irony. Paul Theiner demonstrates how the authors concentrate the audience's attention on the comic element by reducing settings to a functional role. Participating in the same causal connections as the events in these tales, settings are restricted to the moment of action, and they achieve their importance only in that moment.

The final essays deal with pornography and the obscene. Thomas D. Cooke examines certain pornographic fantasies in the fabliaux, such as the worship of masculine potency and virility. He points out that these tales reveal the illusory nature of pornography by fulfilling some of its most fondly cherished dreams only to have this unstable state destroyed in a comic climax that is a return to reality. Roy J. Pearcy believes that the use of obscenities in the fabliaux is much more than the enduring fascination with smut. By comparing the use of obscenities with euphemisms and figurative expressions, Pearcy argues that the authors of the fabliaux were actually embodying the opposition between two different epistemologies, the Platonic and the Aristotelian. Moreover, the movement of these tales toward their comic peripety is frequently one in which an illusion, which is expressed in an abstract euphemism, is replaced by reality, which is expressed in a concrete obscenity.

What we hope is apparent from this brief account of the ten essays is the complexity of a genre that has generally been considered rather simple and naive. From them, it becomes evident that the various fabliaux manifest close involvement with their times, as for example in their parody of other genres, their dramatization of contemporary philosophical questions, and their exposure of shifts in tastes and attitudes. At the same time, these essays argue for a more subtle artistry on the part of the authors than earlier assessments granted them. Clearly, these poets were capable of using tight artistic control to bring about the desired effect. And it is as satisfying as it is curious to discover how many points of agreement there are among the authors of these essays, who all worked independently of the others. As a result of the contributors' independence, several tales are discussed at some length more than once. In order to preserve the integrity of the essays, we have allowed these duplications to remain. Although we have arranged the essays in such a way that they can profitably be read in sequence, they can, also profitably, be read separately.

There is, in spite of their different emphases, one basic point on which all contributors agree and that is the desired effect toward which the authors of the fabliaux were working: humor. That spirit truly pervades these tales, which taken together add up to forty thousand lines, and it molds their diversity and complexity into what might be considered a ribald epic, a medieval Human Comedy.

T. D. C.
B. L. H.
Columbia, Missouri
June, 1974

❧ I ❧

KNUD TOGEBY

THE NATURE OF THE FABLIAUX

I have long wondered why the definition given by Joseph Bédier to the genre of the fabliau, "*conte à rire en vers,*" was so generally accepted and so little questioned. To begin with the last part of the definition: Why "*en vers*"? From what other genre does this element of the definition distinguish the fabliau? There are no Old French *contes à rire en prose*; all literature of the twelfth century and almost all that of the thirteenth was in verse. And if there were such a form as a *conte à rire en prose,* why not call it a prose fabliau? It might be objected that the *Cent Nouvelles Nouvelles* from the fifteenth century are called nouvelles and not fabliaux, because they are in prose, but what about La Fontaine's *Contes,* which are *contes à rire en vers,* but which are not called fabliaux?

My point is that the distinction intended by *en vers* is in reality not one of versification but of chronology. *Fabliau* is the name of a genre of the thirteenth century and hence in verse; it is the form of the short story in thirteenth-century French literature.

Next: Why "*à rire*"? And here we touch the essence of these collected papers. It is evident that most of the fabliaux are intended to be comical and to provoke laughter, but some are not. Serious tales like *La Housse partie* or *La Bourse pleine de sens* are traditionally classed as fabliaux. In virtue of the definition *à rire* one may exclude them from the genre of the fabliau, but where does one put them? They must belong to some genre, and they are in fact short stories like all the other fabliaux. Why not accept the simple evidence that in the thirteenth century, as in all other centuries, short stories might be comical or serious? But one must admit—and stress the fact—that an outstanding characteristic of the short stories of the Middle Ages—not only of the thirteenth century—was that they were predominantly comical.

The superficiality of the term *à rire* may be judged by a comparison of the fabliaux with the fables. Such a comparison must seem natural, if we accept, as I am willing to do, the genre of the fable as one of the origins of the genre of the fabliau. We have in fact comical and serious fables, but the fundamental point is that the genre as a whole includes both types.

The distinction suggested by *à rire* is, in my opinion, of another kind. By this term the fabliaux are distinguished from such twelfth-century short stories as the *lais* of Marie de France. In contrast to the more dignified stories of Marie de France, peopled by kings, queens, knights, and ladies, the fabliaux are on a lower plane, concerned with peasants, priests, clerks, and their like. This is the only reason to place texts like *Le Lai du cor,* which is evidently a *conte à rire,* not among the fabliaux, but in the genre of the *lai.*

I have no objection in the definition of Bédier to the term *conte,* which is synonymous with *nouvelle* (short story). I should thus propose the following redefinition of the fabliau: "*nouvelle de niveau bas du XIIIe siècle.*" This may not sound elegant in French, but is, I believe, precise. It is more common to speak of *style bas,* as opposed to *style haut,* but those terms may have misleading associations. In travesties like *Le Lai du cor* or *Le Mantel mautaillié,* the style may be low, but the characters belong to King Arthur's court and the tales consequently to the higher level.

I purposely avoid the term *realistic,* which has been used

as a distinguishing feature of the fabliau in contrast to the romanticism of the *roman courtois*. *Realism* is the wrong term to use in establishing the relationship of literature to reality. The short stories of Marie de France can be as realistic at their elevated level as the fabliaux at their lower one. The events that happen in fabliaux are most unlikely to occur in reality, and peasants and priests are not more realistic than knights and kings.

A serious or humorous attitude is a distinction which can be made only within the framework of the different levels. A comical tale told on the higher level is called a travesty; a transposition from high level to low level, which is by definition comical, is called parody; and the possibility of other lower-level comical tales exists. We can thus arrange in a table the narrative genres in the twelfth to thirteenth centuries in French literature:

Level	Short 30–40 Lines (Anecdote)	Medium 300–400 Lines (Short story)	Long 3000–4000 Lines (Novel [*Roman*])
Religious		Gautier de Coincy[1] *St. Pierre et le jongleur*[2]	Légendes[1]
High		Marie de France's *lais*[1] *Le Lai du cor*, etc.[2]	Chrétien de Troyes[1] *Aucassin et Nicolette*[2]
High–Low		Pastourelles	
Low	Human fables[3] Anecdotes[4] Exempla[1]	Fabliaux[3] Fabliaux[4] *La Housse partie*, etc.[1]	*Trubert*[4]
Animal	Beast fables[3] Beast fables[1]	*Roman de Renart*[3]	
Attitudes:	1. Serious	2. Travesty	3. Parody 4. Comical

This system has the merit of placing the fabliaux between the three genres from which they have sprung, the travesties on the one hand, and the *Roman de Renart* and the fables on the other. It is only a short distance from travesties or comic *lais* like *Le Lai du cor* or *Le Mantel mautaillié,* in which the conduct of persons of King Arthur's court is on a low level, to parodies like the erotic triangle fabliaux in which the characters are of a low social level.

There is a close identity between the short stories of which the *Roman de Renart* is composed and the fabliaux. Both genres are parodies of the high genre, the only difference being that the transposition moves in the direction of the animal level in the *Roman de Renart,* but toward the low human level in the fabliaux. This close identity is evidenced by the term *fables,* which traditionally refers not only to the beast fables but also to the human ones, both short, and dealing with life on the lower levels.

Such human fables can bear close resemblance to the fabliaux, but they should not be confused with them, not so much because of the moral, which is not obligatory in the fables, but because of their length, which is only thirty to forty lines whereas the fabliaux contain an average of three hundred to four hundred lines. The intimate relation between the two genres must be a sufficient explanation of the etymology of the word *fabliau.*

If the humor of the fabliaux, and consequently the fabliau itself, has its root in the courteous travesties, the *Roman de Renart,* and the fables, the genre of the fabliau must necessarily be younger than the three other genres. The three model genres are, in fact, from the twelfth century, the fabliau from the thirteenth. The first branches of the *Roman de Renart* date from 1175–1176, the fables of Marie de France from about 1180, while the dates of the travesties are more difficult to fix. The existence of *Le Lai du cor* in the twelfth century is proved by the *First Continuation of the Perceval,* and that of *Le Mantel mautaillié* at the same period by the *Lanzelet* of Ulrich von Zatzikhoven.

The fabliaux, on the other hand, do not seem to exist prior to the thirteenth-century tales of Jean Bodel, who is probably the founder of the fabliau as a genre. The use of the word *fabliau* in the prologue of the *Roman de Renart* (1175–1176) has been taken as a proof of the existence of the genre at this early date. In the Martin edition of Branch II we find "et fabliaus et chansons de geste," but the Cangé manuscript published by Mario Roques, which reads "et fables et chancons de geste" (beginning of Branch III), is probably the original version.

The establishment of the social or historical background for the humor of the fabliaux presents a difficult problem. Per Nykrog has effectively questioned the Bédier theory of the bourgeois origin of the genre by the convincing argument that the parody of the fabliaux is to be understood only in a courtly milieu. Such a milieu is obviously even more suitable to travesties.

If we are to venture into this delicate question of the relation between social classes and literary genres, I should like to suggest another social group as a fertile milieu for the creation of the fabliau. A new social group was emerging throughout Europe in the second half of the twelfth century: the students of the cathedral schools, later of the universities. These students created, most notably in Germany, the vagrant poetry. Composed in Latin, the genre seems to have been born of the same comic and parodic spirit as the fabliau. The students were certainly in a position to laugh both at the nobility in the travesties and at the bourgeoisie in the fabliaux. They viewed the world at the distance from each social group which is said to be a necessary condition of comic enjoyment. One of the best examples of this bond between the *contes à rire* and the university milieu is *Le Lai d'Aristote* by Henri d'Andeli, one of the best travesties of the time.

The students, designated as *clercs,* play an important role in the matter of the fabliaux. In the amorous triangle, the young clercs are always victorious over priests, peasants, artisans, and other bourgeois, as the superiority of the student over the knight is a favorite subject of the vagrant poetry. To a large extent the fabliaux are students' wit.

But there is perhaps a more historical than social way of viewing the problem. While the *chansons de geste* were a purely French genre (apparently no *chanson de geste* was composed in England or the areas within its influence), courtly literature was certainly the product of the Plantagenet empire, sponsored by Eleanor of Aquitaine and her numerous children, especially Marie de Champagne. The political opposition between the France of Philippe-Auguste (1180–1223) and the Plantagenet empire possibly affected literature in the creation of French parodies or satires of the courtly literature of England. Here we should think not only of the fabliaux, but also of the travesties. In this connection it is perhaps significant that many of the fabliaux originated in Northern France, for instance those of Jean Bodel. One should certainly be cautious in pressing such a point, but it seems obvious that some specific fabliaux are clearly historical in that their laughter is directed against the enemy. Such is the matter of *La Male Honte* and *Les Deux Angloys et l'anel.*

The humor of the fabliaux is best studied in their historical starting point, the travesties or the parodies. The word *parody* comes from the Greek *para* (beside) and *odê* (song), and thus means "to sing beside, to sing falsely." In literature it is the transformation of a recognized high genre into a genre that is identical yet different in level. It is a kind of devil's mirror, which creates the necessary comic distance. If the persons' milieu is conserved but the subject changed, we have a travesty; if the subject is conserved and the persons changed, a parody.

The travesties and the parodies follow as their model a

whole genre as such or rather its fundamental scheme or skeleton. The consequence is that the humor in these genres springs from the structure of the action, not from the characters or from the subjects as in other comic genres. This difference can be understood from the curious fact that the humor of the fabliaux can be caught from hearing a simple résumé of the action. With all other genres, a résumé kills the work of art; the action in itself is nothing. But the fabliaux, which may be dull reading in their full form, are amusing in their skeleton forms. The humor is attached to the structure itself, to the distance from the model genre, and to the oblique repetition of the scheme of the model genre.

The difference between the fabliaux and the short stories of Boccaccio is that the latter are no longer travesties or parodies but fully developed short stories, comic or serious, in which the scheme of the action is not so significant as the way in which the story is told. A comparison between some fabliaux and Boccaccio's versions of the same themes will verify this difference. It would be one of the surest ways to analyze the humor of the fabliaux.

❧ II ☙

JÜRGEN BEYER

THE MORALITY OF THE AMORAL*

The title which Friedrich Schiller gave one of his shorter esthetic treatises might serve also as the title of this essay: *Thoughts Concerning the Use of the Common and Vulgar in Art.*[1] For what is the as yet unwritten history of the *Schwank*[2] if not the constant attempt to "poeticize," that is, to make worthy of artistic portrayal the vulgar, ugly, and common elements in earthly existence?

The "poetics of vulgarity" attained perhaps its greatest success in the last decade of the twelfth century. If one tempo-

*This essay summarizes fundamental aspects of a comprehensive examination by the author. The substantiation and discussion of individual results of this study may be found by referring to the complete work: *Schwank und Moral. Untersuchungen zum altfranzösischen Fabliau und verwandten Formen, Studia Romanica,* 16 (Heidelberg: Carl Winter, 1969). I am grateful to Dr. Linda S. Pickle of Columbia, Missouri, for her careful and excellent translation of this article.

1. Friedrich Schiller, "Gedanken über den Gebrauch des Gemeinen und Niedrigen in der Kunst," in *Ausgewählte Werke,* Ernst Müller, ed. (Darmstadt: Port, 1954–1959), V, 111–18.

2. The word *Schwank* as it is commonly used in German literary criticism is controversial because of its being virtually undefinable. Two main directions in attempts at definition may be determined. By one definition, *Schwank* designates any genre of coarse (for example, obscene) content; by the other, it refers to a definite historical genre (for example, the fabliau) that primarily treats coarse material. A combination of both definitions of the word does not circumvent the dilemma. Rather, as is the conviction of genre theoreticians among literary critics, one must always consider the specific activity of the spirit (André Jolles, "Geistesbeschäftigung," *Einfache Formen,* 2d ed. [Tübingen: Max Niemeyer, 1958]) and along with this the specific view of the world that underlies a

rarily omits the *Richeut,* which is a questionable member of this genre, the eight fabliaux written at that time by Jean Bodel were Europe's first *Schwänke* in the vernacular that were considered worthy of being set down on costly parchment. Just as "der Stricker" would do almost fifty years later with the Middle High German *Schwank,* so Jean Bodel at this time raised the fabliau in France to the level of an accepted literary genre.

Jean Bodel was neither the inventor of the genre, however, nor was he one of the first to create fabliaux. Curiously enough, the opening lines of the Prologue to the Second Branch of the *Roman de Renart* have been constantly overlooked in the context of the genesis of the fabliau:[3]

> Seigneurs, oï avez maint conte
> Que maint conterre vous raconte,
> Conment Paris ravi Elaine,
> Le mal qu'il en ot et la paine;
> De Tristan dont la Chievre fist,
> Qui assez bellement en dist,
> Et fabliaus et chancon de geste.

> (Lords, you have heard many a tale recounted by many a storyteller: how Paris kidnapped Helen and of the pain and sorrow he experienced; the story of Tristan told so beautifully by La Chièvre; *fabliaux* and *chansons de geste.*)

These verses from the year 1176 show that the fabliau had already taken shape around the middle of the twelfth century.

---

certain genre (for example, the fabliau) and the use of certain material (for example, coarse *Schwank* content). Such an attempt, which avoids an overly restricted method of investigation, is made in the first part of this essay.

The difficulty of defining the concept *Schwank* precludes its satisfactory translation into a single term such as *farce.* Therefore, the German word is retained throughout this study, in the conviction that this discussion will elucidate its meaning and usage.

3. I am grateful to Hans Robert Jauss for this important indication: *Untersuchungen zur mittelalterlichen Tierdichtung* (Tübingen: E. Bouillon, 1959), pp. 178 ff.

Therefore, the oldest European popular *Schwank* is also to be regarded as a product of the creative twelfth century.

As a genre the *Schwank* for the first time took a distinctive literary form in the fabliau although, as many indications show, it existed much earlier as a spiritual attitude toward life, as the expression in comic form of a "vulgar soul."[4] A series of hypotheses have been suggested to explain the origin of the fabliau. The construction of complicated and unverified theories seems futile, however, in view of the fact that the emergence of independent *Schwank* genres in a natural way may be conceived of and interpreted as the spontaneity and literary self-realization of the farcical spirit, which is possible at any time. In addition, the attempts carried out until now to explain the establishment of the fabliau, first in terms of the tracing of motifs (the Orientalists), then later as an expression of *l'esprit gaulois* (Faral), and finally in regard to aspects of form (Nykrog), have remained unsatisfactory. Bédier revealed the instability of the thesis defended by certain Orientalists, while Faral's and Nykrog's hypotheses are contradicted most effectively by the chronology, which in the meantime has been determined more precisely.[5] Since the so-called elegiac comedy, the fabliau, and the *Roman de Renart* all established themselves simultaneously around the middle of the twelfth century, the *esprit gaulois,* which Faral thought to be equally influential in the creation of the elegiac comedy and the fabliau, should not be considered as the genesis of the fabliau but merely as a general source of the farcical spirit. The same is true of the inclusion of *Schwank* material in the *Isopet* of Marie de France.

The farcical spirit always expresses itself in a definite process

4. "Eine niedrige Seele": Schiller, "Gedanken über den Gebrauch," V, 113.

5. Joseph Bédier, *Les Fabliaux,* 6th ed. (Paris: Champion, 1964). Edmond Faral, "Le Fabliau latin au moyen âge," *Romania,* 50 (1924), 321–85. Per Nykrog, *Les Fabliaux* (Copenhagen: Ejnar Munksgaard, 1957).

which, to speak quite generally, is of a reductive nature. It not only "loosens" that which is "bound" (morally or otherwise),[6] but it loosens it always in a constant direction: This process pulls every element down to the level of the human and only-too-human, of the physical and worldly, of the drastic and vulgar. The *Schwank* of all epochs and cultures can do nothing but show "all human reality without transcendence."[7] Some critics have seen this characteristic as a complete denial of all reason in man, while others have seen it as the exact opposite, a "progression toward 'rational' man."[8] The truth may be simpler; it may lie where Ranke placed it: in "a basic drive of our being: man cannot bear the solemn and grave for long," a trait even more evident "the more pressing the demands of these moral categories (*religio, humanitas, societas,* and so on) are."[9] From this premise Ranke defines the *Schwank* as a reduced level (*Schwundstufe*) that parodies positive values and allows them to be swallowed by the negative, a "reduced level conceived as the result of psychic and rational types of behavior which issue from the resistance of the soul and the tendency of the spirit to be disillusioned."[10]

6. Jolles, "Gebundenes,": *Einfache Formen,* pp. 247 ff.

7. "Menschliche Realität ohne Transzendenz": Leo Spitzer, "Die Branche VIII des Roman de Renart," *Archivum Romanicum,* 24 (1940), p. 216.

8. "Ein Fortschreiten hin zum 'vernünftigen' Menschen": cf. Bédier, *Les Fabliaux,* p. 430, and W.-E. Peuckert, *Deutsches Volkstum in Märchen und Sage, Schwank und Rätsel* (Berlin: W. de Gruyer, 1938), p. 168.

9. "Ein Grundtrieb unseres Wesens: der Menschen kann auf die Dauer das Getragene nicht ertragen, [und dies um so weniger, je] dringlicher die Forderungen dieser sittlichen Kategorien (religio, humanitas, societas, etc.) sind": Kurt Ranke, "Schwank und Witz als Schwundstufe," *Festschrift für W.-E. Peuckert* (Munich: Erich Schmidt, 1955), pp. 41–59; here: p. 41.

10. "Schwundstufe als Ergebnis psychischer und rationaler Verhaltensweisen aufgefasst, aus der Resistenz der Seele und dem Hang des Geistes zur Desillusionierung hervorgegangen": Ranke, "Schwank und Witz," p. 44.

Schwank, understood as the result of a reductive process, does not yet mean a specific literary form but a specific "activity of the spirit" (Jolles: "*Geistesbeschäftigung*") that precedes the formation of any genre and that is not necessarily confined to the limitations of a certain genre. Ranke could therefore draw his examples even-handedly from legends, fairy tales, and anecdotes, from the *Pantschatantra* and the *Völsungasaga*. In them, in fact, may be documented the same process of reduction that, as we shall see, is also peculiar to the *Schwank* material of the *Disciplina clericalis* and of the *Isopet*. Unlike other genres, however, the farcical spirit is not intended to project any fixed or particular picture of reality or of life. In the *Schwank* based on legend, saga, fairy tale, or other material, the specific image of the world presented in those genres is questioned and subjected to reductive corrections. Therefore, according to an extremely pertinent formulation by Max Lüthi, the *Schwank* "as genre is not to be placed merely among other narrative genres, but is to be understood as a possibility of every genre."[11] However, this clear-sighted formulation does not quite suffice to ascertain conclusively the significant differences between a closely constructed *Schwank* genre like the fabliau, for example, and the *Schwank* material of other genres. So this essay will also examine more closely the fact that only the negation of its own code (*Verbindlichkeit*) constitutes the decisive element of the *Schwank* as a genre.

The rise of the fabliau, Europe's first structurally independent *Schwank* genre, created a vessel that could receive and collect the various expressions of the vernacular comic story. We know of the existence of such comic tales through the penitentials of the eighth and ninth centuries, which designated penances for the enjoyment of the *fabulae otiosae* and

11. "Der Schwank als Gattung ist nicht ohne weiteres neben andere Erzählgattungen zu stellen, sondern als Möglichkeit jeder Gattung zu verstehen": Max Lüthi, *Märchen*, Sammlung Metzler, Abt. Poetik (Stuttgart: Metzler, 1962), p. 13.

turpes joci,[12] and we know that in his *Institutio inclusarum,* Aelred von Riedval warned nuns against "tales of seduction which poison the fantasy."[13] Moreover, the Anglo-Norman author Wace indicated a knowledge of orally transmitted *Schwänke.*[14] As a possibility of every genre, these tales of coarse events, facetiousness, and deception also were admitted to genres whose didacticism found them basically foreign, such as the exemplum and the fable, wherein they remain recognizable although in an altered form. They appear more clearly in the *ridicula,* often referred to as "monastery *Schwänke.*" The Pyrrhus story in the elegiac comedy *Alda* mirrors perhaps most clearly the orally transmitted comic tale of the early Middle Ages.

The oldest extant comic tales in written form in Europe have come down to us sprinkled throughout the Latin works of Gregory of Tours (ca. 540–594) and Theodulf of Orléans (ca. 760–821). A first high point may be seen around the millennium. At this time not only the *Schwank* songs of the *Carmina Cantabrigiensia* originated, but also the tale of the peasant, *Unibos,* which is to be counted among the few masterpieces of international *Schwank* literature. Later on, the noticeably intensified interest in typical *Schwank* themes in the twelfth century, especially in the second half of that century, is noteworthy. This interest manifests itself in the *Disciplina clericalis,* the literature of the so-called pseudo-Ovidiana, the elegiac comedy, the animal *Schwank,* the fable, the burlesque lay, and other genres.

That which came together then in the fabliau appears to be a literary vogue which finally found a suitable form for itself in that genre. It is possible that the Arabic tales of the slyness of women, which reached the Occident with the re-

12. Bédier, *Les Fabliaux,* pp. 304 f.

13. Gustav Gröber, *Grundriss der romanischen Philologie* (Strassburg: K. J. Trübner, 1888–1902), II, 1, 610 f.

14. Ibid.

turning crusaders, not only brought new *Schwank* material to Europe but simultaneously brought new esteem to the native comical story with its traditional Christian and clerical misogynism. Without doubt the social and intellectual evolution of the period also played a role in the transformation of the orally transmitted comic tale into the literary genre of the fabliau. Some of the forces for development were the rise of the cities, the transition from the so-called first to the so-called second feudal stage with its refinement of all aspects of courtly life, the battle over the establishment of celibacy for the clergy, the quickly spreading knowledge of such writers as Ovid, and the philosophers' quarrels at the universities. Yet it is correct to warn against a one-sided overestimation of either the bourgeois or aristocratic influence on the fabliau, which is evident in the complementary works of Bédier and Nykrog. It cannot be denied that Nykrog's investigations represent a necessary corrective to Bédier's study, which emphasized too strongly the supportive role of the bourgeoisie in the development of the fabliau.

Rychner succeeded in his expressed purpose of adding a dimension to Nykrog's synthesis.[15] By taking into account the conditions for production of literature in the Middle Ages, Rychner showed that by virtue of its purpose and its public the fabliau is an independent genre adaptable to any class. This adaptability is scarcely to be unexpected in a genre of reductive nature, for as such the fabliau naturally has a much stronger integrating power than, for example, the courtly romance. The fabliau may find points of departure for its reductive process everywhere: in the erotic or other conditions of the lower classes as well as in the doctrine of courtly love, the rules of logic of language, philosophical concepts, ecclesiastical relationships, and theological ideas. This possibility of integration is supported by the general world view of man's

15. Jean Rychner, *Contribution à l'étude des fabliaux*, 2 vols. (Neuchâtel and Geneva: Droz, 1960); here: I, 146.

experience and knowledge of his animal nature. It is a non-moral view of the world that ironically reduces all idealistic and enlightening concepts of life and literature to the "real" conditions of earthly existence and that in turn allows us to speak of the fabliau as a completed genre which can assume an independent role in the hierarchy of literary forms. Acknowledged or not, it was always this amoral element which guaranteed the fabliau lasting interest, even earlier than the more elevated genres of the Middle Ages, although in its literary value it usually lagged far behind those genres.

In this connection the morals that were often attached to the fabliaux deserve special attention. Are they, as the majority of earlier critics would have it, merely superfluous appendages, or are they the remains of a constitutive but primarily formal (that is, structural) aspect of the genre that, according to Nykrog's hypothesis, reflect the rise of the fabliau from the fable? In either case, the question of the function of the morals remains unanswered. But in the relationship between *Schwank* narration and morals one can deduce the conditions that first made possible the "use of the common and vulgar in art" in the Middle Ages. Obviously because of the mighty influence of the medieval church, the comic intention, which Schiller from the esthetic perspective of a later epoch regarded as the only significant factor, was at first not strong enough to compensate for the vulgar elements. At least four hundred years elapsed before the comic *fabulae otiosae*—due to the literary acceptance of the fabliaux toward the end of the twelfth century—overcame the odium of sinfulness which had caused them to be confined in the ecclesiastical penitentials since the eighth century. Only then, encouraged by the various conditions cited, did that attitude become prevalent in the society of the twelfth century which Schiller expressed in the following terms: "As soon as the poet is merely concerned with creating a comic work and desires nothing other than to amuse us, we can then allow him to use even vulgar elements; only he must never evoke indignation or disgust."[16] At this point the fabliau accomplishes the decisive breakthrough. From now on it appears on costly parchment, equally accepted with the higher genres of the period. It has become literature. This acceptance makes understandable the pride—always greeted by literary scholars with uncomprehending amazement—with which Jean Bodel, who had become famous in higher literary genres, introduced himself as *.I. rimoieres de fabliaus* (*MR*, V, 191).

The European *Schwank*'s laborious climb toward success, its battle against the odium of sinfulness, may be observed wherever *Schwank* material was able to slip into already recognized literary genres. The most significant of these stages will be outlined in the following section, and two questions may be answered there: Of what type were the comic tales of the oral tradition? and What were the conditions that made possible the amoral, farcical "activity of the spirit" in the Middle Ages and its fulfillment in the fabliau? In other words, in these stages the process that leads from the *Schwank* as a possibility of every genre to the *Schwank* as an independent literary form, the fabliau, becomes evident. Like so many spiritual and intellectual processes, this one by no means develops in a rectilinear manner. Our arrangement therefore corresponds to a sort of inner chronology, the criterion for which is supplied by the morphological stage of development of the respective works.

* * *

The *comœdia elegiaca*, which arose simultaneously with the fabliau around the middle of the twelfth century, is quite close to the latter chronologically, but is morphologically and

16. "Sobald es der Dichter bloss auf ein Lachstück anlegt und weiter nichts will, als uns belustigen, so können wir ihm auch das Niedrige hingehen lassen, nur muss er nie Unwillen oder Ekel erregen": Schiller, "Gedanken über den Gebrauch," V, 114.

structurally very dissimilar.[17] For chronological reasons alone, therefore, this genre may not be considered one of the possible ancestors of the fabliau. Nevertheless, Faral's method of investigation deserves consideration in that it draws attention to this peculiar genre of medieval literature, a genre distinctly different from other Latin writings because of its authors' preference for coarse and farcical plots. The development of the *comœdia elegiaca,* although it takes place at the same time as that of the Old French fabliau, is often unnoticed. The direction it takes is completely different from that of the fabliau. This genre, which originated from late Latin prose versions of dramas of late antiquity, has indeed been "epicized" outwardly, in that the inherited stage elements of prologue, epilogue, and the final formulation of the *acta placent* have been quickly eliminated. At the same time, however, it undergoes a development in the direction of a pronounced pseudodramatic form. With this development it becomes increasingly distant from the narrative genre of the fabliau in its essential structural elements. Even if one disregards the Latin in which it is written, there results a genre of extremely sophisticated attraction which was accessible only to the learned public of the famous monastery schools along the Loire.

The authors of the fabliau, to be sure, were also among the cultured individuals of the age, but they did not, as Faral believed, merely popularize the *comœdia elegiaca* in order to arrive at the fabliau, for there are other differences in addition to the already mentioned structural distinction. For the fabliau there is no example of a direct material filiation from the elegiac comedy. Nor is the inverse true. The figure of the cunning woman who is victorious in spite of all obstacles, and without whom the fabliau could not exist, is almost completely unknown in the elegiac comedy (in her place stands the

17. Gustave Cohen, ed., *La "Comédie" latine en France au XIIe siècle,* 2 vols. (Paris: Société d'édition "Les Belles-Lettres," 1931).

male servant figure, inherited from antiquity). The intention of the Latin genre is often that of school satire and is directed above all against the competing school dialectics of Paris. The genre documents a distinct inclination toward rhetoric, which is normally unknown in the fabliaux. Its form is the so-called elegiac distichon. But the most distinguishing feature of these pieces is their lack of any moral implications, which, by the way, would not have advanced the satiric intention of the genre in any case. It is obvious that the respectability of the Latin tongue and the learned rhetorical, decorative style as well as the satiric intention of these pieces helped to make acceptable their often quite coarse themes and to present them as literature, thereby making them worthy of preservation in writing.

Chronologically also very close to the fabliau are the nine *Schwank* fables of Marie de France. Except for one, they are all in the so-called appendix to *Isopet*,[18] and it is assumed that much of the material in the appendix was borrowed from the oral tradition. The *Schwänke* that folklorists discovered in the oral tradition show, if they happen to belong to the same archetype as the *Schwank* material of Marie de France, a rudimentary but intact plot framework. (For this reason and others, the same traits may be assumed for the orally circulating *Schwank* narrations of the Middle Ages.)

Yet the *Schwank* material must pay for its penetration into the collection of fables; certain characteristic alterations are required. It must renounce the narration not only of causal antecedents but also of future effects—both popular features that help to make events in the fabliaux more vivid. In addition, the core of the action is broken open and robbed of essential parts, for the genre of the fable does not involve the real or causal nexus of a plot. It is concerned only with the proving of a certain state of affairs, of a certain conformity to

18. Karl Warnke, ed., *Die Fabeln der Marie des France* (Halle: M. Niemeyer, 1898).

"That's how it always is." In order to provide this proof, the *Schwank* material is stylized to the extreme. The continuity of the farcical plot is dissolved; the content loses the character of a true, complete event, which is decisive for a plot; the plot is shortened to a mere incident that reveals some sort of moral. Yet all of this—the omission of essential parts of the plot, the surrender of the principles of reality and causality, the reduction to a significant moment of what is stylistically still recognizable as a temporal and spatial whole—removed from the fable any immanently narrative motivation and even the principle of probability, neither of which was necessary in the Middle Ages for the demonstration of a moral.

And so the *Schwank* material paid dearly for its surreptitious entrance into literature through the back door of the didactic fable genre. But significantly, this opening up to the farcical also raised problems for the fable. To be sure, Marie de France, like so many other medieval authors, believed that a "philosophy" (*philosophie*) could be found even in a *fable de folie.*[19] Even though she had no intention of amusing her audience, she did not always succeed in eliminating from the borrowed *Schwank* material every trace of the comic spirit that contradicted the didactic solemnity of the fable. More telling, however, was the fact that in the *Schwank* fables men instead of animals carry the action. The plot of animal fables is predictable to a large extent. Therefore, the events—and with them the moral—gain the character of natural compulsion, so welcome to didactic works. But in the human fables, the genre reaches its own limitations. It may be shown that, in spite of the use of human characters, the horizon of incalculable, manifold human action and freedom cannot be narrowed to conform with the regular, confined, and necessary behavior of the fable animals. To a certain degree there penetrates into the fable the disturbing and foreign force of the unpredictable, which plays a decisive role in the *Schwank*

19. Warnke, *Die Fablen*, Prolog, vv. 23–24.

and which is injurious to any sort of proof. And finally we must note that, with the appearance of the sly *Schwank* character, elements of a morality of worldly wisdom become active in *Isopet* and begin to weaken the feudal-knightly ethics of the collection. The deep alterations in the structure of the *Schwank* material were not completely able to change the reductive wolf into a piously didactive sheep; the *Schwänke* in the fable permit the reader to perceive the wolf under the sheep's clothing.

The medieval *Schwank* material actually made its first advances into the field of didactic literature much earlier than *Isopet*, namely, at the beginning of the twelfth century. The time of its intrusion is proved by the eight examples of *Schwank* material in the *Disciplina clericalis*[20]—a good fourth of this clerical collection of exempla. As in the fable, the *Schwank* material here also had to be bent to demonstrate a certain moral, in keeping with the intentions and structure of this didactic genre. Also in this use of the *Schwank* there reigns the structural principle of extreme stylization that is characteristic of almost all the didactic genres of the Middle Ages. It might therefore suffice to reiterate for its use in the exempla the fate of *Schwank* material in the fable if it were not for three points which deserve to be kept in mind. First, there is the obvious uneasiness the author exhibits vis-à-vis the *Schwank* material he has taken into his collection. This uneasiness is not only clear in connection with the reproduction of the first three *Schwank* tales (Exempla IX, X, XI), but it also causes Petrus Alphonsi to guard himself, even in the Prologue, against possible criticism by requesting the reader not merely to dash through his work *humano et exteriori oculo,* but rather *subtiliori oculo iterum et iterum relegere.* The fact that the translator into Old French gave the designation of the more lowly genre (*fableaus*) not only

20. Alfons Hilka and Werner Söderhjelm, eds., *Die Disciplina Clericalis des Petrus Alfonsi* (Heidelberg: C. Winter, 1911).

to the three cited *Schwank* exempla but also to the entire collection shows how well founded was Petrus's fear of a misunderstanding arising from a hasty reading. And yet it was not at all unusual, in view of the eclectic use of sources common to the exempla literature, that Petrus also included Arabic tales which tell of the cunning of woman. Such stories were in keeping with clerical misogynism. Finally, Petrus as well as Marie de France believed that a "philosophy" could be found even in a *fable de folie*, although he formulated the idea in a more learned fashion. Yet while Marie, who wrote her fables at a time when the genre of the fabliau had already been formed, could introduce *Schwank* materials with a mere short reference, Petrus, who included *Schwank* material two or three generations earlier, needed to protect himself from possible criticism, which he did by a lengthy defensive disquisition. At the beginning of the twelfth century, the odium of sinfulness obviously was still strongly attached to *Schwank* material, even when it was dressed in the cloak of the moral and didactic.

A second point is also instructive, in that it tells us something about the structure of the colloquially circulating oral *Schwank* tales of the time. After the teacher (Petrus) has offered the pupil (the reader) the first informative tales about the slyness of woman, the latter, who understandably is intensely interested now, wants to know more of this subject. But the teacher refuses; that is enough of this delicate matter. Then the pupil supports his request with the revealing argument that the stories were too short (*pauca sonuerunt uerba*) —as indeed they were—since the *Schwank* material here also succumbed to the pronounced principle of stylization of the didactic genre. In a certain respect, the stylization principle of the exempla is even more radical than that of the fable, for here, not only the nexus of reality and causality and the principle of believability are abandoned, but the *Schwank* characters are reduced to complete abstractions of *quidam* or *quadam.* It may be shown that thus the events are raised into the ideal realm of absolute and abstract unconditionality. Yet the teacher is unrelenting, and he "proves" to his pupil by means of Exemplum XII the necessity, based on the nature of the genre, of this stylization which aims for brevity.

But now the teacher reluctantly permits himself to be cajoled after all and to the best of his ability tells more tales of woman's cunning. This time, tricks are related which have a noble purpose. And lo, now he is no longer laconic. These morally unambiguous tales suddenly increase to a length up to four times greater than that which is usual in the collection. Here we see a rounding out of the exempla to complete narrations that surpass the demands of the demonstrative intentions of the genre and that respect the demands of immanent motivation as well as a certain plausibility. This expansion into complete narrative inhibits the moralistic, didactic power of the genre to convince, however, since it lends the stories too much independent weight and consequently causes the demonstrative norms to recede somewhat into the background. Nevertheless, the demand by the pupil for greater loquacity in the *Schwank* tales and the eventual granting of this wish by the teacher (possible for him only in a morally innocuous area) gives us a notion of the appearance of these tales, which Aelred von Riedval condemned a little later for "poisoning the fantasy," and of the nature of the sinful pleasure in these *fabulae otiosae.* If the wolf in sheep's clothing is more clearly visible in the *Disciplina clericalis* than in the fable, this clarity results not least of all from the difference between free prose and poetic constraint.

Finally, it is necessary to mention a third factor. Precisely those three exempla which must bend their amoral content under the strict yoke of didactic stylization more severely than the other *Schwank* exempla reveal unusual, pointedly ironic endings. It is difficult to discover the meaning of this fact. One might perceive in it a relic of the structure of the vernacular comic tale. But it would also be possible to assert that a cleric like Petrus, who time and again believed it necessary to guard against the misinterpretation of thoughtless frivolity, could justify the representation of farcical, coarse events only by means of irony. It is in any case significant that irony here is relegated to the end of the tale and has not yet attacked the moral, that is, the warning against the sly *mala femina*. As in its didactic relative, the fable, the moral that is to be demonstrated remains protected here from the destructive poison of farcical reduction.

The most arresting facts in the history of the medieval *Schwank* are that *Schwank* subjects gained access to literature before the twelfth century and that this entry was not made by detouring through the accepted moral-didactic genres. Those twenty Latin pieces, which are usually combined under the designation of "monastery *Schwank*" *(Klosterschwank)*, can be traced in part to about 820; further, these early stories lack any sort of moral or didactic justification. Their single intent is to amuse their listeners. For this reason, the designation *ridicula*, which several of the authors chose for their works, is more appropriate than the somewhat misleading "monastery *Schwank*," which evokes the image of a separate, complete genre.

We are dealing here with isolated pieces, widely separated in time, which are quite different as to origin as well as to form, and which have little in common other than their comic intention. Their most commonly shared similarity is their harking back to the structure of the pure joke, that is, a building toward a certain expectation and the concluding pointed frustration of this expectation. The oldest of these pieces already reveal a tendency that has moved so emphatically into the foreground of the later vernacular *Schwank* genres of Europe that it is difficult to recognize the fundamental archetype of the joke. The tendency is for the narrative to extend from the surprising frustration of the expectation toward an independent comic image, which no longer draws its comic elements only from the contrast with the previously created expectation but increasingly from the profusion of independent comic details. In the *ridicula*—and this factor makes them important to us—this morphological development, which possibly corresponds to a historical development, is still clearly visible. With the narrative extension at first of the climax of the joke and soon of the whole tale, the *ridicula* use various sources of comedy. Thus, quite early we find a comic literature of the ugly and the lowly and of human frailty. The introduction of the comic-vulgar detail and its close connection to the possibilities of the joke occurs here, as in the later *Schwank* genres, solely for the sake of the accumulation of comic effects, typical of the *Schwänke* of all times.

But while a representation of the negative sides of life and man was possible in the exempla without any justification, since it was only a means of didactic or moralistic demonstration, the learned authors of the *ridicula* had to choose a more cautious path. The concept "morality through the negative in man" could not be replaced with the formulation "comedy through the negative in man" before the second half of the twelfth century. The lack of moral or didactic intention in this comedy made it necessary to justify its content, which was always evaluated negatively. In the *ridicula*, this justification is achieved through the pretended integrity of the amoral behavior of the *Schwank* hero. Naturally it remains objectively reprehensible when the *ciuis Sueuulus* in the famous *Modus Liebinc*[21] sells his son into slavery, no matter if the youth is the result of an amorous escapade of his wife, or when the peasant Unibos in the equally famous work by that name[22]

21. Walther Bulst, ed., *Carmina Cantabrigiensia* (Heidelberg, 1910); here: carmen XIV.

22. Karl Langosch, ed. *Waltharius, Ruodlieb, Märchenepen*, 2d ed. (Darmstadt: Schwabe & Co., 1960).

drives his enemies and even innocents to their death, no matter if he himself has been threatened with death a hundred times. The integrity of the actions of these *Schwank* heroes is totally superficial. It rests solely on the fact that the amoral acts of the heroes are reactions to deeds that threatened them earlier.

This pseudomoral justification of the negative *Schwank* content is joined by formal and esthetic justifications. Although the mastery of classical rhetoric was a matter of course to the learned authors, its application to lowly subjects certainly was not. And there is more; they did not hesitate to dress this worldly subject matter in literary forms that sometimes, like the Christian hymn strophe of the *Unibos* or the sequence of the *Modus Liebinc,* came from the sacral sphere. In addition to the superficial justification of the characters' integrity, it was the literary value of the *ridicula* which gave their earthy content access to parchment, that is to say, to literature. It is certainly no accident that precisely the oldest versions, for example of the *Modus Liebinc* and of the *Unibos,* are also artistically the closest to perfection.

Similar changes occurred in the folk *Schwank,* to which we now turn. Its written tradition also began in France and soon afterward in Germany with authors of the importance and ability of a Jean Bodel or "der Stricker." In addition, a few fabliau authors expressly emphasize in their prologues the literary character of their works; they say that they made fixed, written narrations (*fabliaus*) from oral tales (*fables*) by rhyming them (*torné en rime*) [*MR,* V, 171]. The word *rhyme* here retains the old meaning of verse or versification. It is rhyme which endows the oral comic tale with the dignity of art and which raises it from mere concern with storytelling to that of artistic representation:

> Des fables fait on les fabliaus,
> Et des notes les sons noviaus,

Et des materes les canchons,
Et des dras, cauces et cauchons. (*MR*, V, 171)

(One makes fabliaux from tales, new sounds from notes, songs from written matter, and hose and slippers from cloth.)

The mere change from oral prose to the simple form of the octosyllabic rhymed couplet was extremely important in the twelfth and thirteenth centuries, for there is evidence that with this change the coarse tales became for the first time fit for recital in better circles, even at noble courts.

It is truly remarkable that the use of rhyme alone made the comic tale fit for polite society and worthy of literary treatment, while much more alteration had been necessary to render it acceptable prior to the formation of the fabliau (from about 1150) and prior to its written tradition (from 1190). Before this formative period the comic tale had only two alternatives. It could bend under an oppressive didactic yoke and thus deny its own character to a large extent (as in fables or exempla), thereby justifying its literary existence; or it could to a degree retain its reductive character by being at the service of clerical scholarly comedy (*comœdia elegiaca* or *ridicula*). In the latter choice the artistic form also had to be much more ornate and the tales themselves satiric—and therefore indirectly didactic—or they had to don the scant cloak of superficial integrity. From approximately 1150, a certain liberalization must have spread through society, for the comic tale now is freer from the earlier constraints. Moreover, the fabliau is clearly set off from the earlier literary traces of the oral comic tale in two respects: It opens itself up to the common and vulgar and especially to the obscene and scatological to a degree hitherto unknown, and it almost completely renounces any sort of moral or didactic obligation, so the "poetics of the ugly" practiced in the fabliau now receives full emphasis. This change does not mean, to be sure, that the reductive power of the low content cannot be usurped from time to time for certain other purposes such as the courtly, anticourtly, literary, or political. The major part of the genre is nevertheless henceforth free of such obvious determinations.

What then is the purpose for creating the fabliau and how do its authors pursue their goals? Which activity of the spirit and which image of the world is expressed in it? The earthy material of the fabliau, seen most sharply in the obscene and scatological tales, and its renunciation of any justification aside from esthetic considerations provide us with one answer.

Strangely enough, it has never been asked whether there are any obscenities in the fabliau. Yet even if one ignores the argument of D. H. Lawrence ("What is pornography to one man, is the laughter of genius to another."),[23] which is valid only for individuals and therefore of no value in literary criticism, one must yet ask the question as to whether the average modern reader does not impose in an unreliable manner his emotional attitudes on a genre that flowered long before (according to a theory of Ludwig Marcuse) the birth of the "post-Christian emotion" of obscenity toward the beginning of the eighteenth century.[24] It may now be shown, however, that Marcuse was wrong, for the norms which determine the evaluation of obscene emotion are drawn according to cultural boundaries and are therefore religious and social conventions; these norms have not changed decisively from age to age. In addition, there are medieval sources which, although they do not mention the obscenity of the fabliaux, do show that the Middle Ages reacted to linguistic obscenity much as present-day readers do, a fact which also refutes the popular belief in the apparent "franchise" and "naïveté" of medieval man. Therefore the fabliaux also stood on trial before the

23. D. H. Lawrence, *Sex, Literature and Censorship*, ed. Harry T. Moore (London: William Heinemann, Ltd., 1955), p. 195.

24. Ludwig Marcuse, *Obszön, Geschichte einer Entrüstung* (Munich: Paul List, 1962).

negative judgment that sought to protect society from sexually generated pleasure. If their purpose was to place sex in the service of literary pleasure, the fabliaux had either to demolish these restrictions or at least to circumvent them more readily. Freud once designated the "technique of overcoming repulsion" as the "actual *ars poetica*" of literature, for it alone is able to attain a psychic gain in pleasure through reading.[25] Freud was thinking here of literature in general; how much more then is this dictum true of obscene literature. In the following, I shall sketch only one of the "techniques of overcoming repulsion" that appear in the fabliau, only one of the possibilities the fabliau may employ to avoid indignation and disgust in art. To be sure, it emphasizes the characteristics that are probably the most important in the *ars poetica* of obscene vulgarity: the expansive and the intensive metaphor.

In addition to direct verbal obscenity, the fabliaux use the euphemistic metaphor generously. One of the authors coined the fitting phrase for this practice: *dire .II. moz à un* (*MR*, II, 112). It is particularly suitable because it indicates that which every erotic euphemism accomplishes: the verbal respect of the taboo content. To express this device in psychological terms: The erotic metaphor leads away from that which is actually meant, and toward an independent field of imagery. In this way the metaphor diverts part of the psychic energy from the taboo content, so some of its repulsive effect is destroyed. The taboo content is thus made more readily acceptable. It becomes enjoyable and free of value judgments. Because of its euphemistic character, however, the fabliaux seldom use this potential in the erotic metaphor. In the interest of farcical comedy they attempt rather to extend the distance between the tenor and the vehicle of the metaphor

25. "Die Technik der Uberwindung der Abstossung" as the "eigentliche *Ars poetica*" of literature: Sigmund Freud, *Das Unheimliche,* Fischer doppelpunkt, 4 (Hamburg: Fischer, 1963), pp. 7–18.

as much as possible, indeed to exaggerate it (for example, a penis becomes a pilgrim's staff). The result is a type of expansive metaphor that is only secondarily euphemistic.

But there is more to the use of metaphor than euphemism. The fabliau's creator knew how to augment the technique of the expansive metaphor into the intensive metaphor, for example in *La Pucele qui abevra le polain* (MR, IV, 199). Such works are nothing other than one basic metaphor, maintained throughout, which establishes the metaphorical realm, the *locus amœnus*. In *La Pucele* the basic metaphor is the identification of the vagina as a fountain. This metaphor of the *locus amœnus* is then expanded, the penis being designated as a thirsty horse, the testicles as the guards of the horse. Since there is no connection between fountain, horse, and guard, and vagina, penis, and testicles, it becomes clear that, in the expansion of the metaphors they have become autonomous and need no longer be appropriate to that which they represent. On the contrary, the greater and the less meaningful the distance achieved between vehicle and tenor, the more effective the work. The more artificially removed the erotic situation, the more intensive is the effect of the final intended return to the actual meaning. This form of the extended, expansive metaphor is in reality an intensive metaphor. It presents a verbal acknowledgment of the taboo while its content simultaneously breaks the taboo, for it presents the sexual act in physical detail. This farcical technique for overcoming revulsion is, if we may also use a metaphor, closest to the unappealing behavior of a man who pulls his traveling companion out of a muddy morass only in order to let him fall back into it again from a greater height and so more deeply.

It is easy to understand that the psychologically disruptive force of taboo-laden obscenity would be especially well suited to the farcical reductive process. Because of its sexual character it was quite suitable for use in the controversy between the advocates of *l'amour courtois* and the defenders of *l'amour vilain,* both of which, it should not be forgotten, were represented at the courts. But the process of reduction through obscenity also attempted to find points of departure outside of the erotic sphere. It could even seek them in Christianity. The obscene profanation of Christian cultic ceremonies (*MR,* III, 178), the grotesquely obscene parodying of the genre of the miracle play (*MR,* V, 201), or the obscene and scatological persiflage of the biblical story of Creation[26] all testify to the effectiveness of this use. Basically, every high form of thought, morality, literature, etc., represents a challenge to the low form of the *Schwank* and its reductive activity of the spirit; the fabliau rejected few of these challenges of its period. But—and this point should be clarified briefly in conclusion—it accepted these challenges with no intention to prove the contrary. The fabliau presented no moral of any type, unless it might be an emphatically worldly, nonidealistic one. Its intention, *por faire la gent rire,* had an immediate and simple goal. The author of an obscene fabliau describes this goal in a clear and unmistakable manner:

> Fablel . . .
> . . . grant confortement raportent
> As enovrez et as oiseus,
> . . . .
> Si lor fait il grant alegance
> Et oublier duel et pesance,
> Et mauvaitié et pensement. (*MR,* VI, 68)

> (A fabliau . . . brings great pleasure to the workers and to the lazy. . . . It makes them happy, causes them to forget their sorrow and trouble, and takes their minds off unpleasant things.)

It is sometimes difficult for the modern reader to see why "redeeming" laughter should originate in—of all things—an obscene object. The existence of the fabliaux and the evi-

26. *Fabliaux et contes des poètes françois des XIe, XIIe, XIIIe, XIVe et XVe siècles* . . . , ed. Etienne Barbazan and M. Méon (Paris, 1808), IV, 194.

dence of the wide acceptance of *paroles crasses et doilles* (*MR*, III, 141) speak a clear language. In laughter, if anywhere, that which opposes moral solemnity is made acceptable and restores the unity of the world. This conviction of a contemporary philosopher[27] finds manifold confirmation in the fabliaux.

At first glance, my assertion that the fabliau has no purpose beyond its stated self-justification (relief from care, sorrow, and worry), that its humor is therefore worldly and free of any concern for value, does not seem true, for no fewer than two thirds of all the works draw a lesson from the tales, in many instances by attaching a moral. Too often, also, the authors point to the didactic or proverbially instructive character of their works, which no lesser figure than Henri d'Andeli reduced to the pregnant formula: *Ci vous di example et proverbe* (*MR*, V, 258). The disagreement concerning what one is to think of such claims is as old as the fabliau.

A detailed analysis of the range and function of the proverbs and morals is not included in this discussion. Such a discussion would begin with consideration of the proverb itself. Various investigations in recent years[28] have shown that the proverb is incapable of transmitting norms of behavior, since it is limited to an amoral, empirical knowledge of facts, and it can claim validity only for a certain isolated instance—and then only in retrospect. A careful analysis of the use of the proverb in the fabliau supports this conclusion. A comparative glance at the didactic genre of the exemplum, which characteristically uses maxims rather than proverbs, reinforces it. The use of a proverbial moral in the fabliau could then have the purpose of protecting its daring material and its author from possible attacks: "Look, just like Marie, Petrus, and others, we also

27. Joachim Ritter, "Uber das Lachen," *Blatter für deutsche Philosophie*, 14 (1940–1941), 1–21.

28. I have indicated here only the study that is probably the best, the work of Jolles, *Einfache Formen*.

are drawing a useful *philosophie* from a *fable de folie*." Certainly the use of proverbs must have played this protective role now and then, for in the Middle Ages proverbs had the undeserved reputation of being a useful means of moralizing.

The decisive difference is, however, that in the fabliau the farcical reduction does not stop short of the lesson, but in most cases destroys it. The most conclusive proof of this effect is found in those works which appear to do nothing other than demonstrate a proverbial teaching as in *Jouglet*, but it is not a teaching comparable to that of the didactic exempla. Rather, the metaphorical thesis is taken literally and in this way results in a disagreeable, scatological fabliau, which is then concluded sanctimoniously by its author with the proverb, *Teus cuide cunchier autrui / Qui tout avant cunchie lui* (*MR*, IV, 127). With this unexpected conclusion the "truth" of the proverbial moral is cleverly made absurd. The scatological reduction of this fabliau consequently is directed against nothing less than one of the most fundamental convictions of the Middle Ages, namely, the belief that a useful lesson could be derived from every event. The fabliau, although it destroys this belief, does not offer an alternative. The same is true of other works which also "demonstrate" a proverbial teaching in plastic imagery. Many of these fabliaux omit any type of concluding moral reference, with which they document their lack of interest in a moralization of what they have presented, or they draw a different and totally unpredictable lesson from the tale, so it can be said: The moral actually documents the unfitness of the fabliau for moralization.

In addition to the indicated uselessness of the proverb and the author's obvious lack of interest in moral questions, the fabliau's unsuitability for moralization has a structural basis, which was intimated during the discussion of the *Schwank* exempla. For the *longa uerbositas* is not only the effluence of its attempt to accumulate comic details but also the result of its effort to anchor the events firmly in a concrete situation.

At this point in the literary discussion if not long before, the often refuted but seemingly indestructible reference to the ostensible "reality" of the fabliaux customarily emerges. Actually, the moralizing is a matter of a (pre)novella narrative intention, as may be derived from a close reading of the preface to the fourth day of Boccaccio's *Decamerone*.

Such an analysis leads to the conclusion that the (pre)-novelistic narrative intent of the fabliau contrasts with that of the exemplum. It removes the events from the exemplary world of ideal conformity and transposes them into a world determined by concrete types and situations, thus injecting more material into the tales than could concisely be resolved into a moral. In addition, the action loses its character of natural compulsion and regains the power of the unexpected. This alteration plays a dominant role in the most common of the three archetypes of the *Schwank*, that in which one character outdoes another. Obviously, clear moralization is no longer possible in this type of action, which is characterized by the unpredictable reversal of events. It is not surprising, therefore, that the fabliaux often contain morals that are constructed according to the principle of a chain of morals, the individual links of which refer to the various contradictory aspects of the concrete events and thereby become relative to one another.

Even in those fabliaux which are called *exemples*, a relative moral has replaced the unequivocal moral of the exempla. Like the proverb, this form of moral can claim validity only by reflecting on the respective, individual, concretely presented story. Making the action concrete prevents the disclosure of generally valid and forward-directed perspectives. The morality has ceased to be moral. It is, like the proverb, merely a retrospective commentary which plays with the form of morality, primarily by exposing it to laughter. With respect to poetic effect, the authors of the fabliaux renounce most emphatically in their final commentaries any possible—however incongruous—moralization. No moral at all is, in many stories, better than such a moral. Thus, it speaks for the consistency of the genre that, in respect to one of its essential stylistic principles—the erotic metaphor—as well as in respect to its morals, it may be stated that the form is realized but the contents and value are depleted.

The image of the world that is presented in this genre may be sifted out from the sum total of the subject matter and the morals. It is a genre that is permeated by the conviction of the inability of man to learn and the unimprovable creature qualities of the human being, man or woman. Like the author of the vehement tract *Les .XV. Joies de mariage,* who raised his voice soon after the fabliaux authors grew silent, the *Schwank* authors also do not believe that man can escape from the prison of his physical being. Yet, whereas the ecclesiastical author could only fall prey to pessimism when confronted with the unchangeable corruption of woman and the unteachable, compulsive desires of man, the fabliaux suspend the Christian consciousness of sinfulness for a while in order to be able to laugh about a world constructed in such a fashion. They are content with the comically distorted confirmation of the facts of physically bound existence; they do not develop from their retreat behind the didactic and idealistic genres any binding counter-ideal, not even a hedonistic one. One could define the fabliau as a genre for which the world behind the wall of the famous garden of love in the *Roman de la Rose* is at an end. It sees only the vices found on this side of the wall, but it refuses to recognize the virtues on the other side, for beyond the wall lies the unreal realm of the ideal. In this way the fabliaux offer their listeners a respite from the strenuous idealism of the good and noble. They show the experience of daily life, that is, that which is uncertain and negative in existence. They show this experience with a semblance of seriousness ("That's life!"), but only in order jokingly to destroy this appearance and to laugh about this world without ideals, because otherwise one could only weep.

With the fabliaux the farcical activity of the spirit found its first unlimited access to literature in Europe. The long, arduous, and complicated path along which the lowly, ugly, and vulgar had to toil in the service of foreign masters had ended. Yet the *Schwank,* this possibility of every genre, found in the fabliau not only its own form of expression, but also its purest expression. By refusing to project any sort of counter-ideal, the reductive activity of the spirit denied nothing less than its own code. This refusal is not changed by the fact that also in the fabliaux the reductive power of vulgarity was usurped for certain purposes from time to time. In the fabliaux, the wolf discarded his sheep's clothing, and a closer view reveals that the long-feared beast is relatively harmless. His being consists of the denial of his own nature; his mock bites leave no deep wounds.

III

STEPHEN L. WAILES

VAGANTES AND THE FABLIAUX

Years ago Joseph Bédier called attention to the role of *vagantes*, familiarly known as "wandering scholars," in the creation of French fabliaux: "We think it assured that a large number of fabliaux were written by *clercs errants*. . . .With which group of clerics are we concerned? No doubt, with the *déclassés*, veteran students, monks *manqués* or defrocked who make up the 'family of Golias.' "[1] Although Per Nykrog, in his influential monograph,[2] left the *vagantes* no special role as he stressed the courtly character of fabliaux, German scholars have recently brought up the relation of *vagantes* to the Middle High German *Märe* or *Versnovelle*, a large group of tales which are nothing other than fabliaux in German. They cautiously speak of "certain traces" of this group in the genre (Hanns Fischer), or formulate with reference to the French tales: " 'Students' (*clers lettrés*) were certainly involved in the [French] fabliaux to the same degree as in the German" (Karl-Heinz Schirmer).[3] In fact, no separate study of the problem has been made.

1. *Les Fabliaux*, 5th ed. (Paris: H. Champion, 1925), pp. 389–90: "Nous tenons pour assuré qu'un grand nombre de fabliaux ont pour auteurs des clercs errants. . . . A quelle catégorie de clercs avons-nous ici affaire? C'est, à n'en pas douter, à des déclassés, vieux étudiants, moines manqués, défroqués, qui composent la 'famille de Golias.' "

2. *Les Fabliaux* (Copenhagen: Ejnar Munksgaard, 1957).

3. Hanns Fischer, *Studien zur deutschen Märendichtung* (Tübingen: Niemeyer, 1968), p. 208: "Nur die . . . wandernden Scholaren . . . haben gewissen Spuren hinterlassen." Karl-Heinz Schirmer, *Stil- und*

I intend in this paper to make a comparative analysis of the Latin literature of the *vagantes* and the French and German fabliaux. The points of comparison will be themes of humor: first, satiric themes (specifically, simony, celibacy, and criticism of the higher clergy); then, the worldly life of wandering scholars, humorously presented in the poetry as a series of engagements with wine, women, and dice. By studying these topics of humor I plan to establish the agreement or disagreement among the three genres with respect to the traditional content of goliardic poetry; on the basis of these findings I shall then take a position on the role of *vagantes* in the authorship of fabliaux. I have no expectation of proving a negative—that the wandering scholars had nothing to do with fabliaux—but I believe that the evidence for France differs from the evidence for Germany. When estimating the involvement of *vagantes*, reasons will emerge for discriminating more carefully than has been done previously between the fabliaux of these two countries.

We must first consider a problem of terminology. What social group or groups are identified by the term *vagantes*? To call them "wandering scholars" is justifiable but not an adequate identification. In the works of Bédier, Nykrog, Fischer, and Schirmer cited above I have found fourteen terms used in the apparent assumption that they designate one social group—for examples, *vagantes*, *"weltliche" clerici*, *Studenten*, *goliards*. In part these terms reflect the varied usage in medieval documents, but we must suspect that they also reflect a lack of clarity in our concepts. It is probably wrong to equate *goliardi* with *vagantes*; not all men who wrote goliardic poetry were itinerant hedonists. One hopes for more attempts at distinctions like those made by Hennig Brinkmann in his article

---

Motivuntersuchungen zur mittelhochdeutschen Versnovelle (Tübingen: Niemeyer, 1969), p. 326: "Sicher aber sind an den Fabliaux in gleichem Masse wie bei den deutschen Schwänken 'Studenten' (clers lettrés) beteiligt gewesen."

"Goliarden" and Edwin Zeydel in his article "Vagantes, Goliardi, Joculatores: Three Vagabond Types."[4]

I shall proceed on the assumption that goliardic poetry is a literary tradition defined both formally and thematically. Proof that its themes occur in the formally distinct fabliaux must be weighed seriously as evidence of a common social base. For want of more exact knowledge and terms, I shall call this base the *vagantes.*

One of the dominant satiric themes in goliardic tradition is simony and venality, especially as they occur among the higher clergy. The popular "Money Gospel," a parody of the synoptic gospels that attacks the venality of the Roman see, presents, in its twelfth-century form, the poor and rich clerics who seek the Pope's favor without specification of office; the later and more widely distributed version makes the villain a bishop: "A certain cleric flagrantly oppressed by his bishop" and "A certain bishop, fat, simoniac, and very rich."[5] These roles are retained in the fifteenth-century version associated with Lübeck. They reflect a view from the lower levels of the clerical pyramid, like that in *Carmina Burana* no. 39,[6] which assails the venality of bishops, papal lawyers, and Church administrators. The poem "Goliae versus de praelatis" harps on the dereliction of prelates from pastoral concerns because of the allure of royal courts, and another attack on the venality

4. Hennig Brinkmann, in *Germanisch-Romanische Monatsschrift,* 12 (1924), 118–23; cf. William Powell Jones, *The Pastourelle* (Cambridge, Mass.: Harvard University Press, 1931), Appendix C: "Clerical Jongleurs and the Goliards." Edwin Zeydel, in *Helen Adolf Festschrift* (New York: Frederick Ungar Publishing Co., Inc., 1968), pp. 42–46.

5. Paul Lehmann, *Die Parodie im Mittelalter,* 2d ed. (Stuttgart: Hiersemann, 1963), p. 185: "Quidam clericus ab episcopo suo manifeste opressus . . . quidam episcopus pinguis simonialis . . . valde dives." See Lehmann's discussion of the relation of *vagantes* and the parodies, pp. 19–21.

6. In the edition of Alfons Hilka and Otto Schumann (Heidelberg: Winter, 1930——). *Carmina Burana* cited by number refer to this edition unless otherwise specified.

of prelates, "Sermo Goliae pontificis ad praelatos impios," may reveal the poor *clericus literatus* as author:

> Permit me, and I will say unheard-of things. The poor man
> is driven far away from the altar when the bishop realizes he
> can't give anything. No one supports a poor scholar.
> Now the chorus of poets goes begging.[7]

No doubt simony as a satiric theme became increasingly popular the further one moved in the clerical estate away from wealth, that is, the closer one came to the wandering scholars.

The issue of sacerdotal celibacy flared up in England in the early thirteenth century when Innocent III sought to enforce the principle, and several goliardic poems on this theme apparently originated there. We cannot call them apologies for priestly marriage, yet for all the caricature of priests and their dependence on wives and concubines, the tone is good-natured, even jocular, and many other clerical offices are said to share this problem with the priesthood. Again, in the "Concilium sacerdotum," the problem is presented as conflict between bishop and lower clergy: "Clerics and priests were recently taking sad counsel together in the chapter house, and said: 'The bishop wants to take away our girls; what response should we make?' "[8] The famous poem of the Benediktbeuren manuscript "Cum in universum sit," describing the "order" of *vagantes*, explicitly welcomes the priest with his wife ("cum sua matrona"),[9] and further evidence that celibacy was a hot issue in Germany in the thir-

7. Both poems in Thomas Wright, ed., *The Latin Poems Commonly Attributed to Walter Mapes* (London: Nichols, 1841), pp. 40–42 and 44–45; lines quoted, pp. 41–42: "Inaudita dicerem, si liceret fari: / pauper procul pellitur omnis ab altari, / postquam sentit pontifex nihil posse dari; / non est qui pro paupere spondeat scolari. / Jam mendicat misere chorus poetarum."

8. Wright, *Latin Poems*, p. 174: "Clerus et presbyteri nuper considere / tristes in capitulo simul et dixere: / 'Nostras vult ancillulas praesul removere, / quid debemus super hoc ergo respondere?' "

9. J. A. Schmeller, ed., 4th ed. (Breslau: Marcus, 1904), no. 193.

teenth century is the diatribe "Sacerdotes, mementote" in that same manuscript, directed against married priests:

> O you priest, answer!, you whose hands are filthy, who often and cheerfully sleep with your wife and then get up in the morning to say Mass, blessing the body of Christ after a whore's embrace . . .[10]

Finally, the narrative poem "De presbytero et logico," in the traditional goliardic stanza form, contains mutual insults directed at the sexual mores of priest and wandering scholar. "Most lethal of all your innumerable sins," says scholar to priest, "is your priestess (*presbytera*)."[11] Priest accuses scholar of lechery with urban bawds. Both charges interest us.

These themes occur in the French fabliaux. The *Testament de l'asne* of Rutebeuf, apparently a cleric with a university education who supported himself by writing, shows us the simoniac bishop professing to be outraged when he learns that one of his priests has buried a donkey in hallowed ground; he is immediately mollified by the animal's "bequest" of twenty pounds:

> Et dist l'esvesques: "Dieus l'ament,
> Et si li pardoint ces meffais
> Et toz les pechiez qu'il a fais." (*MR*, III, 220)

> (And the bishop said, "May God pardon him and forgive him his trespasses and all the sins he has committed.")

Rutebeuf's satire encompasses archdeacons, canons, prelates, and prebendaries, but he is generally conciliatory toward the humble parish priests—like himself, on the lower rungs of the ladder. Another conflict between priest and bishop appears in *Le Prestre qui ot mere a force* (*MR*, V, 143–150). The

10. Hilka and Schumann, eds., no. 91: "O sacerdos hic, responde, / cuius manus sunt immunde, / qui frequenter et iocunde / cum uxore dormis, unde / Mane surgens missam dicis, / corpus Christi benedicis, / post amplexus meretricis . . .".

11. Wright, *Latin Poems*, pp. 251–57; quoted lines, p. 256: "Et prae tot innumeris quae frequentas malis, / est tibi presbytera plus exitialis."

priest, summoned by his bishop to explain his neglect of his mother and his large expenditures on his mistress, solves the problem by agreeing to care for the former—and keeps the latter arrangement just as it was! The breaching of priestly celibacy is treated as complacently here as in the "Concilium sacerdotum." In fact, authors of French fabliaux acknowledge the existence of priests' wives and concubines without question. The concubine in *Le Prestre et le chevalier* is introduced thus:

> Ne d'omme nul ne li chaloit
> Fors que de li et de s'amie,
> Qu'il avoit biele et eschavie. (*MR*, II, 47–48)

> (The priest cared nothing for anyone but himself and his lady, who was beautiful and elegant.)

Similarly, in *Le Bouchier d'Abeville*:

> Li doiens avoit une amie
> Dont il si fort jalous estoit. . . .
> Qui mout ert jolie et mingnote. (*MR*, III, 233, 237)

> (The priest had a lady of whom he was so jealous. . . .
> She was indeed a pretty creature.)

Furthermore, this lovely lady is mother of the priest's children.

The most notable fabliau with respect to priestly marriage, conflict of priest and bishop, and satire on the higher clergy, is *L'Evesque qui beneï le con*:

> Uns prestes estut en la vile
> Qui mout sot d'angin et de guile,
> Sa fame avoque lui avoit
> Li prestes, que il mout amoit,
> Et mout estoit preuz et cortoise. (*MR*, III, 178–179)

> (There was a very guileful priest in the city with his wife, courteous and prudent, whom he well loved.)

The bishop tries to separate the priest from his wife by enforcing three deprivations, but the priest finds a way around each one by following his wife's advice. The bishop is then trapped during a visit to his mistress, as he performs that lecherous folly conveyed by the title. The real hero of this tale is the priest's wife, the *prestresse.*

These French stories are built on themes prevalent in goliardic literature. What of the themes in German fabliaux? This question is easily answered, for in the canon of 212 titles[12] there is no allusion to clerical simony, no conflict between priest and bishop, and, most notably, no reflection of priestly marriage or concubinage—this, despite numerous comments on the power of lust in all classes. On the points discussed here the Latin and French traditions overlap, but the German is distinct.

Let us turn now to the humorous self-portraiture of the *vagantes* in their poetry. How given they are to gluttony! How they delight in the fat roast and the full beaker (when they can afford them)! An epitaph for Golias states, "He was the slave of his stomach," and though the bacchic theme is usually lyrical, it becomes narrative in several of the *Carmina Burana.*[13] The chief form of recreation in the tavern is gambling—the Archpoet lists it as second of his vices, after lechery, and the "Ribald's Credo" declares that to sit in the tavern by a wench, with three dice in hand, is better than sitting at the right hand of God ("ad dexteram Dei Patris"). And Hugh of Orléans tells us that dice cost him all his money one night, after a treacherous innkeeper had steeped him in wine.[14]

12. In Fischer, *Studien,* pp. 65–70.

13. Epitaph, "Ventris servus erat," quoted by Lehmann, *Parodie,* p. 141. See *Carmina Burana* no. 76 (Hilka and Schumann, eds.) and nos. 176, 182, and 195 (Schmeller, ed.).

14. The Archpoet's "confession" ("Aestuans intrinsecus") may be found in many editions, for example, Karl Langosch, ed. and trans., *Weib, Wein und Würfelspiel* (Frankfurt a.M. and Hamburg: Fischer, 1969), pp. 8–17. See Helen Waddell's translation of the "Ribald's Credo" in *The Wandering Scholars* (Boston and New York: Houghton Mifflin Company, 1927), pp. 192–94, where the original text is cited.

The French fabliaux document these foibles. Gautier le Leu, introducing *Le Prestre teint,* tells of eating and drinking until he was forced to sell his clothing at Orléans, and he blames the innkeeper. (Perhaps this was the same one who cheated Hugh.) All versions of *La Borgoise d'Orliens* comment on the girth of the scholars arriving in the city: "The clerics were big and plump because they ate very well, believe me"—and a little simple arithmetic demonstrates that the cleric traveling from Paris in *Les Trois Aveugles de Compiegne* eats and drinks half again as much as each of the famished beggars he treats at the tavern. We discover the title figure of *Estormi* at dice, and the author assures us that "grant anui" attends gamblers. A game of dice in which the priest loses his money to two vagabonds underlies the plot for *Le Prestre et les deux ribaus*; we learn from *Saint Piere et le jongleur* that dice are the path of redemption for many souls, including, ironically, those of minstrels in general![15]

We may dispose of the German tradition on these counts as swiftly as on the issue of satiric themes. There is no allusion in German fabliaux to the gluttony of wandering clerics, no tavern scene involving a *vagus,* no hint that scholars gambled. One story does concern a drunken student, but a comparison of *Die drei Mönche zu Kolmar*[16] with its French cognate, *Estormi,* shows how colorless and functional the drunkenness of the German figure is.

Hugh of Orléans, "Hospes erat michi," in George Whicher, *The Goliard Poets* ([Norfolk, Conn.]: New Directions, 1949), p. 76.

15. *Le Prestre teint, MR,* VI, 8–23; texts of *La Borgoise d'Orliens* most conveniently in Jean Rychner, *Contribution à l'étude des fabliaux,* II (Neuchâtel/Geneva: Faculté des lettres, 1960), pp. 80–99 (quoted lines, p. 80, A, ll. 13–14: "Li clerc estoient gros et gras, / Quar molt manjoient bien sanz gas"); *Les Trois Aveugles de Compiegne, MR,* I, 70–81; *Estormi,* ibid., 198–219; *Le Prestre et les deux ribaus, MR,* III, 58–67; *Saint Piere et le jongleur, MR,* V, 65–79.

16. For editions of German fabliaux, which are not collected in one place as are the French, see Fischer, *Studien,* pp. 296–378.

If the reader's patience has been tried by the negative findings for the German fabliaux thus far, I promise more concrete results on the final topic—put plainly, the sex life of the *vagantes*. Much of their erotic poetry is simply a conflation of lyrical moments. They observe the beauty of nature and that of young women; there is sighing, dancing, and dalliance with maidens. The actual stories of love, comparable to the fabliaux, concern adventure with women of lower social position, either rustics (in the *pastourelles*) or urban wenches. Unlike the French pastourelles, the Latin pieces never tell of the lover befuddled or rejected, except in *Carmina Burana* no. 79, for which it is doubtful that we have the full text. Showing the careless satisfaction of clerical lust at the expense of country girls, the pastourelles exemplify the counsel offered by Andreas Capellanus in the section of *De amore* titled "De amore rusticorum": use flattery, then force. Even the lament of the pregnant village lass, *Carmina Burana* no. 126 ("Huc usque, me miseram!"), informs us that the seducer has left for France. She thinks he left to avoid her angry father, but we must suspect that the *vagus* is merely returning to school and has offered a convenient excuse. Why would the father expel him rather than compel marriage?

The conventions of the pastourelle occur also in Latin parodistic texts. The "Peasants' Catechism" states that peasants are miserable "because clerics live off their toil and use their women."[17] This lechery is one of the charges brought against clerics in the "Altercatio rusticorum et clericorum": "Besides, they injure us by polluting our daughters and wives."[18] In the parodistic Masses a recurring prayer runs, "O God, who has caused the multitude of peasants to stand at

17. Lehmann, *Parodie*, p. 198: "Quia dolent, quod clerici utuntur de eorum uxoribus et vivunt de eorum laboribus."

18. *Anzeiger für Kunde der deutschen Vorzeit*, N.F. 24 (1877), col.

the service of the clergy . . . grant, we beg, that we may live on their labors and make use of their women."[19]

We find fewer traces of urban wenching in goliardic poetry, although common sense and the charge of the priest in "De presbytero et logico" mentioned above assure us that it took place. Hugh of Orléans wrote of a woman of ill fame whom he entertained, and of his beloved "Flora," perhaps the same person. *Carmina Burana* no. 76 describes a young man's visit to a brothel, the temple of Venus ("templum Veneris").

Now there are a number of French fabliaux in which a young cleric is lover. His conquests are divided almost evenly between townswomen and the wife or daughter of a *vilain.* Four of the five texts involving bourgeois women are set in the university city of Orléans, and there is no doubt that such liaisons were frequent in fact as well as in fiction.[20] The stories that tell of the conquest of peasant women are fully consonant with the goliardic traditions, except that the lovers' slyness obviates resort to force. For example, in the tale of the miller and the two clerics, the miller's daughter mistakes a grimy ring from the fireplace, which is proffered by a cleric as a magic token to preserve her virginity, she and her mother are used, the rustic is thrashed, and the clerics go on their way. We might retitle this story "De rustico et clericis," with ample

370: "Adhuc nobis faciunt res deteriores, / Polluendo filias nostras et uxores." Is there an allusion to priestly concubinage in st. 12–13?

19. Lehmann, *Parodie,* p. 235: "Deus, qui multitudinem rusticorum ad servitium clericorum venire fecisti . . . da, quesumus, de eorum laboribus vivere et eorum uxoribus uti." Cf. pp. 240 and 247.

20. Affairs with bourgeois women: *La Borgoise d'Orliens,* all versions (Rychner, II, pp. 80–99); *Le Cuvier* (*MR,* I, 126–31); *Les Braies au cordelier* (*MR,* III, 275–87); and *Le Clerc qui fu repus derriere l'escrin* (*MR,* IV, 47–52). Affairs with peasant women: *Gombert et les deus clers* (*MR,* I, 238–44); *La Damoiselle qui ne pooit oïr parler de foutre,* Version D (Rychner, II, pp. 121–35); and *Le Meunier et les deux clers,* both versions (Rychner, II, pp. 152–60). Unspecified social class, *La Pucele qui voloit voler* (*MR,* IV, 208–11); chivalric class, *Un Chivalier et sa dame et un clerk* (*MR,* II, 215–34), an Anglo-Norman text which is altogether exceptional.

basis in the Latin literature. Another story, *Le povre Clerc,* in which the cleric is not involved sexually, is developed from the situation of a wandering scholar who must seek overnight lodging with a peasant.[21]

Again, the conventions of goliardic poetry and the French fabliaux agree significantly, although the urban adventures of the latter are with average townswomen, not prostitutes. The German stories give us more material to analyze because there are twenty-five that present clerics as actors. In nineteen the cleric plays the main role, and in all but two he is a lover. Quite unlike the French tradition, however, in not one German story is a scholar sexually involved with a peasant woman. Indeed, only two show conflict between cleric and peasant; both are late texts (fifteenth century), of which one has no erotic element at all, and the other is cognate with and perhaps derived from the French *Povre Clerc.*[22]

The convention of clerical lover as *vagus* is absent from the German fabliaux, but there is another, well-defined, in its place. In a number of texts we find clerics who are well-bred, well-behaved, and eloquent; in style and erotic finesse they remind us of chivalric lovers; they are involved in romance with exquisite and respectable women from the higher bourgeoisie and the aristocracy. To exemplify the difference between French and German traditions on this point, let us compare two cognate tales on the motif of the misplaced cradle, *Gombert et les deus clers* and *Studentenabenteuer B* (better known as *Irregang und Girregar*).

21. *Le povre Clerc, MR,* V, 192–200.

22. I use the numbers assigned stories by Fischer, *Studien,* pp. 296–378. Young clerics (*schuolaere, schrîbaere, studenten*) appear in nos. 4a, 18, 30m, 30q, 37, 41, 64, 67b, 67c, 72, 77, 80, 82, 92, 105g, 107, 109, 111b, 117, 118, 119, 120, 124, 125B (my designation for *Der Sperber* in MS. B^1), and 129. They play secondary roles in nos. 41, 67c, 72, 77, 82, and 92. Though heroes, they are not lovers in 4a and 105g, which show conflict with peasants. The former is unerotic, the latter cognate with *Le povre Clerc.*

The French story begins:

> En cest autre fablel parole
> De .II. clers qui vienent d'escole;
> Despendu orent leur avoir
> En folie plus qu'en savoir.
> Ostel quistrent chiés un vilain . . . (*MR*, I, 238)

> (In this fabliau I tell of two clerics who were coming from school; they had spent their money more on folly than on knowledge. They sought lodging with a peasant . . .).

Thus, in five lines the conventional hell-rake *vagantes* are housed with a rustic, and the bawdy plot unrolls. The German story begins thus:

> Two good youths agreed together to travel abroad, with propriety and not for glory, in order to learn what is available in books. . . . These reputable youths set out abroad in cultivated style, for both were wealthy in worldly goods and could conduct themselves according to their station. How could I describe their breeding better than to say that they made friends wherever they went. . . . I can tell you most assuredly that they were both handsome fellows; whoever saw them spoke only well of them.[23]

It takes the German author 120 lines to conclude that part of the story told by the Frenchman in five, because he seeks a romantic stylization of characters and plot. The German's hero catches sight of the maiden sitting in her "palast," and *Minne* herself drives the dart of Love deep into his heart (we think of Lavinia and Aeneas); the heroes are finally accepted

23. Larry D. Benson and Theodore M. Andersson, trans., *The Literary Context of Chaucer's Fabliaux* (Indianapolis and New York: The Bobbs-Merrill Co., Inc., 1971), p. 127, with original text on facing page. The German text is that of F. H. von der Hagen, *Gesammtabenteuer*, III (Stuttgart and Tübingen: Cotta, 1850), 43–44. On the courtly image of the heroes in this tale, see Theodore M. Andersson, "Rüdiger von Munre's 'Irregang und Girregar': A Courtly Parody?" *Beiträge zur Geschichte der deutschen Sprache und Literatur*, 93 (Tübingen, 1971), 311–50.

as lodgers because their good family and breeding are obvious. We could continue this comparison throughout the related parts of the two texts, but the conclusion may be stated briefly: There is a basic difference in the presentation of story because of a basic difference in the social identity of the clerics and their beloveds.

If space permitted, we would make a close reading of such German fabliaux as *Der Schreiber, Schampiflor, Studentenabenteuer* A, *Frauenlist, Das Rädlein, Die drei Studenten,* and *Die treue Magd* to appreciate the ingenious ways in which clerical lovers are dignified. But two examples must suffice. When two scholars come to dinner with their host and his daughter, the author quotes Hartmann von Aue's romance *Iwein*—the passage in which the questing Kalogrêant takes dinner with his host and the host's daughter. Thus the author sets in parallel the quest for adventure of clerics and knight.[24] In another story a young man is advised regarding three estates of society—clergy, chivalry, and women (a humorous twist on the usual triad: clergy–chivalry–peasantry). He decides to become a cleric, because "one should serve gracious women and there are no more devoted servants of courtly women than those men who are educated." This youth then sets out for Paris, and on the way has an affair with the wife—of a knight.[25]

The clerical lover of German fabliaux has no precedent in

24. *Studentenabenteuer* A, Wilhelm Stehmann, ed. (Berlin: Mayer and Müller, 1909), ll. 267–271 (my italics): "Nu was der wirt ein hövescher man / und behielt sîn suht daran / *daz ers der megede niht verstiez / und si guotlichen hiez / mit dem knaben ezzen* . . .". Hartmann von Aue, *Iwein*, ed. G. F. Benecke and K. Lachmann, 6th ed. (Berlin: De Gruyter, 1959), ll. 353–363: "dô ich mit ir ze tische gienc, / der wirt mich anderstunt enpfienc. / . . . hie mite sô übergulterz gar, / *daz er mich ir nie verstiez / und mich sô güetlichen liez / Mit der juncvrouwen ezzen.*

25. *Die treue Magd* in *Gesammtabenteuer*, II, 317–18: "ok so horde ik sagen / . . . dat man zarten vrauwen denen sal; / und nener lude man mer vint, / den der, de geleret sint, / de dat vorwar menen, / dat se hoveschen vrauwen denen.

goliardic poetry, but we do find a model for him in another group of texts (Latin, French, and Anglo-Norman) associated with the clergy: the "debates" on the relative merits of knights and clerics as lovers.[26] It has long been recognized that these texts present an image of the cleric that reflects affluence, intelligence, and erotic *savoir-faire*. The women in the "debates" who champion clerics as lovers sum up their virtues with the term *courtliness* (*curialitas, cortoisie*). Obviously, these texts transmit a convention of the clerical lover which is quite unlike that of goliardic literature, though it resembles the notion of the intelligent and well-bred clerk which underlies the dialogues in Andreas's *De amore*. Thus the two contrasting images of the clerical lover in Latin literature, the goliardic and the courtly, are reproduced in the dominant images of such lovers in the fabliaux: The French stories present the goliardic stylization, the German the courtly.

We are able to conclude that the literature of the *vagantes* is much like that of the French fabliaux in all the areas of humor we have examined, but that in all these areas the German fabliaux are dissimilar. Our problem now is to move from observed differences of literary traditions toward a theory of differences in the social groups that supported these traditions. We may assume that medieval authors chose the matter of their stories and their style of treating the matter to appeal to the experience and taste of their audiences. It then appears that the audiences for German fabliaux had greater experience of and taste for the tradition of clerical lovers shown in the "debates" than for the goliardic tradition. Nevertheless, it does not seem possible to accept Hanns Fischer's idea that the literary portraiture in these stories is a form of auctorial self-recommendation[27] and thus to conclude that the authors of these German fabliaux were themselves affluent and urbane.

26. Conveniently collected in Charles Oulmont, *Les Débats du clerc et du chevalier* (Paris: H. Champion, 1911).

27. Fischer, *Studien*, p. 208.

There is no necessary connection between the status of an author and that of his subject, but there is such a connection between his subject and his audience.

I believe the German audiences in question were composed in significant part of comfortable and reputable clerics, secretaries, jurists, or diplomats in lay or ecclesiastical courts, clerks, agents, and notaries in chancelleries or businesses, teachers, tutors, and probably members of the higher clergy as well—deacons, provosts, and bishops. I am sure the misadventures of the cathedral provost in Würzburg, narrated in two stories, were especially entertaining to his peers, and we know that the blood-and-thunder farce *Heinrich von Kempten* was written by Konrad von Würzburg, a refined intellectual, on commission from Berthold von Tiersberg, provost of the cathedral in Strassburg.[28] It was in these circles that the traditions of clerical wooers represented by Andreas Capellanus were familiar, and no doubt cherished; and it was for these circles that the courtly cleric of the German fabliaux was devised.

Experience of and taste for the goliardic escapades depicted in the Latin poetry and French stories surely arose where the students swarmed. Until the end of the fourteenth century, Germans went to France (and northern Italy) for university education, and German audiences for literature lacked that daily experience with *vagantes* which made Paris and Orléans and the towns along the routes of access so amenable to stories about them. Paris is the only university town used as setting for German fabliaux before the fifteenth century. A thirteenth-century German version of *Le povre Clerc* replaces the scholar with a farmboy, but a fifteenth-century version restores the *clericus vagus* to his role.[29] I believe the circumstances of university development in Europe help explain the differ-

28. *Frau Metze* and *Das Bildschnitzer von Würzburg* involve the Würzburg provost. On Konrad's patron, see Fischer, *Studien*, p. 165, and the article by Edward Schröder cited there.

29. See Fischer, *Studien*, p. 122*n*57.

ences between the French and German fabliaux of clerical adventure.

What conclusions does this discussion develop about *vagantes* and fabliaux? The shared literary traditions of Latin and French texts suggest a shared sociological basis, one that was more likely in authorship than in audience because of the different languages of composition: I suspect one group of authors appealed to two publics. These authors were able to exploit traditions of a Latin literature before audiences that were not familiar with Latin because they were familiar with the social milieu from which these traditions derived—the life of the scholastic proletariat in and around the French university cities. The dissimilarity of German fabliaux which depict clerical adventure may be explained by the lack of such audiences in Germany. Clearly, these fabliaux were composed for audiences of different tastes and expectations—audiences in which cultured and reputable members of the clerical estate were prominent but whose experiences were different.

I do not believe we can identify the authors of the German stories as a group. We know they were witty and familiar with the notions of clerical *curialitas,* but whether they were *vagantes, goliards, Studenten,* or "*weltliche*" *clerici,* educated ne'er-do-wells or tonsured courtiers, continues to elude us.

⁂IV⁂

PER NYKROG

COURTLINESS AND THE TOWNSPEOPLE THE FABLIAUX AS A COURTLY BURLESQUE*

The *Disciplina clericalis*, the famous collection of some thirty tales of Oriental origin, translated into Latin by Petrus Alphonsus in the twelfth century, contains three stories about women who play clever tricks on their husbands in order to save their lovers. The collection is cast in the narrative framework of a dialogue: A father tells the stories to his son and admonishes him to draw lessons from them. This the son does, but as is sometimes the case in listening to moralizing, the enthusiasm of the young man varies in degrees—quite notably so in one of the French translations, a rather free adaptation of the work from the early thirteenth century.[1] In the sequence of the stories about adulterous women, the young man seems most remarkably keen to learn; he eagerly asks for a fourth example of feminine deception, so he can be on his guard against them (1146: *Por saveir mei d'eles garder*), but the father, who apparently shares the reader's doubts concerning the boy's real motives, refuses flatly.

The remarkable factor in this passage is that the boy refers to these three tales, exclusively, as *fabliaux*. He seems to have

*This article is based on my book, *Les Fabliaux: Etude d'histoire littéraire et de stylistique médiévale* (Copenhagen: Ejnar Munksgaard, 1957); rpt. with Postscript, Geneva: Droz, 1973.

1. A. Hilka and W. Söderhjelm, *Petri Alphonsi Disciplina Clericalis*, III Französische Versbearbeitungen (Acta Soc. Scient. Fennicæ XLIX, 4 Helsingfors, 1922). The reference is to Version A.

an exceptionally precise definition of that word—as well as a pronounced liking for that sort of tale.

In his *Art of Poetry*, written in Latin shortly afterward, probably in the 1230s, Jean de Garlande exposes the current medieval theory of levels of style by means of the so-called Vergilian Wheel: a set of concentric circles divided into three sections, one for high, one for middle, and one for low style.[2] Each circle carries the object or the notion typical of its style in some domain, the examples being taken from Vergil's three major works, hence the name of the device. Style is thus defined as a set or a system of settings (places), objects, and human types; level of style is identified with social level.

Though the treatise seems to refer to composition in Latin only, the examples it gives of correct and defective plots clearly refer to literature in French, and in a most illuminating way. All four of the specimens given of high and middle style deal with Charlemagne or Roland, the high style with their warlike virtues, the middle with their household virtues in times of peace. But when he comes to the low style, which theoretically should correspond to the Bucolics, Jean takes the reader into an unexpected world. A "correct" distichon in *stylus humilis* might be:

> In tergo clavam pastor portat, ferit inde
> Presbyterum, cum quo ludere sponsa solet.

> (The shepherd carries a stick on his back, and with that he strikes the priest, with whom his wife is accustomed to having fun.)

An "incorrect" one might be:

> Rusticus a tergo clavam trahit et [bertonso]
> Testiculos aufert, prandia laeta facit.

2. Edmond Faral, *Les Arts poétiques du XIIe et du XIIIe siècle: recherches et documents sur la technique littéraire du moyen âge* (Paris: Honoré Champion, 1923; reprinted 1958). The reference is to p. 86ff. (with figure).

(The peasant carries a stick on his back and he castrates the tonsured one, then lunches happily.)

There is nothing Vergilian about lecherous priests more or less savagely punished by outraged husbands, be they shepherds or farmers, but what leaps to the eye is that the learned Paris professor conceives low style, not as bucolic and tender, but as coarse and comical, and that whatever comes to his mind in that connection has the plot type of a fabliau.

In thirteenth-century usage the word *fabliau* designates a short story, written in rhymed octosyllables (though a couple of closely related tales are in courtly stanzas), mainly of humorous nature (though some are either moralizing or edifying), and intended for entertainment of a certain type. The corpus of medieval manuscripts contains about 150 tales that correspond to that definition (since the definition is rather vague, exact limits of the "genre" are hard to draw, and only a person who enjoys statistics is in need of them), but there are, in the medieval texts, allusions to a few more. However, since most of the allusions we find are to texts we know, it seems that what we have covers the essential body of what was.[3]

Humorous short stories had been current in the twelfth century, but they were isolated, and the word *fabliau* was not applied to them.[4] It appears for the first time in an unquestionable way in the writings of Jean Bodel (interned as a leper

3. The most important, though incomplete, edition is that by A. de Montaiglon and G. Raynaud, referred to throughout this article and collection as *MR*.

4. It has been claimed that the word was in use in the twelfth century, but on insufficient basis. Thus, Jürgen Beyer (*Schwank und Moral: Untersuchungen zum altfranzösischen Fabliau und verwandte Formen*, Studia Romanica [Heidelberg: Carl Winter, 1969], p. 9*n* 4) attaches a great importance to the *Roman de Renart*, version α, which, in the Martin edition reads: "Et fabliaux et chancon de geste" (l. 7). The verse is supposedly written in the 1170s. But the version β, older than the α, reads: "Et fables et chançons de geste" (*CFMA*, II, 16, l. 3739). The metrical identity of the two words complicates an exact discussion of chronology.

in 1210), who wrote seven or eight of them and who refers to himself as "a rhymer of fabliaux" (*MR*, V, 191). He also speaks enigmatically of others *qui de fablel fet grant fable* (*MR*, I, 153), which indicates that he had competitors. The expression does not, however, exclude the possibility that he, one of the most remarkably original writers of his time, was to some extent the inventor of the genre.

The prologues and the epilogues as well as some allusions in the texts, may serve to produce a quite vivid picture of the situations the fabliau writers had in mind when they composed their stories. Repeated references to the audience and to a written text, a not infrequent distinction between the pronouns *him* (or a name: the author), *me* (the recitant), *us* (the assembly), and *you* (the audience, or the assembly minus the recitant), and a few sketchy allusions and descriptions can be joined into a reconstruction of a social occasion, in which a group of people enjoy the entertainment of a recital, typically after dinner. The entertainer may be a traveler who pays in this way for hospitality received in a private home, or he may be a professional performer hired for a celebration of some sort. He may be the author—professional or amateur—of his tale, but he may also recommend himself by emphasizing that he recites the work of some named writer. This latter circumstance is the one that brings about the distinction between pronouns just mentioned. It goes without saying that the possibility of a family owning texts to be used on similar occasions enters into the picture. There are allusions to collecting, and the manuscripts that have preserved the fabliaux must have come into existence as systematically gathered copies bound in volumes of such private collections of small manuscripts with one or more texts on each.

If this particular view of the manner in which this literature was used is projected upon the general background of cultural life in thirteenth-century France, it gains a wider significance. In the preceding century, the typical situations in which literary works reached an audience seem to have been two: popular gatherings in public places where *chansons de geste* were recited or sung (at markets or along the pilgrim routes: Bédier's theory holds true for a period he was not interested in—the middle and the end of the twelfth century, the time when most of his texts were composed); and aristocratic gatherings at the courts of the higher nobility, where lyric poetry was sung and/or romances were read aloud from texts.

The rise of the fabliaux, written in the meter of courtly romance and intended to be read aloud in private social gatherings, seems to follow the appearance of a new type of audience for literature. Jean Bodel, for example, was a citizen of a manufacturing and commercial community of Picardy (Arras), and the picture that can be deduced from the texts of the fabliaux corresponds to a new cultural milieu, that of the townspeople, different from both of the earlier. Jean Renart, who was active until the end of the 1220s, seems to have been the last major writer of his time to have lived comfortably, like Chrétien de Troyes, at the court of a wealthy and noble protector. The typical writer of the succeeding generation is one who, like Rutebeuf, had attended the university, but who then had taken to the risky existence of a free-lance writer, living with his family or by himself in a town and offering, like Colin Muset, his services to whoever wanted them and to whoever could pay in cash or in gifts with an immediate market value.

This noteworthy shift in the pattern of literary sociology provides a sound basis for a distinction between a courtly literature, its apogee occurring in the period 1160–1230, and a bourgeois literature, rising around 1200 and becoming dominant during the major part of the thirteenth century. The distinction does not, however, justify the thesis advocated by Bédier and widely accepted, according to which the bourgeois literature was *sui generis,* distinct from and even opposed to the other strands in the literary life of the time. On the contrary, this literature, enjoyed by the townspeople in the thirteenth century, is essentially derived partly from the courtly literature of the preceding age and partly from whatever had remained in the writers' minds from their carefree days in and around the schools. A close study of the texts does not bear out any hypothesis that makes a sharp distinction between even the highest courts and the milieu of the townspeople in general. Rutebeuf, for example, who, after 1261, became the epitome of "middle class" mentality and tastes, counted Royal Highnesses among his patrons.[5]

This complex background to our corpus of fabliaux is reflected in the texts themselves. Thus, an analysis of the system of social roles (whatever actions, possibilities, and motives can be ascribed to characters of a certain social rank and the authors' attitudes toward them) reveals telltale patterns: The unquestionable pet child of the fabliaux is the student (*le clerc*); apart from him, the texts maintain not only a marked deference toward nobility, but also, what is more significant, a considerable contempt for the middle class, a contempt that grows to hateful and bitter scorn whenever the tale is about a bourgeois who transgresses into the world of the nobles, buys a castle, wants to marry a noble girl, or the like. The conception of society as seen through the fabliaux thus remains dominated by the point of view of the old creative alliance between noblemen and men of learning.

Yet many of the fabliaux are merely unsubtle stories written in an unsubtle manner for unsubtle people, whatever their social rank. But ever so often, in the course of an apparently unsubtle story, some detail catches the eye of the cultivated reader, an effect that would have been utterly wasted on an audience consisting entirely of unsophisticated people. Thus, the *Fevre de Creil* notices that his apprentice's anatomical

5. *Oeuvres complètes de Rutebeuf*, ed. Edmond Faral and Julia Bastin, 2 vols. (Paris: A. and J. Picard, 1959–1960). See the introductions to poems 36–39, I, 552 et seq.

manhood has impressive dimensions; he is imprudent enough to tell his wife about it, and so encounters some minor trouble. But look at the wording: the youth had an organ

> Qui moult ert de bele feture
> Quar toute i ot mise sa cure
> Nature qui formé l'avoit . . . (*MR*, I, 231)

> (that was of very beautiful making, for Nature, who had shaped it, had put all its care into it . . .).

This is a direct quotation from Chrétien de Troyes, except that the great *romancier* used these verses in his description of the lovely Enide (the verb had to be changed because of the meter):

> Moult estoit la pucele gente
> Car tote it ot mise s'antante
> Nature qui fete l'avoit. (*CFMA*, 80, 13)

> (The maiden was very lovely, for Nature, who had made her, had put all its attention into it.)

For a good many years the collection of fabliaux by Jean Bodel presented a philological problem. In one text a number of (known) fabliaux are listed as having been written by the same author, and one of these stories indicates the writer's name as Jean Bodel (though a faulty reading and a misunderstanding in the *MR* edition complicated this finding for a long while). But why should this well-known author list only his comical works and make no mention of his more glorious and famous writings (*Les Saisnes, Le Jeu de Saint Nicolas*)? Look at the passage:

> Cil qui trova del *Morteruel*
> Et del mort *Vilain de Bailluel*
> Qui n'ert malades ne enfers,
> Et de *Gombert et des .ii. clers* . . . (*MR*, I, 153)

> (He who wrote [in verse] about the milk-soup [that is, *Le Vilain de Farbu*] and about the dead peasant from

> Bailluel who was neither sick nor ill, and about Gombert
> and the two students . . .)

and compare it to the famous opening passage of Chrétien's *Cligès*:

> Cil qui fist *d'Erec et d'Enide*
> Et les *Commandementz Ovide*
> Et *l'Art d'Amors* en romanz mist, . . . (*CFMA*, 84, 1)

> (He who made *Erec et Enide*, and the *Commandments of Ovid*, and translated the *Art of Love* into French . . .).

It is a direct parodic allusion, and its entire effect would have been lost had the burlesque imitation contained any details other than humorous trifles to match Chrétien's prestigious classics. The milk-soup called *morteruel* is a stock ingredient in descriptions of grotesque meals in the fabliaux, for it is a typical, vulgar peasant dish.

The same *Cligès* is written as a reaction against *Tristan*, in which Iseut agreed to give her body to Marc while her heart belonged to Tristan. Fénice refuses such a compromise and formulates her attitude in two proud verses:

> Qui a le cuer, cil a le cors. (*CFMA*, 84, 94)

> (Who has the heart has the body.)

> Vostre est mes cuers, vostre est mes cors.
> (*CFMA*, 84, 157)

> (Yours is my heart, yours is my body.)

The blacksmith's wife in *Connebert* echoes her when she cries to her beloved priest, who will eventually meet a dreadful fate:

> Vostre est mes cuers, vostre est mes cors
> Et par dedanz et par defors;
> Mais li cus si est mon mari. (*MR*, V, 166)

> (Yours is my heart, yours is my body—both on the inside and on the outside, but my backside is for my husband.)

One of the rare instances of feminine inventiveness protecting a lover in an aristocratic setting (the nature of the plot is, correspondingly, quite dignified) is *L'Espervier*. This rather hybrid story ends, however, on an innocent but precise antiquotation:

> Li *lays de l'Espervier* a non,
> Qui trés bien fet à remembrer.
> Le conte en ai oï conter,
> Mès onques n'en oï la note
> En harpe fere ne en rote. (*MR*, V, 50–51)

> (It is named the *Lay of the Sparrowhawk*, that is very good to recall. I have heard the story about it told, but I never heard the tune to it played on harp or on rote.)

The suggestion that a fabliau could be connected with a sung poem (or with a tune) is preposterous, but compare the phrase with Marie de France's traditional allusion to the lyric poem that accompanies the story retold in her *Lais*:

> De cest cunte k'oï avez
> Fu *Guigemar* li lais trovez
> Que hum fait en harpe e en rote.
> Bone en est a oïr la note. (*CFMA*, 93, 32)

> (From the story you just heard the lay *Guigemar* was composed, which is played on harp and on rote. The tune is good to listen to.)

In courtly allegory the god of Love is pictured as armed with an arrow, but quite often it is said that he also carries a box containing a sweet ointment. Consequently, in *Eneas* and in the *Roman de la Rose*, Love stings and hurts, but he also pours the balm of delight into the wounds he inflicts. In both works the distinguished poets push their allegory dangerously close to the concrete, and one could profitably think of such descriptions while reading the fabliau about *La Saineresse* (*MR*, I, 289): A stupid husband boasts of how closely he guards his wife, and she takes her private revenge against such conceit in a most ingenious way. Her lover masquerades as a "blood-letteress"; the husband personally sends him into the bedroom with the wife, and afterwards she describes in vivid detail to the cuckold what has happened: The "blood-letteress" stung her over and over again, but no blood came out (cf. *Roman de la Rose,* l. 1708 *et passim*); finally, a most delightful "ointment" was poured into the wound (I prefer not to quote her description of the vessel it came out of!). Compare to the *Roman de la Rose*:

> Il a angoisse en la pointure
> Si me rassoage l'ointure. (*SATF*, 62, 97)
>
> (The stinging is anguishing [painful], but the ointment soothes me.)

The story is funny enough in itself, though crude, but placed in the courtly context it gains a third level of reference that makes it even more witty.

Some fabliaux do not make sense if they are not read as comments on courtly customs or on the effects of courtly literature. Thus, a small number of rather similar stories tell about young girls who refuse to have anything to do with young men.[6] Three of them faint every time a certain four-letter word is pronounced, but they are cured by young men who are persuasive speakers: Each pretends a similar respect for chastity and is promptly taken to bed with the girl. As each explores certain regions of his partner's body, he asks, What is this? and What is that? She tells him that *this* is her *fontaine*, and *that* is the "hornblower that guards the spring." He answers in the same way to her questions, and soon his "horse" is allowed to "drink" from the fountain. In the fourth story, the girl's only wish is to "fly in the air like Dedalus," and the young man promises to turn her into a bird by giving her a beak (kissing), a tail (intercourse), and wings—but he never gets that far. The father of one girl, a hapless farmer, addresses his daughter respectfully as *ma demoiselle*. This courtly term

6. *La Damoiselle qui ne pooit oïr parler de foutre,* MR, III, 81; *La Damoiselle qui n'ot parler de foutre qu'i n'aust mal au cuer,* MR, V, 24; *La Pucele qui abevra le polain,* MR, IV, 199; *La Pucele qui voloit voler,* MR, IV, 208.

is a clue to what is wrong with these girls. The diagnosis is the same in all four cases: excessive reading of romantic literature, Arthurian romance (the lady, the fountain, and its guardian: *Yvain*) or Ovidian metamorphoses. These girls are the *précieuses ridicules* of the thirteenth century. It is worth noting that two of the young seducers are described in words reminiscent of courtly knights, and they approach the extravagant young girls as if they were an *aventure* in the knightly sense of that word.

A different situation is presented in two versions of what is basically the same story:[7] A happy young couple gets married and enjoys a passionate honeymoon; then the husband, busy and practical, explains to his wife that courting her is a waste of time, for whenever she grows tender, he is sure to be ready, so she has only to pronounce a certain formula, and he is at her service. She feels insulted but accepts the system. After some time, however, he finds that she uses the cue too often; he reacts by an outrage, then bullies her into silence and submission to *his* whims. The stories can, of course, be read as ironic reflections on a not uncommon development in everyday life. If so, they are remarkable specimens of "naturalism," completely out of their chronological context. But they make sense beautifully if read as a mischievous spirit's study of a phase that is normally left out of focus in courtly literature: A lover is a sublime character, and a husband is an uninspiring bully, but how does marriage transform a sublime young lover into the tedious tyrant depicted by courtly doctrine?

A number of fabliaux tell the story known, from La Fontaine's version of it, as *Le Cocu battu et content.*[8] A husband learns that his wife will receive a lover in such and such a way as soon as he is absent from their home. He pretends to leave

7. *La Dame qui aveine demandoit pour Morel sa provende avoir*, *MR*, I, 318; *Porcelet*, *MR*, IV, 144.

8. *La Dame qui fist batre son mari*, *MR*, IV, 133; *La Borgoise d'Orliens*, *MR*, I, 117; *Un Chivalier et sa dame et un clerk*, *MR*, II, 215.

on a journey, but stays and presents himself disguised as the lover. The wife, however, recognizes him. She asks him to wait in a secluded room, then calls the servants to beat him. The husband takes the beating and remains happily convinced of his wife's unfaltering virtue. *Un Chivalier et sa dame et un clerk,* one of the versions of this motif, is a strange hybrid. Where the other stories are placed correctly according to the social system in a bourgeois setting, this one takes place in a noble family. Accordingly, the lady is actually innocent; her lover is (as in the others) a *clerc,* but he is the son of a nobleman, and during the prolonged sentimental first part of the story, he loves her so intensely and so desperately that he is about to die of his passion. The rendezvous is the only time she is going to accommodate him—she is under pressure to do so from her confessor, who declares that it would be murder to say no to the lover's demands. Technically, this compound story is a most unfortunate enterprise, but it is illuminating to the literary analyst, for he can study the effects of amalgamating a sublime courtly plot type to a fabliau type.

The consequences for the social setting have been mentioned. Another observation concerns the structural relationship between the two plots. Both have the same characters, the eternal triangle. The sublime plot tells about the lover and the lady *only* and keeps the husband in the background as a potential menace. This perspective shifts at the moment we move into the second plot, for this part concerns husband and wife *only* and keeps the lover unseen, as a moving force in the background. One face of the triangle (woman–lover) is sublime, the other (woman–husband) comic. The third face (lover–husband) is cruel, tragic, or dramatic; it is rarely important in the fabliaux, but when it occurs, it results in violence and even bloodshed. One notices that, according to this definition, both examples proposed by Jean de Garlande in his theory are badly chosen. In one respect, however, they are germane, for in a plot in which the woman (or the lover) loses control and the two males are confronted, the lover *must* be a priest. This is a rule that suffers no exception.

This 120-degree turn of the erotic triangle is one key to the nature of the relationship between the courtly types of love stories and the typical fabliau plot type for which the son in the *Disciplina clericalis* had such a liking. A second key is the identification between stylistic and social levels propounded by Jean de Garlande and other academic theorists. As in the seventeenth century, the thirteenth-century world of the nobility is the world of the sublime, and the world of the townspeople is the world of the grotesque and of the comical. In order to understand what the fabliaux are, from the point of view of literary history, one must operate those two keys simultaneously, and all the while keep in mind that these tales are not mere tales and anecdotes; they are works written in the meter reserved for courtly or instructive writings, and they are meant to be read aloud in courtly gatherings. A number of them end in a problem that the audience is called upon to discuss and judge, thus reproducing, in the grotesque vein (what problems!), a typically courtly, or scholarly, pastime.

The corpus of the fabliaux is so heterogeneous that scarcely any formula applies to the whole. About the more characteristic works it may be said, very abstractly, that their essence is that *they are and are not*. They are literary but not literature. They often end, like the fable that was probably their immediate origin, on a moral, but usually a moral that is no moral. The large and typical majority cluster around the courtly themes: love, adultery, or seduction (by verbal persuasion), but they are doubly uncourtly, for the erotic triangle is presented from the wrong angle, the arguments of the seducers are incongruous, the lovers are people excluded socially from the world of courtly love, and their actions amply demonstrate that such exclusion is justified. Yet they persist: Craftsmen's wives yearn for lecherous priests, unscrupulous students use their wits to get at appetizing country girls or Junoesque bourgeoises, and all the characters involve themselves or someone else in more or less undignified situations.

All through these disordered loves flows the language of courtly love, in telling or in talking, spiced with unveiled four-letter words, which are often emphasized by the addition of "three times," "four times," or "very vigorously," or with detailed descriptions. This interplay between the two levels is a constituent trait in their essence as tales. In one of them, a merry tale about the unfortunate love affair of a priest with a cobbler's wife, written in lyric stanzas, the whole system is pinpointed in one happy verse whose two halves form a preposterously incongruous combination:

D'amer par amours fame à Çavetier. (*MR*, II, 30)

(To love by true love the wife of a cobbler.)

This delicate balance—which, more often than not, becomes an indelicate imbalance—is maintained beautifully in the opening scene of *Aloul*, a long story whose subsequent plot (farmhands chasing the lover through the house in the depth of the night) is remarkable because of a strange open-endedness, accumulating one fantastic, improbable, and unnecessary scene upon another, all of them told with epic exaggeration. The beginning is a brief exposition: Aloul, a wealthy farmer who lives in town, jealously guards his wife, a nobleman's daughter, very strictly; she suffers from this crude treatment.

Longuement fu en cel escil,
Tant que li douz mois fu d'avril,
Que li tens est souez et douz
Vers toute gent, et amorouz;
Li roxingnols la matinée
Chante si cler par la ramée
Que toute riens se muert d'amer.
La dame s'est prise à lever
Qui longuement avoit veillié;

> Entrée en est en son vergié;
> Nuz piez en va par la rousée . . . (*MR*, I, 256)
>
> (For a long time she was in this alienation, until the sweet month of April when the weather is pleasant and sweet to everybody, and full of love. In the morning the nightingale sings so clearly in the branches that everything is dying with love. The lady, who had been lying awake for a long time, rose from her bed, she entered her orchard, barefoot she walked in the dew . . .).

So far so good; we are transported into the exquisite world of pure sensual beauty; Marie de France wrote nothing more tender. A few verses later, a priest makes his entrance, and the reader begins to feel apprehensive. The tale, however, continues in the style of Marie (cf. *L'Austic*, v. 35 et seq., *CFMA*, 93, 121):

> Il erent si très près voisin,
> Entr'aus deux n'avoit c'une selve.
> Moult ert la matinée bele,
> Douz et souez estoit li tens,
> Et li prestres entra léenz
> Et voit la dame au cors bien fet.
> Et bien sachiez que moult li plest
> *Quar volentiers fiert de la crupe* . . . (*MR*, I, 257)
>
> (They were so close neighbors [that] between them were only some trees. The morning was very beautiful, the weather was sweet and pleasant, and the priest came in there and saw the lady with the shapely body. And you must know that that pleased him greatly, *for he likes to strike with his loins* . . . [my italics]).

Truly, we had been warned, but it is nevertheless a shock to be thrown with such carefully prepared brutality from the delicate refinement of courtly tenderness into the harsh but energetic world of the *stylus humilis*.

⁂ V ⁂

BENJAMIN L. HONEYCUTT

THE KNIGHT AND HIS WORLD AS INSTRUMENTS OF HUMOR IN THE FABLIAUX

The knight is not normally treated as an object of humor in medieval French literature. His courage and his loyalty to God and his "seigneur" are emphasized in the *chansons de geste,* while in the *romans courtois* he is often judged by his adherence to a rigid chivalrous code stressing valor and perfection in the service of his lady. There are apparent exceptions, if one is inclined to view *Le Pèlerinage de Charlemagne, Aucassin et Nicolette,* and the *Lancelot* of Chrétien de Troyes as rather elaborate parodies of both epic grandeur and courtly attitudes and conduct. But in the fabliaux the knight is consistently subjected to the same comic treatment accorded members of every level of society. The literary techniques employed to reduce the typical knight of epic and romance to his more earthy and perhaps more human counterpart in the fabliaux comprise the subject matter of this essay.

Per Nykrog, in his excellent study of the fabliaux,[1] has acknowledged the presence of courtly parody in the genre, and indeed it was his research which suggested a closer examination of the specific comic devices employed by the fableor in the humorous treatment of the knight in the genre. Nykrog has, however, perhaps gone a bit too far in viewing ridiculed knights or those who act inappropriately as outcasts of courtly society. He does this, to be sure, in order to make their conduct

1. Per Nykrog, *Les Fabliaux: Etude d'histoire littéraire et de stylistique médiévale* (Copenhagen: Ejnar Munksgaard, 1957).

more acceptable to the aristocratic audiences for whom he suggests the fabliaux were conceived and written. But were aristocratic audiences incapable of laughing at themselves? I think not. It is certainly not my intention to dispute Nykrog's view that the tales originated in courtly circles. I would merely suggest that Jean Rychner's research on variant versions of individual fabliaux[2] has quite sufficiently validated a view of the fabliau as a genre which probably originated in courtly circles, but which was intended to amuse audiences from all levels of society.

Ironic contrast and opposition are basic features of the parodic humor centered around the knight. Although I shall not ignore the extent to which the conduct of the knight in the fabliau is at comic variance with his role in epic and romance, I am particularly concerned here with an internal type of contrast. The conduct of a knight, for example, may conflict dramatically with his character as it is depicted in descriptive passages, or exemplary behavior in one section of a story may be negated by crude and vulgar actions in another section. It has been pointed out that such disparities serve as an indicator of irony. In my judgment, these carefully planned changes and contrasts, which may sometimes result in the sudden metamorphosis of a quite courtly tale into a rather ribald fabliau, are indeed the nuclei of the ironic humor in these stories. The skillful use of such technical and structural devices enhances the literary merit of the fabliaux and suggests that their contribution to literature consists of much more than the provision of pleasantly comic diversion.

Such contrasts are most dramatically evident in several of the more obscene tales, in which the grossest of disparities exist in the juxtaposition of courtly ideals and crude reality. In the notoriously obscene *Le Chevalier qui fist parler les cons*, rather delightfully rendered in a recent English translation as

2. Jean Rychner, *Contribution à l'étude des fabliaux*, 2 vols. (Geneva: Droz, 1960).

The Knight Who Conjured Voices,[3] a squire named Hugh attempts to steal the expensive clothing of three maidens bathing in a pool, as part of his plan to obtain the money necessary for his lord's participation in a tournament. He is, however, severely reprimanded by the knight, who insists that such a crime is not at all in keeping with his code of conduct and that it will contribute nothing to his reputation. His language in fact would seem to be that of a person of the highest moral character, one who is fervently devoted to knightly ideals:

> Li chevaliers en ot pesance;
> Des puceles ot grant pitié.
> Lors a le cheval tant coitié
> Que Huet ataint, si li dist;
> "Baille ça tost, se Dieu t'aïst,
> Cez robes, nes enportes mie;
> Ce seroit trop grant vilenie
> De faire à cez puceles honte." (*MR*, VI, 73)
>
> (The knight was quite disturbed and felt great pity for the maidens. He spurred his horse and having caught up with Hugh said to him, "Drop those clothes at once; God help you, don't carry them away. It would be a great crime to put these maidens to shame.")
>
> "Par foi," ce dit li chevaliers,
> "Ge lor reporterai arriers
> Les robes, comment qu'il en praigne:
> Ge n'ai cure de tel gaaigne;
> Ge n'en venrroie ja en pris." (*MR*, VI, 73–74)
>
> ("By my faith," said the knight, "I will take their clothes back to them, whatever the price. I don't care anything for such a prize. My worth as a knight will not be increased by it.")

How typical of the spirit of the fabliaux that this knight who, in magnanimously returning the clothes to their owners,

3. Robert Hellman and Richard O'Gorman, eds. and trans., *Fabliaux: Ribald Tales from the Old French* (New York: Thomas Y. Crowell Company, 1965), pp. 105–21.

should be rewarded with so crude but useful a gift as the ability to conjure voices from the female pudendum.

Moreover, the knight's idealistic protestations to his squire and his obvious embarrassment on acquiring so extraordinary a gift as a result of his kindness to the maidens are soon completely obliterated by his callous and vulgar exploitations of a priest, a servant girl, and the mistress of a château where he has been hospitably received. His own moral fiber appears to have been affected, for he quickly rationalizes his expropriation of the horse and money of the priest, who is frightened out of his wits at the sound of a voice distinctly emanating from the posterior of his donkey. The priest, however, is described as "avers et chiches" and, considering that the priest is usually ridiculed and deceived by all characters in the fabliaux, we might hesitate to question the caliber of the knight's deportment for this reason alone. But he must be rebuked later for obviously enjoying the discomfort of a poor peasant girl upon whom he exercises his magic power and even more so for his determination to make an extremely obscene display of his outrageous powers at the expense of the wife of the gracious lord who has granted him lodging. Although the lady provokes the incident, the knight seems to relish the opportunity to embarrass her. The humor in this antithesis of statement and conduct is compounded when the story ends with the news that this knight will be forever honored by all who know him:

> Que toz li mondes l'ameroit,
> Et fist puis tant con il vesqui. (*MR*, VI, 88–89)

> (Everyone loved him and continued to do so as long as he lived.)

This same fabliau provides us, in the character of the mistress of the castle, with yet another example of this type of humor. She is introduced into the story in a most complimentary fashion:

En cel chastel avoit un conte
Et la contesse avuec, sa feme,
Qui mout ert bele et vaillant dame: (*MR*, VI, 79)

(In this castle lived a count and the countess, his wife, who was a beautiful and noble lady:).

The lady had been attracted immediately to the handsome knight and, having learned of his strange and miraculous power from the previously mentioned servant girl whom she had indeed sent to the knight as a sort of substitute for herself, she challenges him before the assembled court to demonstrate his extraordinary gift:

La contesse parla en haut:
"Seignors," fait el, "se Dieus me salt,
J'ai oï paller chevaliers,
Serganz, borgois et escuiers,
Et aventures aconter,
Mais nus ne se porroit vanter
D'une aventure qu'oi hier,
Qu'il a çaienz un chevalier
Qui tot le mont a sormonté
Quar il a si grant poesté
Qu'il fait à lui le con paller." (*MR*, VI, 84)

(The countess spoke loudly. "Lords," she said, "God save me, I have heard many knights, sergeants, bourgeois, and squires tell of their adventures, but none could ever boast of an adventure such as the one I heard about yesterday—that there is a knight here who triumphs over everyone because he has the power to make cunts speak.")

Again, note the startling mixture of the noble and the base in that this "bele et vaillant dame" now stands before the court and her husband speaking so derisively of a guest and daring to use such low language. Her husband and his knights are not at all disturbed by this boldness on the part of their lady, and she is even encouraged to continue:

Et la contesse reparole,
Qui n'estoit vileine ne fole: (*MR*, VI, 85)

(And the countess, who was neither coarse nor foolish, spoke again:).

What a humorous paradox for the author to insist in one line that the lady is not at all crude or base and then in the next lines to have her openly involve herself personally in a wager that the knight will be unable to demonstrate any such power. Even though she delays temporarily the victory of the knight by a deceit best left unmentioned, he eventually elicits a reply from that normally mute orifice and the countess is forced to pay the wager.

Thus, a knight who speaks idealistically of knightly honor and merit in the first part of the story does not hesitate to take full advantage of the basest of powers in the second section; a countess whom the author insists is noble and elegant acts and speaks like the coarsest of women. These contrasts provide the most pointed humor in the story. The description of the countess as *vaillant et bele* may be passed off by some critics as a mere formulaic device, but it is my contention that such descriptions are frequently a conscious and integral part of a structured intent to produce humor in the fabliaux.

The author of *Le Chevalier qui recovra l'amor de sa dame* dispenses with introductory descriptive comment and launches into a story that we might first mistake for a *lai* or short courtly tale. The knight, pierced by Cupid's arrows, will perform any deed to please his lady, who is—unfortunately—the wife of another. His love for her is expressed in the most courtly terms. He proves himself worthy of his beloved by defeating her husband in a tournament and is granted an interview with her for that same evening. The knight, weary from the long hours of combat, falls asleep while waiting for his lady, and it is this obvious and amusing contrast between his inaction at this crucial moment and his earlier protestations of total love and devoted service to his lady that abruptly shifts the material proper to the courtly tale to the level of the fabliau. From the very moment of this contrast between word and deed, the knight proceeds to regain his lady's favor by employing the sort of ruse that is completely in the tradition of the fabliaux. Pretending to be the spirit of a knight slain in that day's tournament, he rushes into the bedroom where the lady and her husband are sleeping and bemoans the fact that his soul cannot rest until she forgives him for a wrong he has done her. The terrified husband urges his wife to forgive and forget, thus inadvertently becoming a party to his own cuckolding.

This story demonstrates how contrasts between action, word, and description may mark a turning point in certain fabliaux by occurring at the moment at which the level or tone of the story is dramatically shifted. The ruse itself, in this case, though certainly not representative of the highest standards of knightly conduct, has the ironic effect of restoring the lady's faith in her suitor's bravery and devotion.

Le vair Palefroi exhibits all of the characteristics of the short verse romance until a similar contrastive sequence is related. Elaborate preparations have been made for the wedding of Guillaume's beloved to his own treacherous uncle. The finest horses in the land have been chosen for the wedding procession and Guillaume's *palefroi*, reputed to be the most magnificent animal in the country, has been chosen as a mount for the bride. Herein lies the solution to the problem of the unhappy lovers, for the *palefroi* will leave the wedding procession and stray along the secret but often traveled path formerly used by Guillaume on his visits to his beloved. Other preparations are necessary, however, in order to make the bride's disappearance plausible; it is in the description of these circumstances that the level or tone of the story is altered. A huge banquet is held on the eve of the wedding and everyone drinks his fill. Later, the watchman, his mind and vision befogged with drink, mistakes a bright moon for the coming of dawn and awakens everyone. The party of knights sent to escort the lady to the church, being in their cups and drowsy, do not immediately notice the absence of the young woman, thereby allowing time for the *palefroi* to take the lady to Guillaume. The spectacle of the drunken knights and the laughable improbability of a watchman mistaking moonlight for the break of day form effective contrasts to the general tone of the story up to that moment. It is precisely this humorous sequence that permits the denouement to take place and that at the same time allows us to classify *Le vair Palefroi* as a fabliau. Indeed, the author has quite effectively parodied a nuptial custom ordinarily appropriate to the *lai* or *roman*.

A bizarre intermingling of epiclike passages with a description of the problem caused by limited female companionship available to a group of soldier-knights is a source of parody and humor in *Une seule Fame qui a son con servoit .c. chevaliers*. The first ten lines of the tale might well mark the beginning of a *chanson de geste*, but this section is immediately followed by the introduction of the rather comical sociosexual problem of one hundred knights forced to share two women:

> En ung chastel sor mer estoient
> Cent chevalier, qui là manoient,
> Pour aus et le païs desfendre,
> Par que nus ne les pouïst prendre.
> Chascun jor assaut lor livroient
> Sarrazin, qui Deu ne créoient.
> Par acort furent treves mises
> Entre les parties et prises,
> Tant que chascun à lonc sejour
> Retorna et fist son labour.
> Li chastiaux estoit biax et gens,
> Mais assis estoit loing de gens;
> Deux fames entr'ax touz avoient,
> Qui por aus buer les servoient;
> Assez estoient de bel atour.
> Qui plus plus, qui miex, à son tour,
> D'eles faisient lor volenté. (*MR*, I, 294)

(One hundred knights lived in a castle by the sea in order to defend themselves and their country, so that no

> one could take them. Each day they were attacked by the Saracens who did not believe in God. Finally a truce was agreed upon by all parties so that each one finally returned to his own work. The castle was nice, but it was far away from other people. There were only two women to be shared among the 100 knights. They were pretty enough and each knight in turn had his way with them.)

Arguments naturally ensue, but an equitable solution is achieved by dividing the knights into two groups of fifty, each group to be serviced quite willingly by one of the women. No sooner has the problem been solved than the knights are called once more to battle. The description of these knights who have just been bickering over the question of the women's services as "toute la noble compeingnie" definitely seems tongue-in-cheek.

When a wounded knight who is left behind at the castle by his companions during the battle is persuaded by one of the women to kill the other, the writer leads us to believe that the murderer will be appropriately punished when his companions return. They are, however, more enraged by the loss of their concubine and the resulting prospect of sexual deprivation than with the criminal. There is no concern over the murderer's betrayal of the chivalric code of conduct. He is even exonerated of the deed and set free when the surviving woman assures the company that she is quite capable of serving them all. The blending of courtly tale and fabliau noted earlier in *Le Chevalier qui recovra l'amor de sa dame* and *Le vair Palefroi* is thus paralleled in this disparate mixture of epic tone and earthy humor.

The religious pilgrimage even finds its way into the fabliaux in *Le Provost a l'aumuche,* a tale which begins with a dignified description of a knight beloved and respected in his country who wishes to make the journey as an expression of his devotion to God:

> D'un chevalier cis fabliaus conte
> Qui par samblant valoit un conte,

Riches hom estoit et mananz;
Fame ot, dont il avoit enfans
Si come il est coustume et us.
.XX. ans cil chevaliers et plus
Vesqui sans guerre et sans meslée.
Moult fu amez en sa contrée
De ses homes et d'autre gent,
Tant que .I. jor li prist talent
Du baron saint Jaque requerre. (*MR*, I, 112)

(This fabliau tells of a knight who by all appearances was the equal of any count. He was a rich and respected man. He had a wife by whom he had a child, as was the custom. For twenty years this knight lived in peace and was much beloved in his country by his own men and by others until one day he decided to seek out Saint Jacques [to go on a pilgrimage].)

Confiding the care of his estate to his provost, he departs for Saint Jacques. His pilgrimage accomplished, he returns home, to the joy of relatives and friends, and a banquet is prepared in his honor. Up to this point in the tale, there has been nothing in action or tone to indicate or even suggest that we are reading a fabliau. The banquet scene, however, presents a definite contrast to the first part of the story in that its rapid shift in tone lends an almost farcical conclusion to the piece. As a consequence of the knight's ceasing to be the focal point of the story, our attention is shifted to the provost, a greedy and scheming knave who accidentally at table drops a huge piece of meat that he had concealed in his fur cap (*aumuche*) into the lap of a knight seated near him. Then, attempting to flee the room, he is deliberately tripped by a squire, beaten, ejected, and thrown into a ditch:

Uns vallés devant lui servoit:
Anuiéz fu, trop li grevoit
S'aumuche qui estoit forrée;
D'une verge, qui ert pelée,
Li a jus bouté le chapel,
Et li lars chiet sor le mantel

Au chevalier qui lèz lui sist.
Or oiez que li provos fist:
.I. saut done par mi le fu,
Vers l'uis se tret à grant vertu;
Mès li escuier qui servoient,
Qui l'afère véu avoient,
Li donèrent grant hatiplat,
Si qu'il le firent chéoir plat;
Fièrent en teste et en l'eschine;
Li keu saillent de la cuisine,
Ne demandèrent que ce fu,
Ainz traient les tisons du fu,
Si fièrent sor lui à .I. tas;
Tant le fièrent et haut et bas,
Que brisiés li ont les rains.
Aus bastons, aus piez et aus mains,
Li ont fet plus de .XXX. plaies,
Et l'ont fait chier en ses braies.
A la parfin tant le menèrent,
Que par les bras le traïnèrent
Fors de la porte en .I. fossé . . . (*MR*, I, 115–16)

(A servant boy who was serving in front of him [the *prévost*] was bothered by the fur cap. Taking a stick, he pushed the cap aside and the meat fell out on the coat of the knight seated next to him. Now listen to what the *prévost* did. He jumps up as if he were in the middle of a fire and retreats toward the door. But the squires who were serving and who had seen the entire affair gave him such a great smack that he fell flat on the floor. They beat him on the head and the back. The cooks who came running out of the kitchen to ask what was going on grabbed pieces of wood and they all began to beat him at once. So hard did they beat him, both high and low, that they hurt him badly with the sticks, their hands and their feet. There were more than thirty wounds on his body and they made him shit in his pants. Finally they dragged him out by the arms and threw him into a ditch . . .).

This slapstick routine is in complete contrast to the loftier tone established at the beginning of the story. Once more it seems obvious that the background of knightly pilgrimage upon which this farcical element is imposed provides exactly the comic disparity typical of the fabliau.

One could justifiably assume that illustrious knights such as Yvain, Kay, Ydier, and Gawain would be blessed with loving and faithful wives and sweethearts. The contrast between such an assumption and the reality of mass unfaithfulness revealed in *Le Mantel mautaillié* provides a basis for humorous contrast in that tale. Each knight believes that the magic mantle will fit his beloved perfectly (an ill fit indicates lack of constancy), and each in turn is embarrassed as he is proved wrong. The protestations of each knight in support of his lady's virtue serve only to underline or dramatize the lady's misconduct and thereby to increase the comic effect as the mantle is passed from one to the other.

Kay (*Kex*) is the most boastful and self-assured of all:

> Kex en a apelé s'amie:
> "Damoisele, venez avant;
> Oiant ces chevaliers, me vant
> Que vous estes leaus par tout,
> Que je sai bien sanz nul redout
> Vous le poez bien afubler;
> N'i aurez compaingne ne per
> De leauté ne de valor.
> Vous en porterez hui l'onor
> De ceenz sanz nul contredit." (*MR*, III, 14)

> (Kay calls on his sweetheart: "Lady, come forward. Hearing these knights, I boast that you are the most loyal of all and that I have no doubt that the cloak will fit you perfectly. You will have no peer in loyalty or worth. You will be honored above the others without any objection.")

How comic his boasts appear when the lady tries on the garment:

> Et la damoisele le prent;
> Voiant les barons, l'afubla
> Et li mantiaus plus acorça
> Aus jarès et noiant avant,

Et li dui acor de devant
Ne porent les genouz passer. (*MR*, III, 15)

(And the lady takes it; seeing the assembled knights, she put it on and the coat came up to the back of her knees behind and hung down in front.)

As to Yvain, the author enumerates the knight's best qualities and refers to his noble parentage, all in preparation for his humiliation:

Li Rois prist par la destre main
L'amie mon seignor Yvain
Qui au roi Urien fu fil,
Le preu chevalier, le gentil,
Qui tant ama chiens et oisiaus. (*MR*, III, 17)

(The King took the sweetheart of Yvain, son of King Urien, by the right hand, that courageous and noble knight who loved dogs and birds so much.)

Similar adjectives are employed in the introduction of the *amie* of Gawain:

L'amie mon seignor Gavain,
Venelaus la preus, la cortoise . . . (*MR*, III, 16)

(The beloved of Gawain, the noble and courtly Venelaus . . .).

In both instances the comic effect is achieved by the humiliation that accompanies the obvious ill fit of the mantle on each of the ladies.

The supreme irony is reached at the end of the story when a faithful *amie* is finally discovered. In his choice of the less well known Karados Brisebras as lord of the most virtuous lady, the author achieves the final comic contrast in the story, for in so doing the champion knights whose mistresses are faithless receive their final and most disturbing humiliation.

The knight is of course an excellent target for this type of contrasting humor or irony, for he can be brought down from greater heights than the bourgeois, priest, or peasant. When the knights involved are the fabled heroes of courtly romance, the effect is naturally enhanced.

The most obvious contrast of descriptive material and a knight's subsequent treatment in a story is found in *Les Tresces*. The first fourteen lines of this fabliau provide a detailed enumeration of the virtues of the knight:

> Jadis avint c'uns chevaliers,
> Preuz et cortois et beaus parliers,
> Ert saiges et bien entèchiez:
> S'ert si en proesce affichiez
> C'onques de riens ne se volt faindre
> En place où il pooist ateindre;
> Et par tot si bien le faisoit,
> Et à toz sis erres plaisoit,
> Tant qu'il fu de si grant renom,
> Qu'en ne parloit se de lui non.
> Et s'en li ot sen et proesce:
> Il ert de si haute largece,
> Quant il avoit le heaume osté,
> Preuz ert au champ et à l'osté. (*MR*, IV, 67)
>
> (There was once a courageous and courtly knight who spoke elegantly and who was both wise and moral. He was so brave that he never hesitated in attempting anything. Everything he did was done so well and he acquired such renown that his people were always talking about his deeds. He possessed both wisdom and courage. When he was not fighting, he was well known for his generosity. He was valiant both in battle and at home.)

In the lines immediately following, however, we learn that his unfaithful wife prefers a knight from the neighboring countryside to her own paragon of virtue. Is the author soliciting sympathy for the husband in his extremely complimentary description? I think not. This story is just one more illustration of that obvious shift in tone we have shown to be typical of stories about the knight. If the author had intended to make the husband the hero, as his description might indicate, we should then expect his eventual triumph over wife and lover.

Such is not the case, however, for the lady's elaborate ruse succeeds in so confusing the poor man that he is deceived into believing that all the events occurred in a dream and that his wife's misconduct is only imaginary. How amusing the first fourteen lines become, then, in light of the subsequent treatment of the knight in the story!

The description of the knight in *Le Prestre et le chevalier* is also rather inappropriate when we consider his attitudes and actions in the tale:

> A l'entrée .I. homme encontra
> Qui li dist: "Sire, bien viengniés,
> Comme preus et bien afaitiés." (*MR*, II, 49)

> (At the gate he met a man who said to him: "Welcome, courageous and noble knight.")

> . . . Li chevaliers, simples et dous,
> Qui le cors ot plaisant et gent . . . (*MR*, II, 50)

> (. . . The knight, modest and gentle, who had a pleasing and handsome body . . .).

Actually, the positive qualities assigned the knight in this story serve a dual purpose in that they not only supply a humorous contrast to the knight's own actions, but at the same time they also set in motion the opposition or conflict between knight and priest which comprises the central theme of the story. The adjectives *riche, manant,* and *asasé* used in describing the wealth of the priest further underline this opposition.

The conniving knight requests the hospitality of the wealthy priest, intending to take advantage of him. The priest at first refuses but then relents when he believes the penniless knight to be worth a great deal of money, some of which he would like to transfer to his own pockets. A covenant or agreement is reached whereby the knight will be charged what appears to be a reasonable sum for each item he uses and in return he may request anything he desires. The great fuss made over the sacredness of the covenant and the question of honor involved in upholding it provides a most ironic contrast to the manner in which the agreement is exploited by the knight. In exercising his right to request anything he desires, the tricky and lecherous knight not only demands the companionship of both the mistress and the virgin niece of the priest, but he also manages to extort a goodly sum of money as compensation for not violating the priest himself.

There are several fabliaux in which the humor is based on a character's manifestation of moral qualities totally incongruous with the knightly ideals of *courtoisie* and *prouesse* and with the noble role of the knight in other literary genres. The comic effect in these tales is more external than in those fabliaux previously treated, in that we are not specifically involved with contrasts and oppositions within the text itself but with a comparison of internal action or description with an external ideal—the preestablished knightly code of conduct.

The gulf between this ideal and the reality within the tale is widest in the two versions of *Berangier au lonc cul*, for the knight dealt with here is actually a *vilain* who was dubbed only in order to make feasible his marriage to the daughter of a knight. He is completely lacking in those noble qualities expected of the *chevalier*, thus his violation of the code of knightly idealism is all the more blatantly comic. Faced with a lengthy enumeration of the high qualities of the noble ancestors of his wife, he boasts that he is a knight without equal:

> Ge sui chevalier sanz perece,
> Le meillor trestot par ma mein;
> Dame, vos le verroiz demain.
> Se mes ennemis puis trouver,
> Demain me vorrai esprouver. (*MR*, III, 254)

> (I am a knight without equal, the best anywhere. Lady, if I can find my enemies you will see me prove myself tomorrow.)

This is by no means the sole example of his boastfulness in Guerin's version of the tale, but it is the anonymous second treatment of the theme that emphatically stresses this aspect of his character. This weakness serves only to underline comically the knight's complete failure and inadequacy in fulfilling the duties and obligations of his position. His armor, sardonically described by the author as "beles, fresches, et noveles" bears no scars from having been previously worn in knightly combat, and his comic and humiliating reaction when faced with the possibility of such a conflict (he elects to kiss his opponent's behind rather than to meet him in combat) labels him as a coward, the most shameful of all appellations for the knight. Since this character is not a knight by birth, perhaps the humor here derives from the satire of a society in which knighthood might be bestowed on a wealthy bourgeois as a means of financial reprieve for impoverished nobles.

There are five additional fabliaux in which laughter is provoked as a result of flagrant violations of the knight's pre-established proper image: *La Dame qui se venja du chevalier, La Dame escoillée, La Houce partie, Celle qui se fist foutre,* and *Le sot Chevalier.* In each of these fabliaux, a knight is endowed with exactly the opposite of the usual knightly virtues; that is, he reveals in turn fear, a weak will, avarice, vulgarity, and stupidity. In *La Dame qui se venja du chevalier,* a knight who is hiding in his mistress's bed trembles with fear and his teeth chatter uncontrollably as the prospect of discovery by the returning husband increases; the wealthy knight of *La Dame escoillée* places himself in a humiliating position by handing over all authority to his wife and thus becoming a "henpecked" husband; the idea in *La Houce partie* of a knight greedily evaluating the property of a prospective bourgeois bridegroom for his daughter is in comic contrast to the concept of the knight as typically generous and charitable; the voyeur knight of *Celle qui se fist foutre,* feigning shock at his squire's proposal, nevertheless wagers that the squire will be unable to seduce a widow prostrate in grief on the grave of her recently deceased husband and observes all that transpires from the shelter of a nearby tree; finally, *Le sot Chevalier* is a stupid and rather demented knight, recently married and appallingly ignorant of the female anatomy, who must take lessons in sexual matters from his mother-in-law.

It would not be necessary for an audience to be well versed in epic and romance in order to appreciate the comedy in such opposition, for the ridiculing of those in high position is an enduring comic device. Indeed, ironic contrast is at the root of the humor in these five fabliaux.

In summary, since the fabliaux are basically *contes à rire,* the knight and his world as they are depicted in the genre must in some way serve as instruments of the humor characteristic of these tales. I have shown that contrast and opposition are techniques employed by the writers of fabliaux in order to achieve that end. An introductory laudatory description of a knight may be in ironic contrast to his later behavior; high-principled conduct in one instance may be humorously opposed by contemptible deportment on another occasion; abrupt shifts in tone quickly remove us from the atmosphere of the epic or courtly romance to the world of the fabliaux; finally, the knight frequently violates that high standard of conduct cultivated in both epic and romance and therefore expected of one in his position. These features of parodic antiphrastic humor are an essential ingredient of the fabliaux and are basic to their structural design.

VI

HOWARD HELSINGER

PEARLS IN THE SWILL COMIC ALLEGORY IN THE FRENCH FABLIAUX*

Parody is a mode of ridicule usually more comic than moral. In the fabliaux, the parody, to which Nykrog has drawn our attention, of such familiar romance motifs as fairy fountains, Love's arrow, or the elaborate language of *amour courtois* tends generally to confirm our sense of the fabliau as a broadly comic genre free from all but a rough retributive morality.[1] But some fabliaux parody profounder areas of style: the images and methods of allegory by which so much medieval literature conveys its somber moral. The *fableor* tricks out allegory's subtle silences and hidden meanings in the loud colors of obvious rhetoric until they seem no more respectable than the proverbial drunken deacon. But because the essence of allegory is not silence, but cunning, not the covert, but the double statement, such blatant allegory need lose no moral force. The thirteenth-century fableor can respect the moral while mocking the method. For his audience, the unflagging pleasure of discovering the obscure is replaced by the comic realization that they have missed the obvious. The fabliau thus provides an occasion on which the conteur can "let it

*A version of this paper was read at the Sixth Conference on Medieval Studies at Western Michigan University, May 18, 1971.

1. Per Nykrog, *Les Fabliaux: Etude d'histoire littéraire et de stylistique médiévale* (Copenhagen: Ejnar Munksgaard, 1957), pp. 70–79. For an instance of parody comparable to that discussed in this paper, see D. D. R. Owen, "The Element of Parody in *Saint Pierre et le jongleur*," *French Studies*, 9 (1955), 60–63.

all hang out." Though rhetorical training encouraged him to withhold wisdom from the swine, we should not be surprised if he mixes pearls in the swill. As camouflage, after all, it is most effective.

Consider Jean Bodel's simple tale of *Brunain, la vache au prestre* (*MR*, I, 132). The humor of the tale derives from the peasants' foolishly literal understanding of the priest's sermon, for the priest had said that those who give from the heart receive double in return. Taking his words seriously, they naively respond by giving the priest their cow, Blerain. Their motive is not charity, but raw greed, and with worldly practicality they note that she yields, after all, little milk. However comic their action, however simpleminded their response, we may remember that such literal-mindedness is not only foolish, but also, according to Saint Paul, fatal (2 Cor. 3:6). In the tale of *Brunain*, however, the letter does not kill; it instead nourishes, for the peasants' cow Blerain returns home, bringing the priest's cow Brunain with her. The priest is the butt of the tale, but in his loss there is no comedy. The humor of this fabliau derives from its contradiction of the Pauline precept or, more simply, from the unexpected success of literal-mindedness. It is as if Jean Bodel were mocking the allegorist's traditional impulse to scorn the letter.

Dragged through town and country by Blerain, to whom she is yoked, even Brunain, the priest's cow, is an object of laughter. Like Brunain, allegory may originally have been the property of the clergy, but it too was no sacred cow. Secular poets milked it for what it was worth, and the jongleurs in their fabliaux skinned it and turned it inside out.

Allegory turned inside out effectively ceases to be allegory. What was hidden becomes manifest, what was figurative becomes literal, and in the fabliaux that eversion or inversion becomes a source of humor. The most familiar instance is probably Henri d'Andeli's *Lai d'Aristote* (*MR*, V, 243–62). The relationship of man and woman had long been compared to that of a rider controlling a willful horse. The *Lai,* in which the philosopher submits to being bridled and ridden by the damsel for whom he lusts, gives literal form to the traditional figure, but inverts the accepted order of the sexes to reveal the lustful wise man in the role of the bridled horse. The blatancy with which figure is here made fact and the obviousness of the moral are, like the *Lai*'s base matter, in satiric counterpoint to its courtly style. From such discords flows much of its humor.

A less familiar figure is made literal in the tale of *Les Perdriz* (*MR,* I, 188–93), in which, as in the *Lai d'Aristote,* the eversion reveals the effeminizing and bestializing consequences of lust. The incontinent wife of a peasant devours some partridges her husband was about to share at table with the village priest. Inventing a ruse to cover her gluttonous self-indulgence, she sends her husband into the yard to sharpen his carving knife. When the priest, obviously her lover, arrives, she warns him that her husband is preparing to castrate him. As the guilt-ridden cleric flees in fear, the wife cries out that he is carrying off the birds. Her husband, knife in hand, takes off in pursuit, crying out to the priest's dismay, "You won't get away with them like that. You're carrying them all hot, but you'll leave them here if I catch you."[2]

The ostensible moral drawn for us is that women are made to deceive, but it clearly neglects the focus of the tale. Morals too are often made to deceive. This tale is about lecherous men and a gluttonous woman, and partridges, we are meant to bear in mind, were notoriously lecherous birds. According to the bestiary, "frequent intercourse tires them out."[3] Even more appropriate, in light of the dissension sown in the tale

2. I have used the translation of Robert Hellman and Richard O'Gorman, eds. and trans., *Fabliaux: Ribald Tales from the Old French* (New York: Thomas Y. Crowell Company, 1965), p. 125.

3. T. H. White, *The Bestiary* (New York: Capricorn Books, 1960), p. 137.

by Eve's daughter, is the bestiary's report that male partridges "fight each other for their mate, and it is believed that the conquered male submits to venery like a female."[4] In this beast fable in reverse the peasant and the priest clearly resemble two lecherous birds fighting over a hen. In fearing castration the priest apparently anticipates that, like the vanquished partridge, he will be unmanned. But according to the terms of traditional allegory his unchaste life has already rendered him a spiritual eunuch.[5] When, at the climax of the tale, we laugh at his misinterpretation of the husband's threat, we should be responding not only to bawdy error, but to the clear truth that bawdy error reveals—how comically right that the figuratively sterile should fear literal castration.

This explication may seem excessively subtle for a simple tale, but only, I think, because for us allegory is hard and unnatural. If, however, courtly literature was allegorical—perhaps more frequently allegorical than scholars have as yet acknowledged—then in the fabliau, which Nykrog terms the burlesque caricature of a sublime genre,[6] we should not be surprised to find burlesque forms of allegory. The tale of *Les Perdriz is* a simple tale, and the wiles of a gluttonous woman and the misapprehensions of a fearful priest *are* the sources of its humor. We only deepen—but not muddy—those sources if we recognize that the people in the tale are acting like the birds in the title and that the brandished knife threatens to bring the priest's physical nature into accord with his spiritual state.

Sexual transgressions by the priesthood are of course a common subject of the fabliaux, but the frequency of that accusation is not a literary distortion; the incontinence of priests,

4. Ibid.

5. *Glossa ordinaria,* Migne, *PL,* cxiv, col. 148, cited in Robert P. Miller, "Chaucer's Pardoner, The Scriptural Eunuch, and *The Pardoner's Tale,*" *Speculum,* 30 (1955), 180–99; rpt. in Richard J. Schoeck and Jerome Taylor, eds., *Chaucer Criticism: The Canterbury Tales* (Notre Dame, Ind.: University of Notre Dame Press, 1960), p. 226.

6. Nykrog, *Les Fabliaux,* p. 70.

for example, was one of the most common complaints registered by Eudes Rigaud, Archbishop of Rouen, during his diocesan visitations.[7] The Archbishop treated the offenses seriously, and so, despite his use of gross comedy, did the contemporary jongleur. In the tale *Le Prestre et le leu* (*MR*, VI, 51), the peasant who has dug a pit for the wolf that is preying on his flock finds that he has also caught the priest who is his wife's lover. In its account of the villain's chastisements the conclusion of the tale constructs obvious rhetorical balances:

> A ceus avint grant meschaance,
> Et au vilein bele chaance.
> Li prestres honte li fesoit;
> Li leu ses bestes estrangloit;
> Chascun d'eus acheta mout chier,
> Cil son deduit, cil son mengier. (*MR*, VI, 52)

That is, freely translated:

> Both of them came off badly
> And the peasant, very gladly.
> The priest had dallied with his wife,
> The wolf taken his cattle's life.
> Each of them paid like a sinner,
> One for his pleasure, one for his dinner.

Such amusing rhetoric seriously asks us to recognize beast and priest as analogous predators upon the innocent. But the tale really is not very funny. One cut below the Punch and Judy of most fabliaux, it affords us only the pleasure of seeing sanctimonious deceit cruelly revealed and chastised. If there is any finer humor in the tale, it is again in the rapprochement of figure and fact. The sinful pastor is literally caught in the same trap as the beast from which, figuratively, he should be protecting his flock.

7. Sydney M. Brown, trans., and Jeremiah F. O'Sullivan, ed., *The Register of Eudes of Rouen* (New York: Columbia University Press, 1964). In the twenty-one years from 1248–1269, hardly a month passed without Eudes noting of some priest that he was "famed of incontinence." The customary punishment was deprivation of his benefice.

After we have responded to the comedy of its gross action (Aristotle's embarrassing posture, for example), each of these tales requires that we recognize in it the further humor of figurative commonplace embodied (the rational man as rider of the willful feminine horse). The figure may be inverted, as in the *Lai d'Aristote* or *Le Prestre et le leu*; the figure may also be embodied more or less directly, as in *Brunain* or *Les Perdriz*. What matters in our response is our perception of the dead bones of allegory forced back into living flesh. Relatively simple tales such as we have considered so far may focus on the embodiment of a single figure; in the more complex tales to which we now turn the elements of comic allegory may be subordinate or incidental parts of the narrative.

The figure of priest as shepherd, older than the Church, was commonplace in the thirteenth century. Robert Mannyng's version of William of Waddington's *Manuel des Peches* carefully explained that, "As þe gode shepard kepyþ hys shepe / So shalle þe prest, hys parysshenes kepe."[8] Given the tendency of fabliaux to make commonplace figures into literal facts, we should not be surprised that in Eustace d'Amiens's tale of *Le Bouchier d'Abeville* (*MR*, III, 227–46) the bad priest is also a negligent shepherd. From the moment we hear of him the familiar accusations against the priesthood begin to accumulate. "There is no wine in this town," explains a woman to the butcher who is seeking shelter on his way home from market, "except at the house of our priest, Gautier, who has two barrels in his cellar which he got at Noientel. He's always well stocked in wine."[9] We are told that the priest is proud, but that the butcher is a good man ("sages, cortois et vaillanz / Et loiaus hom de son mestier") who was not

8. Robert Mannyng of Brunne, *Handlyng Synne*, ed. Frederick J. Furnivall, The Early English Text Society, O.S. 123 (London: Kegan Paul, 1903), p. 338, ll. 10895–10896.

9. Quotations in English are from Hellman and O'Gorman, *Fabliaux*, pp. 31–44.

stingy when his poor neighbors were in need. He asks the priest for shelter "par charite," but that niggling literalist replies that "no man not in orders may sleep in this house." Insults fly until, with an ironic invocation of the celestial gatekeeper, the angry priest concludes the argument: "By Saint Peter, you'll never lodge in my house." Scene set and characters introduced, the tale proper is ready to begin.

On his way out of town the butcher comes upon a flock of sheep "in front of a ruined house with a fallen roof." The sheep, says the shepherd, belong to the priest. We are dealing, in the most obvious of allegorical terms, with that most common of clerical abuses, a nonresident pastor. The spiritual costs to the Church of that nonresidence are here revealed by the dilapidated barn for, as Johannes Bromyard suggested toward the end of the fourteenth century, "Ruin in ecclesiastical houses signifies the absence of God."[10]

Given this opportunity, the good butcher assumes the role of divine scourge. He steals a sheep, returns to the priest, and offers to barter good mutton for a night's lodging. The priest's joyous acceptance blatantly mocks Christ's parable (Matt. 18:13), for we are told the priest preferred one dead sheep to four living. Corrupt priests who in like manner devour their flocks were repeatedly denounced by the Old Testament prophets. "Woe unto the shepherds of Israel, that have fed themselves," says Ezekiel (34:2–3), "Ye did eat the fat, and ye clothed you with the wool, ye killed the fatlings; but ye fed not the sheep." The Lord's promise to punish His people through such cruel and self-serving pastors (Zach. 11:15) was understood by medieval commentators as a threatening reference to the coming of Antichrist.[11] The destruction of such

10. Cited in C. R. Owst, *Literature and Pulpit in Medieval England*, 2d ed. (New York: Barnes & Noble, Inc., 1961), p. 263.

11. Cf. *The Lanterne of Liȝt*, ed. Lilian M. Swinburn, The Early English Text Society, O.S. 151 (London: Kegan Paul, 1917), p. 15. Commenting on the Lord's words to Zacharia, "Adhuc sume tibi vasa

evil was said by Jeremiah (23:1–5) to await the promised off-spring of David.

David, in fact, is the butcher's name, and when he appears before the priest's door with the sheep slung over his shoulder, he must look very much like the conventional image of the Good Shepherd.[12] This irreverent apparition may remind us that a good butcher is a bad shepherd; it should also reveal as a bad shepherd in a profounder spiritual sense the priest who welcomes him. Of either a sardonic moralist might mutter, "He doesn't feed his sheep, he's feeding on them. Instead of considering the miseries of the young or ailing in his flock he's busy estimating the quality of their milk and fleece. That's how he returns with the lost lamb on his shoulders." Those accusatory words are not my invention, but are from the late twelfth-century "Apocalypse of Bishop Golias," attributed to Walter Mapes:

> . . . non pastor ovium sed pastus ovibus.
> Non tantum cogitat ille de miseris,
> de claudis ovibus, aegris vel teneris,
> quantum de compoto lactis et velleris;
> sic ovem perditam refert in humeris.[13]

The appropriateness of these lines to *Le Bouchier d'Abeville* suggests a close connection between the literal details of the fabliaux and the allegorical commonplaces of anticlerical satire. As the apparition of the Good Shepherd reveals, these allegories may have been used irreverently, but not irrelevantly.

---

pastoris stulti. Quia ecce ego suscitabo pastorem in terra, qui derelicta non visitabit . . ." (Zach. 11:15), *The Lanterne of Liȝt* says, "Þat is to seie . . . I schal suffre antichrist to be rerid vp in lond. Þe which shal not visite hem þat ben forsaken . . .".

12. The early-Christian image of the Good Shepherd had disappeared from the iconography of the high Middle Ages, and was not revived until the Renaissance, but as Walter Mapes (note 13) makes clear, the image was not unknown in the twelfth century.

13. Walter Mapes, *Poems*, ed. Thomas Wright, Camden Society, 19 (London: John Bowyer Nichols and Son, 1861), p. 8, ll. 132–136.

After dining on the lamb the priest retires for the night with his mistress; the resourceful butcher, by promising her the sheepskin, finds company with the serving girl. Lecherous priests being commonplace in the fabliaux, there is nothing remarkable here in the priest's possession of a concubine. It is noteworthy, however, that early the next morning the priest rises to say Mass. Although Pope Urban II had carefully explained that the Masses of married men were not invalid,[14] popular literature judged such celebrations tainted and made them a constant cause of complaint. Walter Mapes, for example, claims that few are as sinful as those who go from a carnal bed to the celebration of the body of Christ:

> O sacerdos, haec responde,
> qui frequenter et jocunde
> cum uxore dormis, unde
> Mane surgens, missam dicis,
> Corpus Christi benedicis,
> post amplexus meretricis,
> minus quam tu peccatricis.[15]

William of Waddington's *Manuel des Peches* and Robert of Brunne's *Handlyng Synne* repeated the assertion:

> Also a preste þat goþ, syngeþ hys messe,
> Þat yn dedly synne ys,
> An hunder folde he synneþ more
> Þan ȝyf he a lewed man wore.[16]

Thomas Brunton of Rochester tells of a priest who was afraid to say Mass "because he had been sleeping that same night with his concubine,"[17] and *The Lanterne of Liȝt* attributes to Saint Augustine the idea that "He þat is on þe nyȝt the louer of leccherie / & in þ morne a sacrar. of þe maidenes sone /

14. See C.N.L. Brooke, "Gregorian Reform in Action: Clerical Marriage in England, 1050–1200," in *Change in Medieval Society*, ed. Sylvia Thrupp (New York: Appleton-Century-Crofts, 1964), p. 52.
15. "Versus de sacerdotibus," in *Poems*, p. 49.
16. *Handlyng Synne*, p. 316, ll. 10147–10150.
17. Cited in Owst, *Literature and Pulpit*, p. 247.

God turneþ away hise eeris from suche mennes preiours."[18] The fabliau makes no such explicit condemnation of the priest's action, but its matter-of-fact account of his celebration of the Mass invites judgment by such standards. In a manner common to satire, the disparity of subject and style generates both indignation and comedy.

The corruption of the Mass by sinful priests is more pointedly the subject of what follows. While the priest is gone, the butcher, in a parody of courtly seduction, enjoys the amorous favors of the priest's concubine by promising her the sheepskin. Those pleasures past, he hurries to the chapel where the priest, just come to the "Jube Domine," interrupts the Mass to salute his true Lord, the devilish butcher come to sell his sheepskin for the third time. The "Jube Domine" is a prayer for a blessing, to which the butcher's offer is a markedly ironic response. Since priests were not supposed to interrupt the service, since laymen were not supposed to intrude, and since the priest ought not to have been in a state of sin, his service is clearly tainted.[19] Despite the serious consequences of these priestly derelictions, the episode itself is clearly comic. Understatement invites us to overlook the corruption and then provokes in reaction both amusement and indignation.

The possibility of moral judgment of the story's action corresponds to the possibility of allegorical interpretation of such incidental details as the dilapidated sheepcote, the butcher named David, and the interruption of the Mass at the "Jube Domine." Both serious moral and allegory seem incompatible with the surface triviality usually thought to be characteristic of these tales. The immoralities are so gross, the allegories so open, we are apt to overlook them, but their very incongruity

18. *The Lanterne of Ligt*, p. 60.

19. Aemilius Friedberg, ed., *Corpus Juris Canonici* (Leipzig: Tauchnitz, 1879), III, dist. ii, c.xxx, "Quando celebratur missa, presbyterium laicus ingredi non praesumat"; and I, dist. xxxii, c.vi, "Non est audienda missa presbiteri, qui concubinam habet," which reads in part "Missam non cantat, nec evangelium legat nec epistolam ad missam."

is the source of a significant vein of humor whose object is not character or situation, but style. We laugh at both the unlikely or inverted allegory and at our initial failure to perceive it. With that perception we also discover our near escape from, and sudden return to, the world of moral judgment—a discovery that is itself a further source of delight.

Such readings of fabliaux as we have presented assume the fableor's familiarity with the devices of allegory and his willingness to subject them to parody. That assumption, compatible with what little we can learn of these poets, gains particular confirmation from the tale of *Le povre Clerc* (*MR*, V, 192–200), for there the clerk of the title is just such an exploiter of the comedy of obvious allegory. Having dropped out of the university for financial reasons, this wandering scholar seeks shelter for the night at the home of a peasant, but he is rebuffed by the surly lady of the house. On his way out he passes a priest, who receives a good welcome from the lady. In the street once more, the outcast laments his plight; he is overheard by the peasant himself, who, returning home, brings the poor clerk with him. The peasant instructs his wife to prepare dinner, but she, anxious to relieve the distress of the priest, whom she has hid in the cupboard, says there is no food. The peasant tells her to do what she can, and while they wait for their meal he asks the clerk to tell some tale to pass the time. As Jean le Chapelain explains at the beginning of *Le Soucretain* (*MR*, VI, 117), it was the custom in Normandy (and presumably elsewhere) for a guest to tell a fabliau or to sing a song. Our poor clerk has to apologize, therefore, that he knows no fabliau, but he will recount a fearful adventure he has had. His host finds the substitution acceptable, because he knows that the clerk is not a fableor. These disingenuous warnings that what we are about to hear is not a fabliau serve to alert us.

Earlier that day, the clerk begins, he had passed an unguarded herd of pigs and had seen a wolf carry off one as fat as the piece of pork in the kitchen. "What!" exclaims the peasant. "Is there pork in the kitchen? Wife, why didn't you say so?"

When the wolf tore into the pig, the clerk goes on, the blood that dripped from his jaws was as red as the wine brought into the house when first he came seeking lodging. "What!" cries the peasant. "Is there wine? How fortunate!"

He found a large stone, continues the clerk, with which to strike the wolf, but the cake in the kitchen is even larger. "What's this, wife? Do we have cake?" For the third time she reluctantly admits the clerk's statement is true, and the husband rejoices in the fortunate effects of the tale.

But the tale is not quite finished. When he picked up the rock, the clerk explains, the wolf looked at him just as the priest is looking at him now through the holes in the cupboard door. The priest is discovered, and the clerk is rewarded with the priest's cloak and hood.

This clerk's tale efficiently and pleasantly reveals the truth, for neither we nor the peasant are tempted to take it literally. Although we may call it clever, it is really a directly obvious narrative whose humor stems from its disingenuous innocence. We may wisely refrain from calling it allegory, since it is so obvious, but like allegory it reveals multiple truths. On the simplest level (*quid credas*), the tale corrects the wife's assertion that there is no food in the house, a practical lesson as mundane as the morals usually appended to the fabliaux.

But like the other fabliaux we have examined, the clerk's tale suggests, by a parodic use of traditional imagery, a profounder allegory. The abandoned herd of pigs suggests the effects of pastoral negligence upon the priest's flock and the blood resembling wine and the stone resembling cake call to mind the corruption of the sacraments. His final image of the sequestered priest with wolfish look suggests the common accusation that priests preyed on their flock.

The poor clerk lacks the narrative skill of Eustace d'Amiens or even that of his own anonymous creator; he is, in effect, a parody of the fableor. Like his artistic betters he makes allegorical commonplace seem funny by making it seem obvious. Like them he works with obvious protreptic intent. Indeed, he so clearly means to reveal the food in the kitchen that we may take this as his sole intent and neglect the allegorical sense of his words. We are likely to be similarly restrictive in our response to other fabliaux, neglecting the possibility of both moral and allegorical levels.

It has always been obvious that in some sense the fabliaux are moral—upon those persons they scorn they enact a crude and Draconian justice. But when the execution becomes entertainment, justice gets lost in spectacle, and that seems to be what happens in the fabliaux. David, the butcher of Abeville, is so clever we may forget the moral direction of his acts, although it is because his acts are moral—intended as punishment of the corrupt—that we can enjoy them without guilt. The fableor's parodic use of allegorical commonplace, by reminding us of levels of meaning beyond the literal, works to restore entertaining spectacle to a moral context.

VII

NORRIS J. LACY

TYPES OF ESTHETIC DISTANCE IN THE FABLIAUX

Although simple in narrative development, the fabliaux utilize a variety of comic techniques to produce humor ranging from the simple to the sophisticated, from the ribald to the refined. Some fabliaux develop a comedy of language, others a comedy of character or of manners. Despite the variety observable in the range of fabliaux, the humor consistently depends on the poet's establishment of esthetic distance, of the distance separating art from reality. In fact, to the extent that a fabliau is a *conte à rire*,[1] it seems to me that distance is an essential characteristic of the genre. My reasons are easily apparent: The author of a serious moral tale wants his reader to understand it literally, to identify with the proper characters, and to draw moral conclusions and parallels; esthetic distance is thus inimical to his purposes. In most fabliaux, by contrast, the author must deliberately avoid reader identification. The subjects of the fabliaux frequently center on cruelty, deceit, infidelity, and violence. It is thus essential that we remain constantly aware of the fictitiousness of the story; "identification" would destroy the intended comic effect. Although certain authors may go to some lengths to show, for example, the cuckold as an old, avaricious, and cruel person who richly deserves the treatment he gets (thereby excluding identification and sympathy), such techniques are generally unnecessary. Authors of the better fabliaux manage to create this

1. See Joseph Bédier, *Les Fabliaux: études de littérature populaire et d'histoire littéraire du moyen âge*, 5th ed. (Paris: Champion, 1925), p. 30.

distance by more economical means, but the purpose is the same: to make us view the work with detachment, free to concentrate on the story itself and its humor. It is no revelation that a genre which is defined in terms of its comic intent should exploit esthetic distance.[2] Of particular interest here are the *types* of distance established and the variety of techniques used to produce it.

* * *

A consideration which is closely related to the matter of distance is the reader's conventional expectations, that is, the expectations which are aroused by the reader's consciousness of genre. In the criticism of medieval literature, a great deal of attention has been given to the definition of genres, but not so much to the effects of generic consciousness on the medieval mind. As Wayne Booth points out, "When I begin what I think is a novel, I expect to read a novel throughout."[3] A work that is called a novel or that appears to be one presents difficulties of interpretation and especially of reader reaction if it does not correspond to traditional expectations, to traditional ideas of what a novel should be.

Most genres carry certain rhetorical cues that identify works as being of a particular kind. In most instances, these cues are complex, and only a certain number of them may be realized in any single work. In the simplest cases, however, they are brief formulas, of the "once upon a time . . ." variety. The fabliaux are frequently begun by stock introductions, in which the poet gives the reader the necessary cue by referring to his intention to relate a fabliau:

2. In this essay I am discussing techniques that create distance, which in turn facilitates comedy. To an extent, however, esthetic distance is a circular phenomenon: As distance facilitates comedy, so can humor, under some circumstances, produce distance.

3. In *The Rhetoric of Fiction* (Chicago: University of Chicago Press, 1961), p. 127.

D'un chevalier cis fabliaus conte
Qui par samblant valoit un conte. (*MR*, I, 112)

(This fabliau tells of a knight / Whose worth equalled that of a count.)

Ma paine metrai et m'entente,
Tant com je sui en ma jovente,
A conter .i. fabliau par rime
Sanz colour et sans leonime. (*MR*, V, 32)

(While I am young / I will put my energy and my understanding / To relating a fabliau in rhyme / Simply and without embellishment.)

Although medieval poets used a number of terms to designate what we call fabliaux, it is nonetheless clear that an audience, told that a fabliau was to be recited, expected to hear a certain kind of work. The term establishes the genre and its conventions—and consequently the attitude of the audience toward what they were about to hear. It is thus reasonable to suppose that esthetic distance is immediately created by the jongleur who announces that he is going to relate a fabliau. A comparable effect may be produced by the question, "Have you heard the one about . . . ?" The word *fabliau* immediately draws us into the realm of the joke, and our consciousness of this fact precludes identification and prepares us instead for laughter. This preparation is the most basic and the most economical way for an author to establish and control distance.

The generic question is obviously much more complex than these remarks suggest. I have already referred to an additional problem, which is posed by the designation of the fabliau by other terms, such as *conte, dit, aventure,* and *exemple.* Use of such terms, especially *exemple,* would work in opposition to what I have suggested, for they ostensibly refer to compositions of more serious intent. Yet, the choice of such terms may in many cases be deliberate, that is, due neither to a vague notion of genre nor to an imprecise use of terminology. When a story that has been announced as an exemplum develops, as it is recited, comic aspects, the effect may be more remarkable because it is unexpected; the designation of the genre is ironic (the cues are misleading), and esthetic distance is established, not from the beginning, but at the moment the irony is made apparent. It would be audacious to suggest that such generic indications are consciously ironic in every instance, but they most certainly are in many. For example, the irony of calling *La Borgoise d'Orliens* an *aventure assez cortoise* (*MR*, I, 117) ("a very courtly story") would be unlikely to escape the medieval audience.

A similar effect may be created by the moral that concludes many fabliaux. I do not agree that this vestigial moral is in most instances an irrelevant appendage. Rather, I think many of these concluding morals must have been recited with tongue in cheek. An inappropriate moral or even an appropriate but mock-serious one added to a purely comic tale underlines the irony of the moral purpose claimed for the work. For example, the audience is unlikely to find edification in the conclusion of *De la Coille noire*:

> Par cest fablel poez savoir
> Que fame ne fait pas savoir,
> Qui son baron a en despit
> Por noire coille, por noir vit;
> Autant a il de bien, ou noir
> Comme ou blanc, ce sachiez de voir.[4] (*MR*, VI, 94)
>
> (By this story you can know / That a woman does not act wisely / Who scorns her lord / Because of black testicles or a black penis; / Know truly that it is as good black as white.)

The fabliaux are almost universally praised for their economy of narration; Walter M. Hart has called them "the best

4. The inappropriate moral is illustrated by *Le Vilain Asnier* (*MR*, V, 41–42, ll. 48–51): "Et por ce vos vueil ge monstrer / Que cil fait ne sens ne mesure / Qui d'orgueil se desennature: / *Ne se doit nus desnaturer*" [my italics]. ("And by this I wish to show / That he acts neither sensibly nor in moderation / Who by pride goes against his nature: / No one should act contrary to his nature.")

narrative art of the Middle Ages,"[5] partly for this reason. What needs to be pointed out here is that this economy is not an end in itself, nor does the poet cultivate it only because he does not require more detail for the anecdote. Fabliau characters frequently are unnamed (or are given only a first name); they undergo no evolution prior to the anecdote or, usually, during it; they thus remain types or stock characters. In addition, details of time and geography are sparse. This economy and simplicity is effective in the creation of esthetic distance. As a rule, the fabliau succeeds only so long as the author can avoid drawing the reader into the story. Booth has pointed out how prolonged exposure even to a less than admirable character can induce the reader to identify with him (pp. 322–23). The same is true, I think, of an accumulation of narrative detail; in literature, familiarity breeds acceptance, and the more "real" the situation and characters are, the less we can appreciate the humor of the anecdote. Conversely, the necessary detachment can be achieved by the extreme narrative economy. Again, the genre of the joke offers a parallel, dealing as it does with character types and skeletal situations. The farmer's daughter, for example, is a stock character who has neither identity nor existence outside the specific situation of the joke, and reader identification is normally impossible.[6]

Distance is created not only by generic expectations and narrative economy; equally important is the artifice of subject matter or treatment. Despite the realistic descriptions of everyday life in the fabliaux,[7] and despite the poet's frequent asser-

5. Walter M. Hart, "Narrative Art of the Old French Fabliaux," in *Kittredge Anniversary Papers* (Boston: Ginn and Company, 1913), p. 209.

6. The reservation expressed here (by *normally*) is explained in the conclusion to this essay.

7. Hart, p. 214: "Certainly the realism of the fabliaux is one of their most striking characteristics. They give us astonishingly vivid glimpses of bourgeois or peasant dwellings, of the dress and habits and customs of those who lived in them."

tions of the truth of his stories,[8] verisimilitude is not a principal concern of the authors. A single but sufficient example is *Le Chevalier qui fist parler les cons,* in which the artifice designated by the title is elementary and obvious. (See *MR*, VI, 68.)

Thus far I have sketched very briefly a few of the more basic techniques that serve to preclude identification with characters or story. A number of the better fabliaux use in addition remarkably subtle techniques to establish and maintain a distance between audience and story, creating an attitude of bemused detachment. In some, the author depicts what appears to be a genuine, believable, and perhaps touching situation, only to reveal ironically that the emotions and actions in question are themselves artificial. These techniques, which produce an ironic vision of character and plot, can be illustrated by an examination of *La Femme au tombeau* (the Matron of Ephesus fabliau, entitled in the manuscripts *Celle qui se fist foutre sur la fosse de son mari*).[9]

The action of this fabliau is simple. At a man's burial his widow throws herself weeping upon the grave and resists all attempts to console her or to make her leave. Before long, a knight and his squire approach, and the latter wagers that he can seduce her despite her grief. As the knight watches from a distance, the squire greets the widow and is told that her only wish is to die. He reveals that he is ten times as unhappy as she, since he had given his love to a beautiful and courtly lady whom he had later killed. The widow asks how he caused

8. For example, *Les Perdriz* (*MR*, I, 188, ll. 1–3): "Por ce que fabliaus dire sueil, / En lieu de fable dire vueil / Une aventure qui est vraie . . ." ("Being accustomed to telling fabliaux / Instead of a fable I wish to relate / A true story . . .").

9. All references to this fabliau are to my edition: "*La Femme au tombeau*: Anonymous Fabliau of the Thirteenth Century" (diss., Indiana University, 1967). The *MR* text is in III, 118. The euphemistic retitling of the fabliau is Bédier's (p. 438); I retain his title because it has gained some currency.

this death, and he replies that he did so by means of sexual intercourse, whereupon she—the grieving widow—expresses the desire to perish the same way. He willingly does her bidding, but the act brings her pleasure rather than death, and her grief is forgotten.[10]

The author of this work begins in a conventional fashion, but, not content with telling a simple comic tale, he constructs a poem in which from beginning to end the ironic techniques support the comedy and establish a distance between audience and text. There is no suggestion that the lady's grief was initially insincere, but we are told that it will soon be forgotten. This distinction is important, for our primary attention centers then on the transformation of the widow's emotions and on the humorous discrepancy between what we see of her grief and what we know about it.

As the story unfolds, it becomes obvious that she begins to feign sorrow for the sake of appearance. The key to the understanding of the poem is then the fact that the widow's relatives and friends are the ones who are impressed by her constancy. To the audience, however, the author offers knowledge denied to the characters themselves: While the latter see only the protestations and manifestations of grief, we are given additional information about that emotion. This double

10. It may be useful to contrast this fabliau with a work usually considered to be its analogue, Gautier le Leu's *La Veuve* (*MR*, II, 197). Although Gautier describes a widow's grief and her subsequent actions, the two poems function in entirely different ways. With more candor than subtlety, the author of *La Veuve* tells us that the widow is merely feigning sorrow from the very beginning, whereas the woman in *La Femme au tombeau* felt genuine sorrow at first but could not sustain it. As the latter author remarks: "Fame est de trop foible nature: / De noient rit, de noient pleure; / Fame aime et het en trop poi d'eure." (ll. 116–118) ("Woman is of too weak a nature; / It takes little to make her laugh or weep; / She is too quick to love and hate.") *La Veuve* is simply designed to show the utter falsity of woman. There is no anecdote as such, and, as outrageous as the widow's actions become, there is no indication that the moral is not presented in all seriousness.

vision, this contrast between illusion and reality, is the source of the poem's excellent irony.

It is significant that, in referring to the woman's sentiments, the poet emphasizes, not the emotion itself, but the evidence for it. Thus we are told, not that she is grieved, but that her grief is expressed in a particular way: She shows great sadness *par fais et par dis* (l. 8) (in her actions and her words), and the author assures us that such sorrow will not last (l. 13). The contrast of appearance and reality is maintained in the descriptions of her grief up to and during the burial. We see the continued shift of attention from a fact to the circumstances accompanying it. Thus she sets about mourning:

> De grant dolor mener *se paine* [my italics] (l. 17)
>
> (She takes pains to grieve deeply)

and we are told that she goes through these motions consciously:

> Molt i emploie bien sa paine (l. 18)
>
> (She puts great effort into it)

and competently (l. 19). Her actions convince at least the townspeople:

> Ce samble a toz, vers son seignor,
> Ainz fame ne fist tel dolor (ll. 21–22)
>
> (It seems to everyone that never did a woman grieve so for her lord).

Evidence of her sorrow can be seen and heard (ll. 24–32). Finally, as she collapses in apparent grief, the author remarks that:

> A la terre cheoir *se lait* [my italics] (l. 36)
>
> (She lets herself fall to the ground).

As the townspeople become progressively more deluded, we become progressively more enlightened, and the effect of the ensuing events is neither surprise nor dismay, but humor.

A further ironic effect is created by the disparity between the squire's intentions and his speech. He earlier made light of the pity the knight expressed for the widow. Now, after his wager, which understandably shocks the knight, the squire's words to the lady are completely in the vein of courtly diction. The vocabulary, sentiments, and tone are reminiscent of courtly lyrics and romances, as he tells her:

> Je avoie mis tout mon cuer
> A une fame que j'avoie,
> Et assez plus de moi l'amoie,
> Qui ert bele et cortoise et sage;
> Ocise l'ai par mon outrage. (ll. 88–92)

> (I gave my whole heart / To a lady I had / And I loved her more than myself; / She was beautiful, courtly, and wise; / I killed her by my outrageous action.)

The audience, aware of the squire's intentions, can fully evaluate his conversation with the widow, for his language, in contrast to that which he has previously used, is clearly a parody of the courtly style. The encounter with the widow is humorous, not simply because the squire attempts to seduce her—and succeeds—but also because his artifice in this attempt involves the assumption of language and actions that are totally inappropriate to his character and intent and that properly belong to the knight, the proponent of the courtly code, of *fin amour*. The contrast between the two men and the implicit critique of courtly ideals are the primary and perhaps the only justification for the knight's presence in the fabliau. He takes no direct part in the action, but he functions as the backdrop against which the squire plays out his comedy.

After the explanation, in courtly language, of the source of the squire's grief, the widow asks him how his lady died, and he replies with a statement that, by its abrupt change of tone, is indispensable for the full comic effect: "En foutant, voir, ma dame chiere" (l. 94) ("Truly, it was by fucking, my dear lady"). Her reaction to this frankness is just as abrupt; far from showing displeasure or shock, she immediately invites him to inflict the same fate on her. Indeed, he merely presents to her an opportunity which, we suspect, she has been waiting for. The opportunity is perfect. She has taken care to maintain the appearance of grief and to hide her real emotion, and the squire, also concealing his nature behind courtly pretenses, permits her to take her pleasure and thereby wins the wager. The appearance–reality contrast is here applicable to both characters, for each poses as something he is not, and as a result both succeed in satisfying their real desires.

As this analysis indicates, the humor of the fabliau is consistently based on an incongruity introduced into the work. The seduction here is in sharp contrast to the outcome a widow's lamentations should normally suggest. Furthermore, the fabliau utilizes for its effect the discrepancies between the manners of the knight and the squire, between the normal speech of the squire and the tone of his words to the lady, between this courtly tone and the sudden return to his usual style ("En foutant, voir . . ."), and, finally, between the widow's expected response to this statement and the desire she expresses to meet a similar fate. Thus, the author's success is due to his repeated focusing of attention on an aspect of the story and then resolving this attention in an unusual or unexpected manner. The work depends on the opposition of illusion and reality and on that of expectation and resolution. These discrepancies establish the distance that is essential to the poet's design.

In my discussion of this fabliau, finally, I suggest also another means to create distance—authorial intrusion. The medieval poet, and the fabliau author in particular, is not overly concerned either with impersonality or with a fixed narrative point of view. In *La Femme au tombeau*, for example, the poet facilitates his task by speaking directly as author to reader to assure us that the widow will not grieve for long. The result of this technique, whereby the author divulges the conclusion before developing the story, is the creation of a kind of dramatic irony. In a work that requires economy, this device is frequently the most efficient means of making the audience privileged observers of the action.

* * *

Art is by definition artifice. While writers in some genres can succeed only by effacing, as far as possible, the reader's consciousness of this artifice, the fabliau author exploits it systematically. Reader identification must be avoided at all costs, and a sharp distinction drawn between reality and illusion. These requirements may explain in part the frequency of fabliau themes that involve disguises and mistaken identity. Although the poet may go through the motions of drawing a moral, the distance he has created enables the reader or audience to suspend moral judgment, even when the poem treats of anticlericalism or antifeminism, infidelity and explicit sexuality, deception and physical violence. This statement requires immediate qualification. Although we cannot deny "the power of artifice to keep us at a certain distance from reality" (Booth, p. 122), sensitivity to certain themes nonetheless has the power to bridge that distance and negate its effects. Obvious examples of this phenomenon are reactions to ethnic, racial, and—more recently—antifeminist stories. Yet, if the author can successfully establish and maintain distance, subjects that are potentially sensitive or shocking become nothing more than ideal material for a *conte à rire*.

❧VIII❧

PAUL THEINER

FABLIAU SETTINGS

The ambiguity of my title has been deliberately sought after and will be just as deliberately cultivated. We should perhaps agree without great difficulty that there is a sense of the term *setting* that deserves here at least to be called primary: setting as the locus of fabliau action.[1] Nevertheless, over this fundamental there plays a series of rich overtones, all of which contribute to what we actually perceive in the fabliau. There is the authenticating setting,[2] the establishment of a trustworthy relationship between the world of the fabliau and the world outside this fictive enclosure, which the audience would perceive without question as the real world. There is also the presentational setting, the frame in which the fictive world is established in its relationship to the audience. There is finally the setting of fabliaux (and even of the fabliau as genre, unless we exercise great care) into the complex of relationships, developments, and moments that comprise literary and, more broadly, cultural history. Nor are all of these overtones aspects of fabliau setting; they are instead the integrated constituents of our perception as readers of fabliaux, and it is as such that we must consider them.

Where to begin, then, given such a formidable complex of

1. The term *locus of action,* as well as the impulse to think about its implications for literary analysis, is derived from Charles Muscatine's brief essay, "Locus of Action in Medieval Narrative," *Romance Philology,* 17 (1963), 115–22.

2. The notion of authentication in the senses in which it is employed here is based on Morton W. Bloomfield's "Authenticating Realism and the Realism of Chaucer," *Thought,* 39 (1964), 335–58.

structures? It might be logical to assume that, having given some attention to the definition of the notion of *setting* as it applies to fabliaux, we might proceed to an attempt at defining the other term of the title, *fabliau*. It seems best at this point to retreat to the relative safety of a couple of stipulations, neither of which need to be considered definitive of the genre as a whole. First, the fabliaux I have in mind demonstrate an interest on the part of the authors in the presentation of plot; there is always an action of at least some rudimentary physicality. This is not to deny the existence of such pieces as *Le Sentier battu* nor to bar them from fabliau status, but simply to set them aside. More importantly, I choose to apply the term *fabliau* only to those tales whose materials give evidence of having been deployed for a comic purpose, because the generation of humor is what I wish to stress in my discussion of settings. This stipulation will allow for a compactness that would have to slacken badly to accept a piece like *L'Enfant qui fu remis au soleil*; for the moment this concision is more useful than broad inclusiveness.[3] The field of vision, then, ideally covers all of the contents of Montaiglon and Raynaud not excluded by the stipulations. As a practical matter, however, I shall allude to only a few of the better-known fabliaux and concentrate for the most part on the sharply drawn and exquisitely controlled *Borgoise d'Orliens* and the episodic hackwork of *Aloul*.

Any reader of fabliaux will readily observe that many of these tales are localized at the outset, always in a perfunctory way and often even vaguely:

> Or vous dirai d'une borgoise
> Une aventure assez cortoise.
> Née et norrie fu d'Orliens,
> Et ses sires fu néz d'Amiens. (*MR*, I, 117)

3. The action in *L'Enfant* . . . can be described as the product of a more or less warped form of monkish humor, but my anticlericalism does not extend that far; such an explanation can follow only upon the assumption that what we have before us *must* be funny.

(Now I will tell you a very courtly tale about a city wife. She was born and raised at Orleans, while her husband came from Amiens.)

The indeterminate quality of this opening to *La Borgoise d'Orliens* is both typical and instructive. Unlike some such passages in other works, its relationship to the action of the poem is rather casually left to the guess of the reader. A few lines later, when the story is getting under way, we find a quartet of scholars entering "la vile," and soon after that we find them comfortably housed "en la vile"—but which "vile" of the two mentioned in the first four lines is never made clear, nor does it really need to be. For whether the reference is treated as casually as it is here, or specified as neatly as the place names in *Le Bouchier d'Abeville*, the setting named does not function as the locus of the story's action. The care exercised by Eustache d'Amiens may obscure this point somewhat in the *Bouchier*, but it is clear that our inability to identify the locality of the *Borgoise* in no way interferes with our reading of the tale. The story is not located in either of the towns named, nor indeed in any setting as large and palpable as a town. The citing of these places by name belongs, not to the localization of the action, but to the fableor's authentication of himself and his materials. As such, the naming of a city serves the same function as the author's naming himself, which often happens either at the beginning or at the end of a fabliau or in his account of the circumstances of the story's transmission.

This authentication, as Morton Bloomfield has so brilliantly shown,[4] is vitally important to any genre that bases its claim to our attention on the consequentiality and palpability of its realism; in this regard the fabliau is quite insistent. The

4. Bloomfield's argument is not confined to the description of the particular kind of authentication I am discussing here but is a wide-ranging and broadly based theoretical and practical study of authentication as a contribution to literature.

fableor sets his tale into the ongoing sequence of fabliaux, which is a real sequence in the most naive sense of the term; we have heard other fabliaux, so we recognize the existence of the class; the story we are about to hear falls into that class.

On a similar level of naivete, the authenticity of the fabliau is often sustained by appeals to universal knowledge, especially of a proverbial sort. If we all agree on the truth of the principle enunciated, we can scarcely find fault with the "realism" of that individual feature that does not so much confirm the saying—because its freedom from the need for further confirmation is assumed in the first place—as provide us with an instance. This is a trick. The sly and playful banter of a Eustache or a Jean de Condé, with its frequently heavy-handed insistence on its own truth value, has about it the tone of that conspiracy against the ordinary truth values of the world that we recognize as humor.

It is as vain to ask whether the fabliau audience was actually drawn into faith in the authenticating levels of its tales as it is to suppose that the modern comedian's audience believes that the anecdote he relates deals with an event that actually happened "on the way to the studio." In both genres performer and audience agree to participate in a mutual stipulation of truth values that the audience can approach as essentially harmless, at least to themselves.[5] The ease with which this agreement can be reached is shown quite clearly by the truncation of most of these authenticating features in any given single example:

> Seignor, oïez une merveille,
> C'onques n'oïstes sa pareille,
> Que je vous vueil dire et conter;
> Or metez cuer à l'escouter.

5. I do not wish to say that their acceptance of such an arrangement may not stem from malice on their part, or that such malice or other factors related to it are intrinsically harmless to everyone: witness the current furor over *All in the Family*, and the recent one over *Bonnie and Clyde*.

Parole qui n'est entendue,
Sachiez de voir, ele est perdue. (*MR*, III, 227)

(Good lords, listen now to a wondrous tale, the like of which you have never heard before; I'd like to tell it for you now, so be especially careful to pay attention to it. The word which is not heard, as you must surely know, is simply wasted.)

This, the familiar opening of *Le Bouchier d'Abeville,* relies for its effect not only on our tacit agreement in the game of authentication, but also on our having as secure a grasp on the conventions of the game as the author. Once we have joined him in the game, we can follow his lead into the actual story, secure in the knowledge that the whole performance has been properly placed in the schema of reality.

When we do arrive in the narrative itself, we discover that it is scarcely located at all; employing a dramatic metaphor, we might say that the stage is nearly bare of scenery. The narrator, having first seen to it that we are both aware of the separateness of his performance from outer reality and willing to lend our assent to the proposition that there is to be some sort of congruence between these two worlds, now begins to establish what that congruence will consist in: elemental identity. The stage is bare of scenery, to be sure, but it is not devoid of props, and these props have both a solidity and a simplicity of the sort that has always commended itself to Western ontology.

What exists in the fabliau world has been admirably described by Charles Muscatine, who has also interspersed in his description some hints that lead toward the understanding of the structure composed of these elements.[6] His version of this structure is, I think, somewhat misleading, and that in two different, but related, ways. First, on the phenomenal level, his enthusiastic and sharp-eyed descriptions of "smoked

6. Charles Muscatine, *Chaucer and the French Tradition* (Berkeley and Los Angeles: University of California Press, 1957), pp. 60 ff.

eels and pieces of lard, of hot irons and frying-pan rings, wash-tubs, barrels, baskets and chests, bats and clubs, loads of dung and thick, white goose sauce" as well as of "peasants and bourgeois, clerks, priests, nuns, jongleurs, miscellaneous rascals of all kinds and . . . some knights and courtly ladies,"[7] are superb, but they give the misleading impression of a density in the structure of the fabliaux that few fabliaux are capable of bearing out. All of these things and people—and a good many more besides—belong to the fabliau world if we are considering that world as the composite of the constituents of all fabliaux. But the typical single fabliau is as economical in its use of them as the genre is egalitarian in its criteria for their admission.[8] Muscatine relates this misleading impression to a rather more serious failure to account for these phenomena in a way that will help us to understand the artistic and philosophical principles that underlie fabliau narration.

When Muscatine introduces the series of items quoted above, he says that "the fabliau cosmos is defined and limited by [their] important presence," a statement which, when combined with the convincingly thingish density of the list that follows, leads us to think of them also as constitutive of the reality of that cosmos. A page or so earlier, when he is opening his discussion of "the realistic style of the bourgeois tradition," he states, "The literature of the bourgeois tradition is 'realistic' *or* 'naturalistic,' but it neither attempts nor achieves the reportorial detail of the modern fiction describable by these labels" [my italics]. And a few lines later: "I use the terms 'realistic' and 'naturalistic,' then, loosely—for lack of better ones—to indicate that for the Middle Ages, and particularly in contrast to the courtly tradition, this literature

7. Muscatine, *Chaucer and the French Tradition*, pp. 60, 61.

8. I have characterized this as *misleading*, rather than *mistaken*, because Muscatine makes quite clear at other points in the same general discussion that he views the typical scene of the fabliau as economical and spare, and he does not actually refer to the items in the list as *constitutive*.

has a remarkable preoccupation with the animal facts of life. It takes, in the ordinary sense, a realistic view of things."[9] Certainly there is the possibility for some confusion here. Even those who do not ordinarily care to quibble about the use of literary labels will probably agree that, in this discussion, sharpening our awareness of the implications of the terms *realism* and *naturalism* might well lead us to a clearer understanding of the bases of fabliau art. It will, provided that we decline to demand an explanation that simply selects one of these terms as the "right" one and rejects the other; there is not much evidence to suggest that thinking like a fabliau character will lead us to a better and more comprehensive view of the genre.[10]

The fableor—in his role as fableor, that is, not to be confused with the same man in other roles—is a realist in the sense that he lives in perfect ease with the assumptions about reality that his art proceeds from. He would remain to that degree a realist even if the assumptions were not so commonsensically confined to the here-and-now, the touchable and graspable as they obviously are. Naturalism, by contrast, is programmatic and, above all, tendentious. A realistic novelist —Balzac, for example—proceeds with a certain spareness to employ the objects that are real for him as props, to make them serve the action he is primarily dealing with. In much the same fashion, in *Le Pliçon*, the garment named in the title does not exist in the story until the precise moment that it is to be used. There is no way in which *Le Pliçon* can be described as being about a *pliçon*. For a naturalistic writer, on

9. Muscatine, *Chaucer and the French Tradition*, p. 59.

10. The following discussion does not take issue with Muscatine's right to use these terms in a general way; it merely points out that the closer analysis of what *realism* and *naturalism* mean in the practice of nineteenth-century French fiction can be useful in sharpening our view of what the fableor does and/or does not do. The obviousness of the debt owed to Georg Lukacs at this point should not prevent my acknowledging it.

the other hand, the world that the realist assumes so blithely as his subject has slipped away, to be reclaimed only by the most diligent verbal reconstitution, the most pointed insistence on the rightness of that view of reality. Whereas the action of a realistic narrative determines the use of the articles that appear—so that use and appearance become functionally synonymous, the latter never occurring without the former—the objects themselves limit, even determine the action in a naturalistic story. It is difficult to say which is more telling in Zola's art, the painstaking constitution of a world detail by detail, or the uncompromising insistence that no real world can be otherwise constituted; neither the detail nor the insistence has any analogue in fabliau creation. The fableor can easily be imagined kicking a stone in refutation of Berkeley, but he cannot be seen trying to prove that stones are all; among other things, the former activity is a joke played on Thought, while the latter is Thought itself.

Like naturalism, the fabliau is magnificently disdainful of ultimate causes or, indeed, of any causes other than the most obviously proximate. This prejudice, if you will, is extended with equal malice in the direction of both First Causes and teleological explanations, so that any sort of rational activity that attempts to bridge nonadjacent entities, to create mental structures of any sort, is excluded from the fabliau world. It is possible, in the absence of any fabliau characters who speculate themselves into perdition,[11] to see this distrust as a form of benign realism, much alike in kind to the easy assumption, rather than the aggressive assertion, of realistic data that characterized the fabliau view of being. Still, given the character of medieval philosophical preoccupation with essences and

11. As opposed to those who simply act stupidly in fabliau situations. It might be objected that both Nicholas and the carpenter in the *Miller's Tale* are counterexamples, but Chaucer's manipulations of the fabliau's artistry are so complex that I prefer to leave them out of the present consideration altogether.

eschatology, not to mention Aristotelian causes, it seems best to regard mere avoidance of these modes as disdainful, if not belligerent. What we are left with in any case is a view of a fabliau framework which, with its realistic ontology and its naturalistic insistence on the proximity of causes, will help us to understand both the constitution and function of the fabliau setting as the locus of fabliau action. We are, in summary, ready to accept the constriction of fabliau space and the contraction of fabliau time on their own terms. We need merely to remember that these terms do not include advocacy of a world view, but quite the opposite: the contrivance of a fictive world in which the constrictions and constraints can be put to comic use, together with the genial willingness of the audience, at the minimal urging of the fableor, to enter into the spirit of the fiction.[12] Our awareness of the presence of a certain kind of fiction, of a structure designed to determine comic actions, is a prerequisite to our comic response. The fabliaux, like other comic forms, are not participated in, but observed.

What we see in a fabliau setting is confined to the moment of the action, in both the temporal and mechanical senses of the term. The corollary of this statement, to extend the word-play to another dimension, is that what is not seen is of no moment. If we look at *La Borgoise d'Orliens* (*MR*, I, 117–25), a fine example of a tightly organized, well-constructed fabliau narrative, we can easily and economically see both the workings and the implications of this kind of setting. We have already noted that the town, be it Orleans or whatever, is not the locus of the action.[13] There are, to be sure, genres or subgenres of realistic narrative—the modern spy story, for example

12. When this willingness is withheld, comedy is not possible. In a fabliau that even hints at any coerciveness in urging our acceptance of its view as Truth, comedy melts away instantly; I believe that this factor accounts for the basic noncomedy of *L'Enfant qui fu remis au soleil*.

13. See text, pp. 120–21.

—in which real cities function as the loci of action, but the definition of setting creates an artistic symbiosis between action and place inimical to the comic purposes of the fabliau, which must show the action dominating all other forces in the story. Characters must be conventionalized and settings functionalized. The actual setting in the *Borgoise* is never at any time larger than a space that could be covered by a spotlight, and the theatrical metaphor is strikingly apt. Not only is the dramatic character of fabliau action commented on by almost all critics, but whatever is not in the spotlight is for the time being out of all existence, just like a character who has left the stage. Therefore, the setting for the *Borgoise* as a whole cannot be characterized at all. If we say something like "the house and grounds of a certain burgher," we verge toward precisely that sense of place that the story tries so strenuously to avoid. *La Borgoise d'Orliens* consists of 248 lines, but it is not until line 52 that the action—as opposed to the loosely localized ("chies .I. borgois") background to the action—begins, significantly with the tale's first lines of dialogue:

> Dame, fet-il, il me covient
> Aler en ma marcheandie.
>
> (Good wife, he said, I have to go away now, on a business trip.)

This speech sets the plot in motion (aler) and from that point to the end of the tale (less than 200 lines) the scene changes more than fifteen times.[14] We move from the house to a place, ".III. liues de la vile," to the "uis du vergier" and "par le vergier" to a "solier," back to the "uis del vergier," up to her "chambre" and so on, often doubling back and forth, never lighting for more than a moment, and never acquiring any

14. My actual count was seventeen, but I have rounded it off against the possibility of disagreement over what might constitute a scene shift in every case; the essential point, that the tale is in constant motion, should remain unscathed by this evasion.

characterization of place except in terms of action. Therefore the loft is not dark, nor drafty, nor rat-infested, but ".I. solier dont j'ai la clef," because the key in question is to be handed over, nearly 100 lines later, to the gang of household ruffians the wife dispatches to cudgel her husband. Even the one-line characterization of the bedroom—"Ou li dras furent portendu"—falls into this category: the room is not so much comfortable as *ready*. In cinematic terms, we might say that the shots were cut to the rhythm of the plot, with longer views—house, town—employed only in the process of moving in from the authenticating introduction to the action and back out again from the action to the fade-out, which is accomplished by shifting the scene from reality to the vague, extra-narrative territory of the clerk's (unspecified) native land.

Likewise, there is no simultaneity to clutter up the naturalistic view of monocausation; the proprieties of unity and simplicity observed in the fabliau's treatment of place extend as well to the tale's location in time. Even when events occur that we may logically infer are taking place at the same time, the text discourages such conclusions by linking the events with connectives that do not make precise time relationships easy to discern. We get sequences like this one, which begins with the end of the scene in which the servants beat up their master:

> Hors le traient com .I. mort chien,
> Si l'ont sor .I. fumier flati,
> En la meson sont reverti;
> De bons vins orent à foison,
> Toz des meillors de la meson,
> Et des blans et des auvernois,
> Autant com se il fussent rois;
> Et la dame ot gastiaus et vin,
> Et blanche toaille de lin,
> Et grosse chandoile de cire;
> Si tient à son ami concile
> Toute la nuit dusques au jor. (*MR*, I, 123–24)

> (They dragged him outside like a dead dog, and after flinging him onto a dung-heap, went back into the house. There they had their fill of good wine, the best the house had to offer, white and red alike, just as if they were kings. And the lady of the house got together some cakes and wine and white linen napkins and a good fat wax candle; and she and her lover closeted themselves together all night long until the break of day.)

Here the actual linguistic forms connecting the parts of the sequence are minimal enough to suggest that each isolated portion is to be joined to its neighbors only by our inference and not by the narrator's disposition to order. Does the wife eat upstairs at the same time that the servants are feasting downstairs? Does she eat downstairs at that time and then go up to hold her night-long meeting with her lover? These details are not entirely enigmatic, but the hints toward their unraveling come from our own notions of the action's requirements and proprieties, not from the manipulations of the narrator.

Also, the overall narrative is played out to the sense of a sharply restricted field of time. Just as our fabliau has no extensiveness in space, neither does it involve more than a fleeting succession of individual points in time. Within the action, each shift in scene points to a cut in time as well, which is the detail the movie-editing metaphor was designed to explicate. The action neither covers a long period of time, as epic and romance necessarily do, nor does it proceed from or lead to any sense of time as a continuing and containing factor. The fabliau is perfectly self-contained, isolated from any other events in time or place—ongoing wars, famines, festivities—unless they come directly into the story. There is no way for such events or continuities to be related to the story; this fabliau has in its comic austerity severed all connections, all affinities, all affects.

Naturally, not many fabliaux are such perfect models of

austerity as *La Borgoise d'Orliens*; this fact in no way compromises my use of it as a classic model. More to the point is the fact that even among fabliaux that stray considerably from the restraint we have just observed, the elaboration and digression seldom touch on the time and place coordinates of the setting, which still functions as a locus of action in much the same way that the moving locales of the *Borgoise* did. A good case for comparison is that of *Aloul* (*MR*, I, 255–88), which lies much closer to the *Borgoise* in Montaiglon and Raynaud (as well as in the manuscript from which they derived both texts) than it does in its overall form or in our critical estimation. Yet we find that, although it has placed different emphases on the function of the authenticating setting and in connection with these emphases has developed a somewhat stronger tendency to cultivate the presentational setting, its locus of action resembles what we might have projected from our classic model.

Aloul is similar in overall plot structure to *La Borgoise d'Orliens*. Both concern the adventures of clerk–lovers who succeed in spite of awareness on the part of cuckolded husbands in carrying out their nefarious schemes with the aid of the wives—a plot shared with many other fabliaux. Within this framework are other common features: encounters in gardens, the drubbing of the husband by his own allies, the scene, and its relation to the action. But in these items there are differences: The garden encounter in *Aloul* occurs prior to the onset of the deception plot; there is more than one drubbing, and they are not all administered to the husband; not only the lover but also the comic underlings take their lumps. In general, we might say that the writer of *Aloul* is doubling up. Not willing to take chances on the success of one tried and true device, he repeats himself. The overall structure thus loses in balance whatever it gains in intensity.

The authenticating setting, which in the *Borgoise* is rather cleverly and deceptively colored to resemble an action setting, is here reduced to zero, to be replaced by the crudest of authenticating formulas:

> Qui d'Aloul veut oïr le conte,
> Si com l'estoire nous raconte,
> Sempres en puet assez oïr,
> S'il ne le pert par mesoïr. (*MR*, I, 255)
>
> (Whoever wants to hear the story of Aloul, just as it was told to us, can very well hear it right off, if he doesn't bungle it by hearing it wrong.)

This opening, with its jangling *oïr*'s, is not even perfunctorily connected to the beginning of the narrative, which proceeds immediately, as follows: "Alous estoit uns vilains riches." In spite of this offhand beginning, the narrator expends considerable effort on securing alert attention from his audience, both by editorial pushiness and through the sure device of catering to what he perceives as their notions of entertainment. Whereas the *Borgoise* fableor resorted sparingly to the use of asides and limited them to the sententious remark that is intended to bolster the truth value of the action, the writer of *Aloul* is constantly busy. When he resorts somewhat laconically to a *sententia*: "Male chose a en jalousie," he is quick to follow up the brief action based on that remark with a pointer:

> Or est Alous toz sos provez,
> Qui s'entremet de tel afère. (*MR*, I, 255)
>
> (So Aloul was shown to be a complete fool, to meddle in such things.)

These editorial asides are sprinkled throughout, our fableor being a very aggressive teller. "Diex, c'or ne set cele aventure / Alous, qui en son lit se gist!" ("Oh God, if only Aloul, now tucked away in his bed, knew about this business!"); "Or est la dame decéue, / S'ele ne se set bien gaitier" ("Now the lady is going to be taken in, unless she knows how to look out for herself"); "Bien le demaine jalousie, / Qui de lui fet tout son voloir" ("Jealousy had control of him, making him do everything she wished"), and so on. All these comments occur within less than 100 lines.

He is also quite generous with actions, including a fight between the priest and a watchdog; a fight in bed between Aloul and the priest; a fight in bed between Aloul and his wife; a shouting match between the "vieille bajasse," Hersent, and the rest of the household; a mistaken-identity brawl between Aloul and his servants; a fight involving the servant, Rogelet, and the priest; an epic struggle in which the priest and the entire cast, Aloul included, participate; the fight between Robin and the priest; ditto with Dan Berengier; and finally, more violence between the priest and the whole assembly. Sexual encounters are not only much more graphic and numerous than in the *Borgoise,* they are introduced with a minimum of plot motivation: The old hag, Hersent, appears out of nowhere: "Or avoit-il enz en l'ostel / Hersent . . ." ("There was also in the household one Hersent . . ."); she heads straight for the barn: "En l'estable s'en vient tout droit" ("Went straightway into the barn") without any light to see by: "Tous sanz lumiere et sanz chandeille" ("With no light and no candle"); the whole mysterious trip is finally enlightened by the teleological reason for it: It allows us another view, quite gratuitous but apparently not expected to be unwelcome, of the priest's "coilles granz et enflees, / Qui pendoient contre val jus" ("his balls, enormous and swollen, which hung down so far they touched the ground"). This description leads to an extra coupling, again with visual aids.

Should we stop here, with a by no means complete account of the sheer busyness of *Aloul,* there would be no mistaking the differences in artistic intention and method—not to say sensibility—between our two authors. Nevertheless, in spite of this obvious divergence, almost all of our observations concerning the fabliau setting as locus of action serve *Aloul* as well as the *Borgoise.* The moment of action in each determines the extent of the visible setting, and that setting is no wider than before. It consists of largely undifferentiated portions of the "house and grounds" seen one at a time and briefly. There is a bit more emphasis on things as things in *Aloul*, with implements like a sword, a bucket, or a flail being introduced from time to time. These items come into view only on cues from the action, however, and in the immediate vicinity of that action.[15]

In *Aloul* the essence of the plot is motion as in *Borgoise*, even though the neat, rhythmical "cuts" of the latter are replaced, in the former, by a much more ragged pacing. Both the general extent of time covered and the quality of time isolation from any possible historical context, or any time context involving a *longue durée*, are precisely what we saw in the first instance. In the *Borgoise* the very spareness of the action set against no backdrop, the very bleakness of a timed action set against no external standard of time provide the means for a play of wit that seems built into the setting itself. In *Aloul* the joke is also inherent, but it has been all but forgotten in the rush for other effects: the scatology, the raucous sexuality, the violence, and the parodic echoing of courtly values that inform most of its more nearly successful scenes. This last device has not been mentioned up to now because it does not figure prominently in the use of settings, being confined as it is to gesture, to language, and to characterization. Now, however, this mock-courtliness serves to point up a remark made earlier, in connection with the world view of *La Borgoise d'Orliens*,[16] namely, that the world view of the fabliau is not in itself a corrective to the values of romance, or epic, or organized religious or philosophical tenets. It is a strategy for eliciting laughter. It

15. The exception here is obviously the *coillons* and other accoutrements that are introduced only by the fableor's deliberate distortion of the plot line. This particular form of exhibitionism, however, is his only fall from narrative grace in this regard.

16. See text, p. 127.

perhaps affronts some of these values and tenets, but certainly no more seriously than its own world scheme. After all, it runs up against its own limitations in providing us with a fictive world in which no serious action, no connected thought, no human continuity, and no affect is possible. Its humor is neither bleak nor black because it does not for a moment permit itself the solipsism of assuming that its Truth is anything but contingent upon our willingness to accept it as part of a game: a gloriously witty and astringent game in some texts, rather more of a mess in others, but a game nevertheless; a game necessarily played on somewhat the same field in all of its versions, despite some quirks in the ground rules.

This leaves one version of the notion of "fabliau settings" still unexplored; namely, the setting of the genre in the context of cultural history. A great deal has already been written in this line by Bédier, Nykrog, Rychner, and others, but I should like to advance some cautionary observations that I think may be drawn from my discussion of fabliau structure. First, let us consider a condensed version of what we have identified as the comic framework of fabliau action: The fableor creates a fictive world whose purpose is best seen as rhetorical, a setting in time, place, character, and action that will determine and sustain a certain kind of humor. This is done, in brief, by atomizing this world into time and place fragments that are isolated from every affect of association, idea, sentiment, or atmosphere, so the only remaining human causality possible is that of a series of successive, mechanical actions, each pushing its predecessor forward. What is achieved in this way is the automatization of fabliau characters and their fictive lives in a miniature deist world. As a strategy for prompting laughter, this world demands no assent on the part of the audience save their acceptance of its effectiveness as an artistic means. In fact, as we have seen,[17] any more substantive assent to its reality is ruinous to the art

17. See note 12.

form. Finally, this framework continues even when the particular fableor, as in *Aloul,* veers off in search of other effects, just as the structure of the Morality Play of the Old West continues to inform modern television westerns whose surface values have expanded to comprise sociology, psychology, or the cult of violence.

With respect to literary history in particular, a cautionary note springs from the analogy between the fabliaux themselves and the atomized world of their settings. Individual fabliaux are notably isolated in themselves. They do not interconnect, develop, or use cross-reference except as they relate generally to the personification of a craft in the figure of the fableor. Thus, it is difficult to characterize the movement that must give life to literary history if it is not to remain in the status of annotated list. It is difficult to imagine a theory of literary influence being generated by the extant fabliaux alone. It is equally difficult to imagine a literary historical ordering of the fabliau materials on internal grounds, that is, on grounds intrinsic to the fabliau as a literary form. In these senses of the term *history,* we must conclude that the fabliau has no history.[18]

What the fabliau quite clearly has, however, is a social history, which, in one way or another, has usually been taken as its History. With this view it is difficult to be out of sympathy, provided we realize that such a history is not a literary history and that it is only part of a cultural history. In brief, there is a danger in assuming that the fabliau's form and values are determined genetically through its cultivation by one class or another at one particular point in history, even as there is a danger in assuming that the world of the fabliau is the world of any nation, class, or fableor.

18. This factor does not prevent its being analyzed, typed, described, catalogued, defined, etc., nor does it impugn any of these processes.

IX

THOMAS D. COOKE

PORNOGRAPHY, THE COMIC SPIRIT, AND THE FABLIAUX

Sexual relationships form a significant part of the subject matter of the Old French fabliaux. In most of the tales of this genre there is some mention of sexual activity, in many the structure itself is a sexual encounter, and in not a few there is a detailed and vivid account of a seduction. Despite this emphasis, the fabliaux are not usually considered pornographic, yet I believe that there are present in some of these tales definite tendencies in that direction. It might be said that some of them are potentially (but never actually) pornographic. Definitions of pornography vary from the extremely narrow, which label as pornographic almost any description of sexual activity, to the broader, which deny that any such description is pornographic. I do not take sides in this debate, but rather acknowledge that it is possible to point to certain distinctive features of literature dealing with sex, to make some general observations on that literature's attitudes toward sex, and then to give those attitudes a name.

I shall, at the beginning of this essay, outline the basic points of one recent study of pornography, which can be used as a paradigm for an examination of pornographic attitudes in the fabliaux. Almost all the other studies that I have read express a militant liberalism in their approach, and however valid that attitude might be, it has not allowed for an in-depth study of the literary and psychological aspects of this phenomenon. Steven Marcus's *The Other Victorians: Sexuality and Pornography in Mid-Nineteenth-Century England*[1] focuses on those aspects more clearly and with more success than any other work I know.[2] Principally it is a study of Victorian pornography, but from his reading of that material Marcus establishes a general theory, which he summarizes in his concluding chapter entitled "Pornotopia," and which may legitimately be applied to certain features of the fabliaux. As a literary genre (if it can be called such), pornography took form only with certain historical events in the eighteenth and nineteenth centuries, the rise of the novel and the private reading audience the novel assumes. But it surely must be allowed that the interest in and desire for a genre that can be called pornography does not begin at such a late date in history. It seems safe to say that the novel merely gave fuller expression to an interest that had always existed in less complete form. That interest is complex and so it will be necessary to examine at length the principal ideas in *The Other Victorians,* although they apply directly to a literature seven centuries later than the fabliaux.

According to Marcus, pornography is basically a masculine phenomenon, written by and for men. (There are a few "pornographic" works by women, but they are radically different.) In the usual pornographic work there is an overwhelming concern with the physical aspects of sex, particularly with the penis, its size and potency. In the land of Pornotopia, all heroes have huge penises and are capable of an unlimited

1. Studies in Sex and Society (New York: Basic Books, Inc., 1967).

2. The severest criticisms of Marcus's views have been made by Morse Peckham, *Art and Pornography: An Experiment in Explanation,* Studies in Sex and Society (New York: Basic Books, Inc., 1969). Peckham points out some important exceptions to Marcus's theories, yet I find those theories to be generally valid. All the other studies of pornography that I read in preparation for this study show a surprising amount of agreement with Marcus's main points; unfortunately, they lack his sensitivity to the literary values involved. But see also Susan Sontag's essay, "The Pornographic Imagination," in her *Styles of Radical Will* (New York: Dell Publishing Co., 1969), pp. 35–73.

number of erections and ejaculations. Marcus theorizes that this idea is not simply masculine, but more particularly *adolescent* masculine. Affected by this same adolescence is emphasis on masculine aggressiveness, a typical feature of youthful notions of virility. The male overpowers the female sexually, and she is awed by his masculinity. Marcus believes that sexuality in pornography is almost totally aggressive and that women not only tolerate aggressiveness, but desire it and respond only to sexual dominance. According to him, they even enjoy being raped. In keeping with this notion of sex roles, the male characteristically thinks of his penis as a weapon.

Given this view of masculine sexuality in pornography, it is little wonder that the attitude toward women is limited. They are merely objects to be seduced, actually mere extensions of the penis. Women are usually anonymous, even in those works which claim to be factual, as unnamed as those parts of their bodies which are the only concern for the male. So unconcerned with the female is the male that he can project his own misconceptions and fantasies onto her sexual responses. Even such an experienced seducer as the author of *My Secret Life*, who, according to his own word—which Marcus believes to be honest—made love to over twelve hundred different women in his life, even he had misconceptions about female sexuality. He claimed, for example, never to have met a frigid woman; all were satisfied by his sexual prowess. His boast can, however, be interpreted as meaning that *he* was always satisfied and did not really notice how the woman was reacting. Another of his fantasies was that a woman ejaculated in intercourse in exactly the same way that a man did. Finally, he believed that women are always ready for intercourse, a belief based upon a biological view of women, not a personal one. In short, women in pornography are generally not treated as persons but as objects.

As a consequence of these attitudes toward men and women, the relationship between them is impersonal. The concentration on the sex organs does not allow for any exploration or development of the total human experience. At times the organs are viewed as supernatural objects, sources of all life and happiness. Marcus quotes from *My Secret Life* as an example of this deification: "After the blessed sun, surely the cunt ought to be worshipped as the source of all human happiness. It takes and gives and is twice blessed" (p. 193). This is actually a reversion to the primitive attitude toward sex, an emphasis on the physical instinct and processes themselves rather than on the persons involved. The result of this reversion is, frequently, that persons are regarded as attached to the organs, as appendages to them, rather than the other way around. It is the penis and the vagina that are considered as performing intercourse, not the persons.

There is also occasionally found in pornography a mechanistic attitude toward the sex organs, as can be understood from another quotation from the author of *My Secret Life*. He is describing one of his seductions: "In short she was a machine (like any other piece of machinery) obeying the impulses of the key that so potently set her in motion" (p. 214). Although these attitudes toward the sex organs may seem radically different, they actually are the same: They regard the organs as having their own power and existence, becoming the dominant and controlling forces in the relationship, and hence forcing the human and personal into subservience and stagnation.

Since the sex organs have a life force of their own in pornography, the sex drive cannot be resisted; it is uncontrollable. Far from being a lamentable situation, however, it is desirable, for the ideal state in Pornotopia is constant sexual excitement. It is not enough to experience a strong, healthy sexuality; the goal is hypersexuality. The hero of pornographic writings wants sexual activity constantly, and the pressures of this ruttish state require that he be satisfied with any woman—actually, any vagina. This desire, however, boils over into even more impersonal forms of sexual conduct, for invariably there arises a desire not only for every kind of partner and position, but also for all the less usual sexual practices: homosexuality, sodomy, bestiality, flagellation, and on and on. The crowning delight in this kind of literature is to enjoy every variety of sexual experience at the same time and all the time: An orgy in which everything sexually possible is experienced while the individual affords every possible experience to others would be paradise. This state is one of total eroticism, in which the whole body and every part of it is viewed as an erogenous zone. Nowhere, however, can the impersonality of this attitude be more clearly seen than in an orgy, in which distinctions not only between people but between sexes are obliterated in the mass of indistinguishable heads, torsos, arms, and legs. Commenting on this confusion, Marcus observes that in orgies "clitorises become penises, anuses are common to both sexes, and everyone is everything to everyone else" (pp. 275–76).

The final result of this impersonality is the absence of any continuing relationships in pornography. The drive toward total sexuality prohibits the heroes and heroines from entering into a deep relationship with one person. In fact, they flee compulsively from one sex object to another. Consequently they deny, implicitly or explicitly, any notion of personal love, a love that would bind two people together in a meaningful and lasting relationship.

This attitude toward the union of the sexes is the exact opposite of that found in the respectable literature of the nineteenth century, in which the ideal relationship between man and woman was deeply personal and enduring. It can certainly be argued that the veiled treatment of the physical aspects of sex in the approved literature of the Victorian period forced them to a desperate and exaggerated life of their own in underground literature. Because this dichotomy between respectable and underground literature is not one of peaceful coexistence but rather one of smoldering antagonism, there are many examples of attacks back and forth. Since one of the most powerful forces of the Establishment in the nineteenth century was the Church (although there was, certainly, conflict between the ecclesiastical and secular within that establishment), there is a great deal of anticlericalism in pornography, which views the Church as suppressing the natural desires of mankind. (What is curious, however, is that pornography often attacks the Church by portraying the clergy as being the most lecherous of people.)

If pornography concentrates on the physical aspects of sexual relationships while the respectable literature concentrates on the more refined, spiritual aspects, we might ask which is the more realistic. Pornography frequently attempts to justify itself as being faithful to the raw facts of life. Admittedly there is an excessive refinement in the more traditional Victorian literature that all too often makes it seem ethereal. Actually, neither literature does justice to a complete and total view of human sexuality, a division Marcus believes has tragic implications. I sense, however, an awareness in the respectable literature that is consciously refined and delicate. On the other hand, pornography seems to be almost militantly realistic, claiming frequently to be a record of facts and using some of the standard techniques of literary realism. For example, there is the first-person narrator, a technique that helps to establish a more immediate relationship between author and reader. The style of pornography is rapid, curt, and nonreflective (who has time for or interest in reflections during sexual activity?), concentrating principally on actions. Reflection and long descriptive passages do not build sexual excitement, so they are not used.

Despite this attempt at realism, Marcus believes that pornography lives in a fantasy world, a land of promised plenty, in which sexual juices have replaced milk and honey. He believes that this fantasy exists because pornography is a projection of infantile and adolescent attitudes. Besides some of the adolescent concerns already mentioned, Marcus notes that orgies could be informed by an infantile theory of anal intercourse as well as the belief that a woman is a castrated male with a hidden penis. Marcus suggests that this belief might be one reason why pornography is so compulsively repetitious, as its hero moves from one affair to another; it reveals that the hero (ultimately the author) is looking for something he cannot find because it does not exist. Although some might question the psychological assumptions upon which Marcus relies, it is still difficult to deny that there are some strongly incompatible drives at work in pornography. If nothing else, the sadism and masochism into which so much pornography evolves reveal an unhealthy attitude toward sex. Marcus believes that pornography ultimately manifests a desire to return to the bliss of infancy: "Inside of every pornographer there is an infant screaming for the breast from which it had been torn" (p. 274).

The fantasies in pornography take many forms. One that Marcus finds to be prevalent is the portrayal of dreams as the revelation of hidden desires. In one pornographic novel, *The Lustful Turk*, a young and virtuous maiden who has just been violently deflowered is visited by her attacker, who watches her, in her sleep, go through all the motions of being seduced, but with a radiant smile on her face.[3] She is dreaming, of course, and her dream reveals her true but unrecognized feelings about being sexually overpowered. The author of *The Lustful Turk* is expressing two attitudes here. One is the masculine fantasy that women enjoy being violently seduced and raped, even though they cannot admit it to themselves. The other is that this fantasy is revealed in the fantasy world

3. "It should be observed that this scene of dream, awakening, and then continuation and fulfillment of the dream in reality soon becomes a convention in pornographic fiction. I have noted at least a dozen subsequent instances of it." Marcus, p. 211*n*3.

of dreams. The masculine fantasy is projected onto the woman, not as awake or conscious, but as she fantasizes in a dream. This motif shows again just how confused are the attitudes in pornography, and now the genre must resort to some kind of make-believe in order to make its beliefs convincing.

This confusion of fantasy and reality is carried to its furthest extreme by the author of *My Secret Life*. As he aged and began to lose his potency, he would attempt to excite himself sexually by lying in bed with a woman and reading from the diary he had kept of his earlier affairs. Marcus comments on the circularity of this activity: "His accumulated fantasies, written down in the form of recollections of his experiences, now feed back into the reality of the present, heighten that reality, infuse it with further fantasies, and stimulate him to act out everything all over again in a frenzy of reading, feeling, acting, imagining, and going on and on" (p. 187).

Some of Marcus's best insights, I believe, are into the nature of the language of pornography. He finds that it actually is a burden: "At best, language is a bothersome necessity, for its function in pornography is to set going a series of non-verbal images, of fantasies, and if it could achieve this without the mediation of words it would" (p. 279). Hence one finds many clichés and hackneyed phrases, for they have been proven to evoke the desired responses. Taboo words are used for different reasons, however, for they achieve their force from the belief, found in primitive societies (but living on in the modern consciousness) that, somehow, saying the word is magically connected with doing the deed. Marcus puts it this way: "Their [the taboo words'] primeval power has much to do with the fact that in our minds these words are minimally verbal, that they are still felt as acts, that they have not been dissociated from the tissue of unconscious impulses in which they took their origin" (p. 240). Ideally, then, in pornography, the use of certain words causes instant sexual excitement in all who hear them. Mind over matter, indeed! A similar attempt is found in the use of metaphor in pornography. Instead of its ordinary use, which is an identification of two objects into a new verbal unity that gives fresh insight into reality, metaphor in pornography "seeks to *de-elaborate* the verbal structure and the distinctions upon which it is built, to move back through language to that part of our minds where all metaphors are literal truths, where everything is possible, and where we were all once supreme" (p. 280). In its use of clichés, taboo words, and metaphors, the language of pornography tries to present the reader with a direct and immediate relationship with sexual phenomena; it does not try to form, control, and make personal those phenomena through the human use of language.

The structure of pornography betrays a curious ambivalence. On the one hand it reveals a desperate need for variety and change, as the hero moves compulsively from one sexual encounter to the next. On the other, this change is in name only, since the hero is interested only in satisfying an urge that remains unchanged. Thus the change and variety is ultimately monotonous and ritualistic. Like the language of pornography, its actions become formulaic; the variety finally becomes circular. This need for variety and change prohibits any meaningful development of narrative structure. But there is something even more curious about the structure of pornography. As noted above, the ideal state is one of constant sexual excitement. There is no desire to achieve total gratification—normal in a sexual relationship—for complete satisfaction would mean the end of sexual excitement. The ideal pornographic novel would involve perpetual sexual arousal—for the man, an eternal erection. Hence, there tends to be something formless about pornography in its attempts to achieve this ideal state. There is no growth or development in this form, except the kind that is found in *Fanny Hill,* where every male the heroine meets has a larger penis than the previous one.

Finally, Marcus believes that pornography is basically a sad literature: "We tend to think of honesty as invigorating; we forget that often it can be depressing. The literature of sex, in all its branches, is not a particularly joyful or happy literature. It is on the whole rather grim and sad; even at its most intense moments there is something defeated in it. Something in the nature of its subject, one may reflect, dictates this prevailing tone" (p. 162). I believe there are some exceptions: One thinks of Terry Southern's *Candy*, which according to popular testimony is both hilarious and pornographic, although one wonders about the depth of its comic vision. Still, I think Marcus is generally correct in this observation. Almost every statement he makes about pornography leads to that conclusion: The severe limitations on deep personal relationships, the view of sex as aggression, the reality-distorting fantasies, the compulsive need for change within a pattern of endless repetition, these and all other limitations could hardly create a joyful vision.

* * *

Like Victorian pornography, the Old French fabliaux flourished in a society where the more respectable literature—the romances, epics, and *chansons de geste*—characteristically omitted explicit details of sexual acts. The natural interest in and curiosity about such matters seem to have been somewhat satisfied by these ribald tales. It is surprising, however, to view the directions such curiosity took, for many of the fabliaux, some in part and some almost in their entirety, exhibit definite pornographic elements. These tales are finally saved from being pornographic by their humor, which flows out of the surprise endings and redirects the pornography into comic channels.

The authors of these tales were, with one exception, men—frequently young clerics—whose adolescent viewpoint is betrayed by their persistent attention to the male sex organ.

When measurements are given, they are never anything other than heroic, as in this description of a young squire:

> Gros avoit et quarré le vit. (*MR*, V, 208)
>
> (He had a huge and solid prick.)

The potency of the penis in the fabliaux is generally enormous, the prize, I believe, going to the priest in *Le Prestre et Alison*, who has sex nine times in one night (*MR*, II, 21). This fantasy certainly resembles events in the land of Pornotopia, but the landscape of the fabliau has a way of blending everything into its own scenery. Another fabliau, *Le Vallet aux douze fames* (*MR*, III, 186), uses the fantasy of unlimited potency and lets it play itself out. The young hero of *Le Vallet* deludes himself into believing that he is so potent that he can be sexually satisfied only if he were to have not one, nor two, nor even three, but a dozen wives! His father tries to convince him to try just one, as a test, and he finally, but reluctantly, agrees. But after a mere six months of being married to just one girl, he is so physically exhausted that he is reduced to skin and bones. The comic nature of this tale rests precisely on its destroying the fantasy of unlimited male potency. This reversal of expectations is a typical comic climax in the fabliaux; the climax is the point at which fantasy becomes reality. The reality in this tale, it must be admitted, is limited, since it replaces one fantasy with another—the insatiability of the female sexual appetite.

Aggressiveness is also a part of the sexuality of the fabliaux; the penis is a weapon. One of the more typical verbs used to describe intercourse is *battre* ("to beat"), and its use gives the seductions in some of these stories the semblance of a cudgeling rather than of an act of love. The following quotation illustrates that aggressiveness:

> De la point du vit la point;
> El con le met jusqu'à le coille,

> Dont le bat le cul, et rooille
> Tant, ce m'est vis qu'il ot foutu. (*MR*, V, 61)
>
> (He stuck her with the head of his prick / and shoved it in her cunt clear up to his balls, / and then he beat hard against her bottom, and thrust so / that I believe she really got screwed.)

Reliance on the size, potency, and power of the penis for one's total concept of masculinity and pleasure has its negative side, for if one loses any of those qualities, or worst of all, the whole Priapean trinity, one is lost forever. That fear is dramatized in *Le Pescheor de Pont seur Saine* (*MR*, III, 68), a story about a husband who fears that his wife's chief interest in him centers on his penis. When he asks her if that is so, she denies it, but he is not convinced. One day while fishing he happens to find the dead body of a priest, so he cuts off the penis, takes it home, and tells his wife that it is his. She immediately prepares to leave. A happy reconciliation results when the husband reveals the truth, but their reunion does not resolve the fear that motivates the story. There is clearly a sense of uneasiness at the conclusion of this tale because the climax does not come from the needs the story embodies. It is closer to tragicomedy than to comedy.

Another adolescent masculine motif that is frequently found in the fabliaux is a fascination with farting. There does not seem to be anything unhealthy about this fascination in itself, but it is curious that the fascination blends with what surely is a masculine amazement at the differences between the male and female anatomy. Perhaps the silliest story depicting this strange interest is *Les Trois Meschines* (*MR*, III, 76), a tale about three young girls who are trying to mix some face powder they have bought. They decide to mix it with urine, so one of them gets up on the bowl containing the powder and tries to urinate. Her efforts cause her to fart instead, and the face powder blows all over the other two girls. Her only defense at their outrage is that they must have placed the bowl under the wrong hole! One certainly can envision young medieval lads giggling nervously over that story.

When those boys got a little older, they might have told the one about *Gauteron et Marion* (*MR*, III, 49). This tale combines not urination and farting, but farting and intercourse. Here is another motif that recurs with surprising frequency: a fear that a woman will fart during intercourse. In the very act of consummating their marriage, Marion farts, and when young, naive Gauteron asks her what that horrible stench is, she replies that it is her escaping maidenhead! Gauteron's prayer that may maidens never more preserve their virginity, so bad is its smell, is a comic expression of a rather deep sexual drive in young men, while at the same time it fuses the two distinct orifices into the fantasy world of one. The young men's laughter would be somewhat deeper at this joke.

The portrayal of women in the fabliaux is similar in many ways to their portrayal in pornography. There are as many anonymous women as there are ones with names, and even those with names do not have defined personalities; they are not memorable for themselves but for their functions. They prefer men who are virile and potent, a preference that arouses both hope and fear in men—hope if one is the seducer, fear if the woman is one's wife or daughter. The fears are well grounded, for women in the fabliaux are easily available and generally insatiable. In fact, sex is the universal tonic that can overcome all griefs. The most extreme example of this attitude is the fabliau, *Celle qui se fist foutre sur la fosse de son mari* (*MR*, III, 118). A knight and squire pass near the place where a young widow is grieving on the grave of her recently departed husband. They halt and the squire bets the knight that he can seduce her. He approaches the woman and expresses his sympathy for her plight, saying that he too has just lost his beloved. She asks how his beloved died, and he tells her that he killed her by "screwing her to death." The widow, in her grief for her husband, says that she too wants to die, and so she begs the squire to lead her out of this vale of tears. He obliges her, but, not quite miraculously, she recovers from her grief, forgets her husband, and is restored to happiness. I believe the story is humorous, though admittedly it skirts black humor, but here the humor never really covers up the fears of young men who might be fully aware of the power of sex but not of the emotional stability produced by a deep personal relationship.

Occasionally, however, there is a surprising insight into a more feminine attitude toward sex. In spite of the usual masculine attitude that women delight only in violent sex, there are a few instances in which women actually complain that the man is being too rough:

> Au con trover mie ne faut,
> Lo vit i bote roidement:
> "Vaslez, tu quiers trop durement,"
> Fet la pucele qui sospire. (*MR*, V, 154)
>
> (He found her cunt with no trouble, and shoved his prick in rudely; "Sir, you are being too rough," said the panting young girl.)

Comments like that are exceptional, but they do reveal another way in which the fabliaux can occasionally break through the fantasy world of pornography.

As a result of these unreal attitudes toward sex there is little chance for the development of strong personal relationships in the fabliaux. A few long-lasting affairs are celebrated in these stories, but most of the men and women in them are satisfied with casual sex. Even when the love endures for some time, no real emotions develop between the lovers. The beloved is usually another man's wife or his daughter, so practical difficulties prevent establishing a deeper relationship. But the main reason for the lack of meaningful attachments in the fabliaux resides in the demands of the humor. It would be destructive of the comic climax if the relationship between man and woman should be portrayed as refined and delicate. A good example is *La Gageure* (*MR*, II, 193), a story about a squire and girl who are very much in love and want to marry. The marriage is opposed by the girl's older sister, but she finally agrees to allow the squire to marry the girl if he will first kiss the girl's bottom, a task she feels certain he will not stoop to. The squire does agree to the humiliation, but when the time comes to perform the deed, he quickly and deftly turns the misdirected kiss into a seduction and thus forces the girl to marry him. It is difficult to imagine two young people whose refinement and delicacy had been well established engaging in such an act and maintaining the comic tone of the story. At the same time it does show how the comic climax forms these stories, with results that might superficially seem the same as those found in pornography, but with far more important and deeper differences. Its similarity to pornography could possibly be explained as embodying the anal theory of intercourse which Marcus believes to be the cause of several pornographic fantasies. What seems to happen in *La Gageure* is a comic displacement of that fantasy: what was supposed to be anal osculation and could easily have become anal intercourse if the young squire had been confused about his appointed task and his natural desires, becomes instead a normal act of intercourse.

The emphasis on sex organs is not quite the same in the fabliaux as it is in pornography. Their gradual evolution into machines, which Marcus believes to be the trend in all pornography, is not found in the fabliaux, and this is no doubt due to the primitive and limited nature of machines in the Middle Ages. Nor is there the deification of the sexual powers, even in a blasphemous or parodic way. We do find frequently, however, in these stories the personalization of the sex organs. Several sex organs are named, given human characteristics, and can perform certain functions that only a person can perform. The most observable human function is the power of speech, and so it is with uncanny and no doubt unconscious insight that a certain knight, in *Le Chevalier qui fist parler les cons* (*MR*, VI, 68), is granted the ability to make a woman's pudendum speak. The tendency in pornography to view the organs as persons while the rest of the person is a mere appendage to them here achieves fulfillment. It is, to be sure, an absurd notion, one that would be unimaginable even in the wildest pornographic fantasy, but in being absurd it underscores the illogicality of the fantasy; it shows what would happen if the fantasy were to become reality. Fulfillment of pornographic fantasies is one of the principal narrative modes in the fabliaux, allowing, as in *Le Chevalier qui fist parler les cons*, the fantasy to play itself out *ad absurdum*. Moreover, the fabliaux very frequently, after fulfilling the fantasy, turn around and destroy it before our very eyes. In *Le Chevalier qui fist parler les cons*, for example, one noble lady tries to thwart the knight's power by blocking her vagina with rags. She does not know, however, that he also has the power to make the rectum speak, so when her pudendum cannot respond to his questions, the lady is thoroughly humiliated when her rectum blurts out the the answers. Whatever pornographic fascination there might have been in a pudendum that speaks would be completely destroyed by such a gross reversal. The authors of the fabliaux, it seems, recognize an absurdity when they see one.

If sex organs can be made to talk in the fabliaux, it would not seem improbable that they could also assume a separate existence. In a straight pornographic work this separation would be the means of some incredible erotic fantasy, with minute details about the life and loves of a penis and vagina. There are several fabliaux in which that separation does take place, but, true to the genre's purpose, in strange comic fashion. In *La Sorisete des estopes* (*MR*, IV, 158) a foolish young man marries a girl who prefers to render her virginity to another man. When the naive husband begins sexual foreplay by feeling for his bride's pudendum, she tells him that she does not have it with her; she left it with her mother. The husband quickly gets up and rides off in haste to his mother-in-law's home, who helps with the ruse by giving the husband a basket with a mouse in it. On his way back to his bride, he becomes so aroused thinking about the *con* so close to him, that he decides to make love to it on the spot. When he thrusts his penis into the basket, however, the mouse becomes frightened, jumps out, and runs away into a dew-covered field. The comic tone of the story is evident in the plaintive cry of the rejected husband as he searches frantically for the *con*:

> "Biaus cons, doz cons, tost revenez;
> Tote ma fiance tenez,
> Que mais ne vos adeserai
> Devant que à l'ostel serai,
> Et tant que vos avrai livré
> A ma fame, si delivré
> Vos puis avoir de la rosée." (*MR*, IV, 162)

> ("Pretty cunt! Sweet cunt! Come back! Now! I give you my word that I won't try to screw you until we get back home and until I have given you back to my wife, and have saved you from the dew.")

Frustrated in his search, he returns in despair to his young wife, who meanwhile has been enjoying herself with her lover. When her husband tells her that he has lost her *con*, she tells him not to worry, it has returned and is safely tucked away between her legs. The surprise ending comes when the anxious husband then reaches down to make sure it is there; it is, but it is also wet—a condition that proves to him that it is the right *con*, since it naturally would have gotten soaked while running through the dew-covered field! The ending dovetails all the elements of the story: It allows the wife to escape being caught in her infidelity; it completes the quest of her husband, and it brings full circle the fantasy of the self-existing *con*. The husband's fantasy is a fiction within the fiction of the story, something like a play within a play—possibly the only way that this particular erotic fantasy could have been dealt with. But it is lived fully until it is dissolved at the end. The comic climax of this tale is a perfectly blended consummation of fantasy and marriage.

The hypersexuality that characterizes the heroes of pornography is not found in the fabliaux, whose heroes desire sexual activity, of course, but not frantically. The reason for this difference may spring from the pervasive comic tone of these tales. There is something rather pathetic and frightening about a man in violent heat, and it might be too difficult to present that type in a comic vein. There is one fabliau, however, that depicts a phenomenon which is closely associated with hypersexuality, the desire for the total eroticization of the body, in which the whole body becomes an erotic zone. The story is *Les Quatre Sohais Saint Martin* (*MR*, V, 201), and it tells of a husband who is granted four wishes by Saint Martin. When he tells his wife of his good luck, she asks for one of the four, which he gives her, and she immediately wishes that he be covered all over with penises. Here certainly is literal wish fulfillment! He counters by wishing that she be covered all over with pudenda. Right away they realize how foolish their wishes were, so the husband uses the third wish to get rid of all the *cons* and *vits*, and so they all disappear, including their original ones! Sadly, but necessarily, the husband uses the last wish to be restored to their original normal state. The author of this tale has instinctively brought to realization one of the most cherished dreams of the pornographer in the utmost radical way; if the whole body is going to be an erotic zone, what more basic way than for it to become entirely a sex organ? Just as instinctively the author realizes how impossible such a state of total eroticization is, so he destroys it by allowing the logic of wish fulfillment to take the next inevitable step, total de-eroticization. The inevitability of that step rests on an all-or-nothing-at-all logical structure, which is actually at the heart of pornography: Either life is all sex, or it is nothing. The conclusion of *Les Quatre Sohais* is a restoration of common sense.

Besides total eroticization, pornography aims for permanent eroticization, that is, a permanent erection. Sure enough, there is a fabliau which grants that desire. *L'Anel qui faisoit les . . . grans et roides* (*MR*, III, 51) is about a ring which gives its wearer an unfailing erection. This pornographer's stone, however, is turned to nought in the story, for it is found by a bishop who is embarrassed by his condition and who does not realize its cause. (Here too, perhaps, is a bit of satire on the respect shown for a bishop's ring.) He is finally relieved of his embarrassment when the owner learns that the bishop has the ring and offers to "cure" him for one hundred pounds, plus a gift of the ring the bishop is wearing. There is a curious ambiguity in the tale, for we tend to think only of the bishop's relief and not of the fact that the ring still has its powers, leaving the fantasy intact at the end.

One of the motifs that Marcus believes to be conventional in pornography is the erotic dream, which, when the dreamer awakes, is fulfilled in reality. The story of *La Damoiselle qui sonjoit* (*MR*, V, 208) is basically built on that structure, although with some significant differences. A young man comes to a young girl who is asleep and has intercourse with her four times before she awakens. (The seduction of the sleeping girl in this story may also be an attempt of some kind to give more concrete and believable form to another medieval fantasy: the incubus.) Instead of screaming, however, she tells him that *he* is caught, and then, talking as though he were a foe vanquished in the lists, she orders him to continue. But he is vanquished more than figuratively, for his amatory assaults have left him exhausted and temporarily impotent. She scolds him, but then tells him to get underneath her:

> "Ce n'est pas, ce m'est avis, honte
> Quant homme faut, se fame monte." (*MR*, V, 210)
>
> ("It is not shameful, it seems to me, for the woman to mount when the man fails.")

The narrator then concludes:

> Ainsi torna son songe à bien
>
> (Thus her dream turned out well.)

Although it is essentially the same motif as is found in later pornography, the variations are important. First, the seduction occurs before the dream, and perhaps can be seen as its inspiration. But then there is the very realistic incapacity of the male, which seems at first to ruin the girl's dreams, but since she manages to make them turn out well, her dreams take a strange twist. Her first words on opening her eyes are "*Vous estes pris*" ("You are captured"), and the last thing she does in the story is to assume a superior position. Hence, although the story seems to be fulfilling the male desire for dominance, it literally turns that desire upside down.

The language of the fabliaux is quite similar to that of pornography. There are the clichés and hackneyed phrases that attempt to set off stock responses. There are the obscenities and taboo words, sprinkled liberally throughout these stories, in some being interwoven almost thematically, and in some being restrained until the comic climax, where their shock value is the surprise element of that climax. The general comic tone, however, that flows from that climax brings about a radical difference in the tone of these words in the fabliaux. Frequently their use in pornography is very sad and desperate, coming, as they do, from compulsions that make the speaker seem less than human, as in this passage from *My Secret Life*, which Marcus quotes: "When I once have my rutting fury on . . . I can think of nothing but cunt, and, even when for the time used up by copulation—*Cunt*,—*Cunt*,—is all I think of" (p. 177). The chantlike nature of those words could be taken as an unconscious attempt to evoke the object by an erotic litany. Compare the desperateness of that anguished cry with the following rhapsody, spoken by a sweet and curious young girl whose mother has just reluctantly told her the name of the male organ:

> "Vit," dist ele, "Dieu merci, vit!
> Vit dirai je, cui qu'il anuit,
> Vit, chetive! vit dist mon pere,
> Vit dist ma suer, vit dist mon frere,
> Et vit dist notre chamberiere,
> Et vit avant et vit arriere
> Nomme chascuns à son voloir." (*MR*, V, 103)

> ("Prick," she said, "God-a-mercy, prick! Prick I'll say, no matter whom it bothers, prick, you wretch! Prick says my father, prick says my sister, prick says my brother, and prick says our chambermaid; either prick in front or prick behind, each asks according to his desires.")

It seems to me that this lyrical outburst is as fresh and innocent as its speaker. Part of that tone comes from its formalism, its careful use of such rhetorical devices as *repetitio* and *conduplicatio*, which make it seem more controlled, more human, than the formless and mere obsessive repetition of the anguished cry from *My Secret Life*. The mother's reluctance to tell her daughter the word is based on the primitive fear that there is a direct relationship between saying the word and having the object. The mother comes close to expressing that belief outright:

> "Fille, no soiez mie
> Ne trop parlant ne trop nonciere,
> Ne de parler trop coustumiere,
> Quar à mal puet l'en atorner
> Fame quant l'en l'ot trop parler
> Autrement que ele ne doit." (*MR*, V, 101–2)

> ("Daughter, neither speak too much, nor speak nonsense, nor gossip too much, for one can turn a girl to evil when one hears her say more than she should.")

The girl's paean could be viewed as a defiant attempt to break the taboo, and it seems to work here. Other young girls in the fabliaux are not so lucky; one of them faints whenever she hears the word *foutre* (fuck) (*MR*, II, 81). But even that response is an attack on the primitive attitude toward taboo words. It gives a comic answer to the question that is implied in the taboo: What would happen if saying the word *were* the same as doing the deed? The pornographer's answer would be that saying the word actually brought sexual raptures to all who heard it. Her response is a form of comic displacement; it does not exactly destroy the taboo, but merely laughs at it.

What is even more curious is that these girls, like several others who do not know these taboo words or who cannot bear to hear them spoken, are all willingly seduced. The seduction in each case is accomplished, not by breaking the taboo, but by going around it. In all these stories a young man appears on the scene, hears of the girl's innocence or fears, approaches her, and the two construct an elaborate metaphorical game that allows them to have intercourse. Typical are the metaphors in *La Damoiselle qui ne pooit oïr parler de foutre* (*MR*, III, 81). The girl begins the amatory foreplay, during which she discovers that the young man has a small horse to which is attached a sack of oats. Then the young man discovers that the girl has "the most beautiful meadow in the world," and in the middle of it is a deep fountain. Up to this point the description of the girl's body is almost an exact replica of Marcus's description of the landscape of Pornotopia (pp. 271–72). But the fabliaux escape the limited boundaries of pornography, and so the young man ventures farther afield and discovers the girl's anus, which she tells him is the guard of the meadow and fountain. Sure enough, when the horse gets thirsty and starts to drink at the fountain, the guard sounds a warning; twice, in fact! But the owner of the fountain is not disturbed by the horse's trespass, and instead asks its owner to silence the guard by killing it:

> "Ferez, batez, hurtez, boutez,
> Batez le tant que l'ociez. (*MR*, III, 85)
>
> ("Beat, strike, shove, thrust, strike until you kill it.")

The young man gladly obeys, and the guard sounds no more.

Only on a superficial level are these true metaphors, for they are not used to bring about any new insight into reality, but only to bring about a seduction. The lovers are playing a clever game, and their metaphors are mock ones. They are, admittedly, highly suggestive and erotic, and they have a surface appropriateness, except for that which is most dominant—the anus as guard. The total disparity of that identification jars the reader into a full realization of how foolish is the rest of the metaphoric structure. When the guard sounds a warning, instead of the congruity which a true metaphor should bring, only incongruity results. The humor of the situation is, indeed, that very incongruity. Even though the girl keeps up the game with her request that the guard be killed, the sexual nature of the game is clearly seen and felt in the strong sexual rhythms of that request: "Ferez, batez, hurtez, boutez. . . ." This is the pattern that underlies all these tales of innocence metaphorically seduced; at some point, usually the comic climax, the metaphor is revealed for what it really is: a sham.

The fabliaux also share certain stylistic traits with pornography as defined in the Marcus study. There is an emphasis on action, with almost no long descriptive passages, nor accounts of psychological states, nor lengthy dialogue. One major difference, however, is the complete absence of the first-person narrator within the main structural narrative (there is some use at the beginning of the tale and at the end, but they are invariably comments on the story and not part of the story itself). The device is not used frequently in medieval literature, except in some short lyrics, and it might have been dangerous to use it in these tales which so often come close to being pornographic. According to Marcus, it is used in pornographic novels in order to establish a more direct, personal, and intimate relationship with the solitary reader, a relationship that helps the pornographer in his purposes. Since the fabliaux were recited before a live audience, and usually a mixed one, such a method might have been too immediate and too embarrassing. The use of the omniscient narrator creates a more objective tone and keeps a comic control over any element the audience might find objectionable.

Although the fabliaux are famed for their realism, its exact nature and function are not so well understood. Granted that the overall style is realistic, there are almost no fabliaux that portray completely realistic actions, for they range on a spectrum that moves from the wild or far-fetched through the bizarre and incredible all the way to the impossible or supernatural. The bits and snatches of realistic description and dialogue serve the same purposes as realism in pornography; they shore up the dream castles with a solid base which allows us to enter on a more secure footing. But that is where the similarity stops. In pornography the ideal is to stay in the dream castle, and it is with great reluctance and even despair that one must leave. But the fableors instinctively and invariably know that the dream castle is nothing more than a fun house, which allows them to enjoy themselves and then leave, smiling and laughing.

Consequently, the structure of the fabliaux is very different from that found in pornography. Instead of being formless and episodic, the fabliaux are generally very well knit and tightly formed. They progress and build, not in character development nor in philosophical insight, but in comic movement. These tales characteristically end in a surprise that is so well prepared that the ending, the comic climax, is a deeply satisfying fulfillment. At the moment of the surprise ending, we see the full relevance of all that has gone before, and when we see how the surprise balances the preparation, we are struck by the symmetry and harmony of the tale. This is true, I believe, no matter how chaotic, farcical, crude, or even obscene the story has been. Most of the tales that I have used as examples in this paper prove that theory. What seems truly significant, moreover, is that this structure is frequently—especially in the stories that have erotic elements—a movement from realism to fantasy and then back to realism. Style, structure, content, and vision—all the elements of the fabliaux—reveal a healthy and liberating attitude.

Finally, unlike the bulk of pornography, the fabliaux are humorous. There are many reasons for that difference. Lacking the desperate compulsiveness, the fears, the craving for total eroticization and infinite variety (there are no acts of homosexuality nor any orgies in the fabliaux), and the pathetic fantasies, these tales approach sex as something that is fun and joyful, an activity that almost always brings "grant joie et grant delit." Because the fableors see sex as fun, it is also seen as a game, not only individual sexual acts, but also whole episodes and many of the tales themselves. The erotic element in many tales exists as a game within the total work, a play within a play, and its patently fictional nature has a way of folding itself over and embracing the whole tale. Despite the author's occasional claim that he is telling a true story, the tales are easily recognized for what they are.

The main source of the humor lies deep within the foundation of these stories, in the surprise endings. Unless the word is used ironically, the substantive word *surprise* is something pleasant. Since full appreciation of the surprise depends on seeing how it completes the whole tale, it actually is a recognition, somewhat like the sudden encounter with a friend whom we have not seen for a long time. Further, because of the tension that builds up as a result of the preparation, that recognition is more properly like the experience of suddenly finding someone we have been ardently searching for. Hence the very justifiable joy we feel in reading the fabliaux, despite their crudities and obscenities. But because this recognition is the moment when the pornographic fantasy is smashed, it is also at the same time a movement from servitude to freedom. The dream world of pornography will allow no recognitions, for that would be their death. Truly the comic spirit of the fabliaux transforms potential pornographic tendencies and liberates them with joyous laughter.

❧ X ☙

ROY J. PEARCY

MODES OF SIGNIFICATION AND THE HUMOR OF OBSCENE DICTION IN THE FABLIAUX

When Reason in *Le Roman de la Rose* outrages the Lover by her casual use of the term *coilles,* she initiates an exchange that provides one of the rare opportunities for thirteenth-century attitudes toward obscene diction to be articulated. Despite Reason's argument that the instruments of generation, as created by God and necessary to the fulfillment of His divine purposes, must in themselves be good, the Lover insists that delicacy dictates glossing such referents with "quelque courteise parole":

> Car, tout ait Deus les *choses* faites,
> Que ci devant m'avez retraites;
> Les *moz* au meins ne fist il mie,
> Qui sont tuit plein de vilenie! [1]

> (For even though God made the *things* which you mentioned to me before, the *words,* at least, which are so full of offensiveness, he most certainly did not make.)

The Lover, as spokesman for courtly refinement, sees the issue as essentially stylistic. Reason, impatient with the Lover's fastidiousness, tries to expose his folly in supposing that he objects to the *significans* rather than the *significatum*:

1. Guillaume de Lorris and Jean de Meun, *Le Roman de la Rose,* ed. Ernest Langlois, *SATF* (Paris: Firmin-Didot, 1914), III, 25, ll. 6983–6986. All quotations of *Le Roman de la Rose* are from this edition.

Se je, quant mis les nons aus choses,
Que si reprendre et blasmer oses,
Coilles "reliques" apelasse,
Et reliques "coilles" clamasse
Tu, qui si m'en morz e depiques,
Me redeisses de "reliques"
Que ce fust laiz moz e vilains. (III, 30)

(If, when I assigned to things the names which you now presume to accuse me with, I had called balls "relics," and relics "balls," then you would be making the same sharp and mordant criticisms of "relics" as you made to me regarding "balls," that it is an ugly and churlish word.)

By attempting to show that the Lover's objections are not to the words used to describe things but to the things themselves, Reason shifts debate to ontological grounds. As if to prove her point, Jean de Meun concludes *Le Roman de la Rose* with a graphically obscene description of the Lover's final success, which studiously avoids all use of objectionable terms, but in point of fact Reason is being deliberately perverse in substituting *reliques* for *coilles*. The Lover had intended that she should use as a *courteise parole* some euphemism such as *choses* or *riens*. While Reason's proposed substitution of the unacceptable *reliques* casts doubt on the Lover's assumption that the names of things viewed simply as sounds (*flatus vocis*) are in themselves evil, his apparent willingness to accept such substitutions as *choses* or *riens* undermines Reason's contention that he finds the things objectionable in themselves. We are dealing here with three distinct linguistic phenomena, figurative expressions (*reliques*), obscenities (*coilles*), and euphemisms (*riens*). Although ontological arguments address themselves only to the first two terms and stylistic arguments only to the last two, discussion of obscenity in *Le Roman de la Rose* and in contemporary fabliaux in which the same three linguistic phenomena are of frequent occurrence has been governed by one or the other of these approaches.

The ontological argument remained a live issue for Christine de Pisan, who argued in her attacks on *Le Roman de la Rose* that things good when created by God are not necessarily so after the Fall.[2] Per Nykrog has most recently set forth the stylistic argument, devoting a full chapter to obscenity in a book whose title, *Les Fabliaux: Étude d'histoire littéraire et de stylistique médiévale*,[3] clearly indicates his critical orientation. Unlike some of his predecessors, the value of whose comments is vitiated by the delicacy of their own sensibilities, Nykrog resolved from the start to observe "une objectivité toute médicale" (p. 209) in his investigations. His willingness to confront the phenomenon squarely furnishes a reasonably exhaustive analysis. However, his primary concern—to refute Bédier's view of the fabliau as a bourgeois genre[4]—led him to regard obscenity as a phenomenon potentially prejudicial to his thesis that the fabliaux constitute a *genre courtois*. Noting that the authors of fabliaux frequently employ courtly euphemisms and that when they choose an obscenity they often use it in conjunction with modifiers which aggravate its offensiveness, Nykrog resolved his problem by concluding that in the fabliaux "l'obscénité . . . veut choquer en faisant ouvertement infraction à la décence" and that we are therefore dealing with a "franche et naïve pornographie" (p. 216) which might be enjoyed by members of a courtly society that retained a taste for *gauloiserie*.

Nykrog's explanation of the function of obscenities is not readily disprovable, and indeed for a large number of obscenities it may be the right explanation. It assumes, however, that obscenities are minimally and uniformly funny, whatever the context, an assumption at odds with any sensitive experience

2. *The Epistles on the Romance of the Rose and other Documents in the Debate*, ed. Charles Frederick Ward, diss. Chicago, *Transactions of the Royal Society of Canada*, 8 (1911).

3. Diss. Aarhus, 1957 (Copenhagen: Ejnar Munksgaard, 1957), pp. 208–26.

4. Joseph Bédier, *Les Fabliaux*, 5th ed. (Paris: Champion, 1925).

of the works; it leaves the matter of the obscene use of figurative expressions untouched; and it totally isolates the issue of obscene diction from Nykrog's own concern with the fabliau as "un genre courtois burlesque" or from any other thematic principle.

Since I plan to include figurative expressions in reconsidering Nykrog's view of obscenity in the fabliaux, I have tabulated some occurrences to show the relationship of figurative expressions to corresponding obscenities and euphemisms. The limits for such tabulation are set by accepting as obscene only the four terms that deal with sexual obscenity cited by Nykrog. The possibilities for euphemistic avoidance of the obscenities are limited, and these are fairly comprehensively represented. For figurative expressions, however, the only limit is the authors' ingenuity, and consequently only a representative sampling of such expressions is given. (See table, p. 167.)

The relationship between obscenities, figurative expressions, and euphemisms has other than stylistic implications. With respect to fabliau diction it can best be understood epistemologically, since choices between the linguistic categories potentially reflect different theories of cognition current in the Middle Ages. These choices have direct bearing on issues of falsity and truth, illusion and reality, in characterization, and in the development of fabliau plots. If we choose as our grounds of certitude a pluralistic and concrete external reality and see the process of cognition as moving from objects through percepts and individual concepts to general concepts, then obscenities represent an earlier stage in the process of abstraction than the euphemisms and to that extent more immediately convey the reality they signify. If, on the other hand, we choose as grounds of certitude the single, transcendental source of all being and perceive the process of cognition as dependent on "the light of the mind," which has precognition of the Ideal forms and knows the objects of the external world only as material manifestations of these forms, then our

Obscenity	Euphemism	Figurative Expression
Foutre	Coucher / Gesir avec quelqu'une Mener revel Faire revel / amor / volentez / voloir / bon / talent / delit / plesir Servir à talent / gré Avoir gré / delit / plesir / solaz / deduis / sez	Aforer le tonel a quelqu'une (to broach someone's barrel) Marteler (to hammer) Brochier Ferir un cop (strike a blow) Percier
Coille	Afere Chatel	Forel (satchel) Mailluel (mallet)
Con	Rien	Treu (hole) Plaie (wound)
Vit	Membre Ostil Chose	Andoille (chitterling) Pasnaise (parsnip) Bordoun (staff)

estimate of the efficacy of the signifiers is reversed. The choice between euphemisms and obscenities therefore relates, in however minor a way, to the opposition between essentially Aristotelian and Platonic views of the world, an opposition that, in my view, pervades the fabliaux.

The conflict between Aristotelianism and Platonism was certainly woven into the very fabric of medieval intellectual life. The Platonic view was authoritatively expounded by Augustine,[5] whose influence extended throughout the Middle Ages. Another immensely influential figure, Boethius, contributed to Platonism's early establishment,[6] and it reappears in the writings of Alcuin, John Scotus Erigena,[7] and Bonaventura. Serious opposition to the Platonic viewpoint arose following the rediscovery in the twelfth century of many previously unknown works of Aristotle and with the writings of Peter Abelard. This opposition continued in the work of Thomas Aquinas, and it was fully expressed in an extreme

5. Augustine's understanding of the process of cognition is summed up by Meyrick H. Carré, *Realists and Nominalists* (London: Oxford University Press, 1946), p. 18: "General notions are entirely independent of sensible origin, in the same way as the notions of truth, coherence, equality, and number. Their content comes 'from above.' The mind refers the intelligible norms which it contemplates above it to the sensations and images derived from its commerce with the body and with physical objects. *Scientia* is rooted in perception, but it is not derived from the flux of sensations. And since *scientia*, the farther it advances, is increasingly concerned with the 'reasons,' numbers, and forms of things, it does not require the process of abstraction from particular sensations."

6. Boethius was responsible for conveying to the early Middle Ages such knowledge of Aristotle's logical works as it had. But in transmitting Porphyry's introduction to the *Categories*, Boethius bequeathed, according to Ernest A. Moody, a distorted approach to Aristotelian logic not corrected until Ockham. His interesting discussion is stated in *The Logic of William Ockham* (New York: Russell & Russell Publishers, 1935), pp. 66 ff., where he argues that Porphyry's use of the predicables as a means of understanding the *Categories* fails to distinguish between signification and predication and hence reduces demonstrative science to a dialectical metaphysics: "Porphyry's point of view . . . makes the primary subject of all predication, and hence the object of science, infinite and incapable of being comprehended or signified in determinate manner . . . [74]. Every universal term is an attribute, predicable of 'something' indicated only by other attributes—no determinate concept, but only the indeterminate concept, 'thing' or 'something' or 'being' is the primary subject of attribution."

7. "For him [Erigena] the universal is the essential reality from which the particular is derived; and it is the more real in proportion to its universality. The logical hierarchy of concepts is the scheme of reality, and the most comprehensive abstraction is the fullest Being." Carré, p. 40.

form, at the end of the period when the fabliaux flourished, in the writings of William of Ockham. The fabliaux authors were not philosophers, to be sure, although I suspect many of them belonged to that class of *clerici vagantes* who, in however desultory a way, had spent some time at a university and had acquired some familiarity with the main issues of logic, psychology, and the other disciplines of the conventional undergraduate curriculum. In finding some congruity between the underlying presuppositions of the fabliaux and the expositions of the schoolmen, it is not necessary to assume any direct influence, since we are dealing here with basic, preconscious habits of mind, as likely to be expressed in popular narrative literature as in philosophical disputations. The philosophers are useful for articulating attitudes we must deduce indirectly from the works of the fabliaux authors, but the attitudes are produced in the one as in the other by the cultural environment they share. Much of the humor in the fabliaux can be accounted for in terms of the conflict between the Aristotelian point of view the authors espouse and the Augustinian Neoplatonism they reject.

Medieval discussions of our perceptions of the external world and of the function of verbal signifiers in acquiring knowledge of its nature deal predominantly with the relationship between particular and general concepts of substances, organized in a hierarchy from individuals through species to universals as in the familiar schema of the "arbor Porphyriana." Words such as *con* or *vit,* which signify classes of individual objects, are clearly much less abstract than the words *rien* or *chose,* which signify objects only in respect to their existence as such and are usually classified independently as 'transcendentals,' the "all pervasive attributes of being characteristic of any datum of experience."[8] These tendencies are borne out when the alternative signifiers occur in the context

8. Stephen Chak Tornay, *Ockham: Studies and Selections* (La Salle, Ill.: Open Court Publishing Co., 1938), p. 99*n.*

of the fabliaux. Nykrog has noticed about the word *vit*, "une tendance à l'émployer . . . accompagné d'un adjectif ou d'un complément d'un autre ordre, capable de le rendre encore plus graveleux qu'il n'est à l'état isolé" (p. 211). He cites as modifiers typically insistent on the physical dimensions of this particular object: "plus lonc d'un coutre" (longer than a coulter), *MR*, II, 85; "long et quarré" (long and muscular), *MR*, II, 195; "lonc et gros" (long and thick), *MR*, III, 69; and "gros e plener" (thick and big), *MR*, IV, 128. At the risk of some indelicacy, the characteristic features of these descriptions can be illustrated in an extreme form with the account of the extraordinary *vit* of the vallet Gautiers in *Le Fevre de Creil*:

> Devers le retenant avoit
> Plain poing de gros et .ii. de lonc;
> . . . .
> Rouges come oingnon de Corbueil;
> Et si avoit si ouvert l'ueil
> Por rendre grant plenté de sève,
> Que l'en li péust une fève
> Lombarde très parmi lancier
> Que jà n'en lessast son pissier,
> De ce n'estuet-il pas douter,
> Ne que une oue à gorgueter
> S'ele éust mengié un grain d'orge. (*MR*, I, 231–32)

> (To lay hold of, it was a complete handful around, and two long; it was as red as a Corbueil onion; and its eye was always so open to deliver plenty of juice, that, without any exaggeration, one could have thrown a Lombard bean inside without affecting his ability to piss, anymore than a goose would be stopped from swallowing if she had eaten a grain of barley.)

Such modifiers as are given here, by describing size, shape, and color, restore the accidents of quantity and quality to the abstractive signifier *vit* and endow the concept with some of the characteristics of an original percept, thus moving the signifier further back along the axis of abstraction toward the reality of the object itself. The imaginative re-creation of the sense data associated with earlier experiences of the class of objects denoted, which the words stimulate, is necessarily detailed and particularized. Elaboration in the form of similes contributes to this effect by conjuring up such other immediately significative concepts as fists, onions, eyes, beans, and goosenecks. No comparable phenomenon affects the euphemisms *riens* or *chose*, which are rendered significative merely by the addition of a demonstrative or a possessive pronoun. The object thus belongs to the most general class imaginable —that of all existent things—so the concept is not only devoid of particularizing accidents but is also formless even in respect of the *differentiae* of any particular class of individual objects. Euphemisms of this kind are not used with descriptive modifiers and indeed cannot be so used except to create a deliberate incongruity for humorous effect. An attempt at greater determinateness is sometimes made. The word *ostil* may be used, for example; it identifies the object not only as existent, but also existent as one of a vaguely defined class of objects that have some practical use. Or a relative clause will be attached to the general noun, defining it in terms of some abstractly indicated final cause: "Et si portoit du premier mès / Qu'il covient aus dames servir" (And he carried, of the finest quality, that which is proper to the service of women), *MR*, I, 231. Such devices stop far short of confronting the audience with the physical accidents of particularized concrete occurrence, and they consequently remain quite innocuous.

The use of words to signify actions parallels that of words to signify objects in terms of a graduated determinateness. The plain obscenity *foutre* signifies a specific act and thus conjures a physical image in much the same way as the obscenities that directly signify physical objects. The courtly euphemisms, however, combine the most general verbs in the language (for example, *faire* and *avoir*) with a series of abstract nouns (*revel, amor, volentez, solas,* and *bon*), and the relationship is so inexact that verbs and nouns can be interchanged almost at will. The result is to subsume the particular activity under the general concept of activities related to pleasure or volition in so vague a way that the specific referent is lost sight of completely.

As with the nouns, differentiation of the verbs is also clear, on the basis of their occurrence or nonoccurrence with modifiers. The obscenity is often modified, particularly in respect of the frequency or duration of the action signified. Nykrog cites several passages that illustrate the practice of qualifying how often an action has taken place: "En .i. lit l'avoit estendue / Tant que il l'a .iii. fois foutue" (And he stretched her out on a bed for as long as it took to fuck her three times), *MR*, I, 290.

> Li pautoniers qui ont gros vit
> La fot mout viguerosemant.
>
> . . . .
>
> Et sachiez que en petit d'ore
> La foutit .iii. fois près à près. (*MR*, V, 181–82)
>
> (The vagabond, who had a thick prick, fucked her very vigorously. And be sure that in a short while he fucked her three times in quick succession.)

Specific duration is stated in the following passage, in which the kind of shock effect Nykrog stresses is also achieved through the satiric reference to religion: "Une fois la fout, en mains d'eure/Que l'en éust chanté une Eure" (He fucked her once in less time than it would have taken to say a prayer), *MR*, II, 20. Nykrog says that in about half the instances in which *foutre* occurs it appears in conjunction with "un complément qui insiste très fortement sur le caractère grivois de l'expression" (p. 211). Clearly, the use of the obscene verb does indeed lend itself to further specification in the same way as the obscene nouns. No such modifiers are used with the courtly euphemisms except in a few very rare cases such as the passage cited below, in which the intention seems to be to create a deliberately humorous incongruity: ".v. fois li fist li giu d'amours,/Ains ne se mut nient plus c'uns hors" (Five times he played the game of love with her, and she moved no more than a wall), *MR*, II, 38.

Now it is not an especially startling discovery that greater determinateness of signification correlates directly with greater offensiveness. Such a conclusion, if not explicitly stated, is immediately deducible from Nykrog's observations and consonant with his theory that the obscenities are meant to shock. What Nykrog fails to observe, however, and what I want to stress especially, is that in terms of an Aristotelian theory of signification, which is meant to protect an idea of the concrete, pluralistic, and particularized reality of the external world, there is also a correlation between increased offensiveness and increased efficacy of the signifiers to reflect the reality of the things signified. That such a correlation of euphemisms with the illusory and of obscenities with the real was actually made by the authors of the fabliaux can be demonstrated by examining the use of euphemisms and obscenities in relation to the matters of characterization and plot in their works.

Before I proceed to that, however, figurative expressions must be related to obscenities and euphemisms. This can be done, using William of Ockham's distinction between concepts and words. Concepts for Ockham are the act of the intellect in knowing the sensed objects and are natural signs of the objects as smoke is a sign of fire or groaning of pain. Words, like concepts, also function as signs, either of the objects signified by concepts or of the concepts themselves. Unlike concepts, which as *natural* signs cannot be changed without a concomitant change in the objects signified, however, words are *conventional* signs, so that one word may be arbitrarily used to signify different objects, or one object may be arbitrarily signified by different words. In the figurative expressions that concern us here, a word conventionally used to signify one object is arbitrarily used to signify another—one conventionally signified by an obscenity. Circumstances attendant on the use of the expression and perhaps some superficial physical similarities between the objects signified alert the audience to the fact that signifiers are being used in an unusual way. What makes figurative expressions as offensive as obscenities is that, once the audience has realized that the figurative expression signifies the same object as the obscenity, the figure signifies the object in the same quite determinate way, often in conjunction with the same particularizing accidents.

A good example of the use of a figurative expression occurs in the opening section of *Aloul.* A bourgeois wife is walking in her garden in the early morning. The scene is described in sentimentally romantic terms (Nykrog cites it as an instance of the parody of courtly conventions in the fabliaux), until the wife is accosted by a priest, who responds to her remarks on the salutary effects of the early morning dew with some health hints of his own:

> Mès l'en se doit desjéuner
> D'une herbe que je bien conois;
> . . . .
> Corte est et grosse la racine,
> Mès moult est bone medecine;
> N'estuet meillor à cors de fame. (*MR*, I, 257)

> (But one ought to breakfast on an herb I am familiar with; the root is short and thick, but it is a marvellous panacea; none better is needed for the body of a woman.)

The wife, who, we are told, "n'i entent nule figure" (does not suspect any double meaning), assumes that *herbe* signifies the concept associated with it by convention. But insight into the priest's character and knowledge of his immediate schemes have prepared the audience to suspect that the word *herbe* is here being applied arbitrarily to a quite different concept, a suspicion confirmed by the accidental determinants "corte . . . et grosse" that we have already encountered in a different context, by the causal modifier "[bon] à cors de fame," and, expectedly, by the turn that events in the story take shortly thereafter.

When the figurative expression is a verb, it too is linked with the concept that it signifies on the basis of some purely physical similarity, so that again, once the arbitrary substitution has been recognized, the signification is quite determinate and particularized, as in the use of the verbs *marteler* and *brochier* as substitutes for *foutre*. Such verbs are characterized by the fact that they precisely indicate the relationships between objects involved in the action signified by the verb so as to promote a mental picture of the objects themselves (see, in respect of the verb *marteler* [to hammer] the use of the figurative expression *mailluel* [mallet] as a substitute for *coilles*). Once the idea of substitution for conventional signifiers has been established, it may be extended to any of the objects involved in the action or to associated actions. The result is a kind of allegory—what kind will be discussed in some detail later—since differences between this obscene allegory and allegory as a mode associated with medieval idealism are significant for an understanding of the fabliau ethos. Enough of the conventional signification of the word used in the figurative expression is carried over to identify the concept that it is to signify in the new context. Once the arbitrary signification has been apprehended, the new concept is signified quite precisely, however, and can be further particularized with any attributes it may share with the conventional *significatum* of the arbitrarily applied word.

The process has already been noted in the conclusion of *Le Roman de la Rose*. It may be illustrated for the fabliaux by the story *La Damoiselle qui ne pouvait ouir parler de foutre*, in which the original arbitrary significations are established by the game the mock-modest lovers play in bed. In response to questions prompted by the young man's exploration of her body, the girl identifies her *fontaine*, guarded by a *corne-*

res, and located in "un bos,/Dont li mur sont tres bien enclos/De ma fonteine tot entor" ("a wood, with which the walls around my fountain are effectively enclosed on all sides").[9] Reciprocally, the young man identifies his *cheval*, in turn guarded by *dui mareschal*. The further arbitrary significations and the actual concepts involved in the following exchange, when the young man has complained that his "horse" is "thirsty," are readily apparent:

> "Beveroit il a ma fontaine,"
> Fait ele, "se ge l'i metoie?"
> "Oïl," fait il, "se Dieus me voie!
> Mais li corneres grouceroit."
> "Par foi," fait ele, "non feroit,
> Et se il groce por nul mal,
> Si soient prest li mareschal:
> Si le batent errant molt bien,
> Se il grouce de nule rien!" (Rychner, II, 133)
>
> ("Would he drink at my fountain," she asked, "if I put him there?" "Yes indeed," said he, "as God is my witness! But the trumpeter would grumble." "By my faith," she

9. This story survives in three versions, all of which are printed in *MR* and in Jean Rychner, *Contribution à l'étude des fabliaux* (Geneva: Droz, 1960), II, 120–35. Quotations are taken from Rychner's Version D. (In Nykrog's list, this version is entitled *La Pucele qui abevra le polain* [*MR*, IV, 199].) I have stated that the substitution of conventional signifiers is arbitrary, and in respect of logical signification it is, but a separate essay could be written on the reasons for particular substitutions. Here, clearly, the choice of *fountain* depends on the garden imagery associated with courtly love literature, and it parodies the *garden enclosed* and *fountain sealed* of the *Canticus Canticorum*. The "oingnement [qui] . . . moult par estoit savoreuse" of *La Saineresse* perhaps derives in part from the same source. The use of *fuiron* (ferret) for *vit* in *Le Prestre et la dame* depends immediately on the con/conin (rabbit) pun, but this substitution and that in *Esquiriel* probably owe some force to a more general association that makes small furry animals part of the traditional iconography of sensuality. D. W. Robertson, Jr., has been the foremost investigator of these image patterns: "The Doctrine of Charity in Medieval Gardens," *Speculum*, 26 (1951), 24–49, and *A Preface to Chaucer: Studies in Medieval Perspectives* (Princeton: Princeton University Press, 1962), particularly pp. 112–13 and 190–207.

> said, "no he would not, and if he did grumble without cause, then let the marshalls be at hand and straightway give him a sound beating, if he grumbles for any reason.")

The lovers spin a web of words that in another context would signify concepts associated with chivalric romance (the incongruity is deliberate and humorous), but here the concepts signified are unmistakably of quite another order of experience.

In seduction stories like *La Damoiselle qui ne pouvait ouir parler de foutre* or *L'Esquiriel* no one appears to be victimized, and if the verbal manipulations constitute a trick, then it seems to be the hypocritically prudish side of one or both lovers' personalities that is deceived and circumvented, to their final mutual satisfaction. The characters consequently do not divide clearly into trickster and dupe figures, and use or avoidance of obscenities and euphemisms cannot be correlated with their roles. In other tales where such a division can be made, the use of obscenities and figurative expressions of the kind described characterizes the favored trickster figure, while the use of euphemisms characterizes the dupe, at least up to that point in the story (if it is ever reached) where the dupe discovers that he has been deceived.

Two fabliaux which deal with promiscuous but hypocritical wives well illustrate this point. While the husband's diction in *Le Fevre de Creil* is restrained in comparison with the author's, he is plainspoken to the point of using such obscenities as *vit* and *foutre* in talking with his wife about the sexual prowess of their servant. The wife, however, feigns outrage at any mention of the subject matter, and even as she attempts to seduce Gautiers, she uses the courtly euphemism *ostil* in preference to an obscenity. Still more striking is the situation in *Le Pescheor de Pont sur Saine*, in which the husband, who insists that his wife loves him only because of the sexual satisfaction she derives from their marriage, uses the noun *vit* four times and the verb *foutre* once, while the wife, who insists that sexual activity is merely an annoyance she tolerates, uses the euphemisms *afere, riens,* and *ostil.* Only after the husband has tricked his wife into revealing the justness of his assumptions, and then only after he feigns recovery of what supposedly was lost, does she declare in an unguarded moment, "Mesire a son vit recouvré" (My husband has got his prick back), *MR,* III, 74. Her use of an obscenity here at the conclusion of the story reflects a spontaneous outburst of honesty, a contrast to her earlier hypocrisy.

A slightly different but quite dramatic instance of a contrast between coy hypocrisy and blunt reality that involves a related contrast between euphemisms and obscenities occurs in *Le Chevalier qui fist les cons parler.* When a beautiful young maid-in-waiting named Blancheflor, the subject of the most extended courtly description in the fabliaux, is sent to the bed of the knight referred to in the title, she pretends reluctance to her mistress and tells the knight that she is there only at the insistence of the countess, who would have come herself but for fear of detection:

> "Je suis cousine et damoisele
> Ma dame, qui a vous m'envoie
> Pour vous faire solas et joie;
> Molt volentiers i fust venue
> Ne fust por estre aparceüe.
> De moi pouez vostre bon faire
> Einsis con il vous vourra plaire."
>
> (Rychner, II, 67: Version I)

> ("I am cousin and maid-in-waiting to my lady, who sent me to you to do your pleasure; she would willingly have come herself were it not for her fear of being discovered. You can do with me as you like, whatever may be your pleasure.")

When the knight exercises his bizarre powers, however, he elicits a response apparently more frank and couched in quite different terms:

"C'est li cons qui vous atant ci
Que vous maintenent le foutez
Et en faites vo privautez,
Et se mervoille durement
Que vous alez tant atendent,
Car por autre riens n'iert venue
Ma dame, qui lez vos gist nue." (Rychner, II, 69)

("This is the cunt which waits for you here, that you should fuck it immediately and use it for your private pleasures, and which is greatly surprised that you are dallying so long, for my mistress who now lies naked beside you came for no other reason.")

The use of figurative expressions in fabliaux whose plots turn on intrigue and deceit can be even more readily correlated with trickster and dupe figures, since these expressions are often used with deliberate ironic intent. The dupe understands the expressions in literal terms as conventionally significative, while the trickster and the audience are aware of the new significance the expressions have acquired by arbitrary substitution in their particular context. *La Saineresse* provides perhaps the best example, an extensive allegory rivaling that at the conclusion of *Le Roman de la Rose*. The husband, who supposes that his wife has been visited by a female blood-letter, understands in one sense her description of the "treatment" she received, while the audience, who know that the visitor was in fact a male seducer, understand it quite differently:

"Par .iii. rebinées me prist,
Et à chascune fois m'assist
Sor mes rains deux de ses peçons,
Et me feroit uns cops si lons;
Toute me sui fet martirier,
Et si ne poi onques sainier.
Granz cops me feroit et sovent;
Morte fusse, mon escient,
S'un trop bon oingnement ne fust.
. . . .

> L'oingnement issoit d'un tuiel,
> Et si descendoit d'un forel
> D'une pel moult noire et hideuse,
> Mais moult par estoit savoreuse." (*MR*, I, 291–92)

> ("He made three attempts at me, and each time he placed two of his lancets on my thighs, and struck me such a hard blow; I surrendered myself completely to being tormented, and yet I could not once let blood. He struck me with great and frequent blows; I would have been dead, it seems to me, had it not been for an exceedingly fine ointment. The ointment came from a pipe, and ran down from a satchel with a very black and hideous skin, but it was extraordinarily delicious.")

The scene catches something of the quintessence of fabliau humor. The dupe is here confronted with the reality of the situation, conveyed in an almost brutally direct and detailed fashion, and yet he totally fails to comprehend it, as the husbands who, in *Le Prestre qui abevete* and *Le Vilain qui vit un autre home od sa feme,* witness their wives having intercourse with other men, but are led to deny the evidence of their senses. While he does not actually see what is going on, a husband is also present at his wife's seduction in *Le Prestre et la dame,* and the author describes this incident with an obscene allegory of his own, initiated by his use of the figurative expression *fuiron* (ferret) for *vit*. The seducer, who pretends that his activities are an attempt to lift three persons, the wife plus her maid and her husband lying beneath her, introduces another figurative correspondence, not developed in detail in this instance, but mirroring physically the sort of stratification into different levels of consciousness generated by the verbal ironies. The husband, oppressed and deluded at the bottom of the pile, knows only his own discomfort; the seducer, at the top, has full knowledge of a situation he has engineered and is now exploiting; and the women in between are functionaries, the maid coopted and oblivious to what is happening, the wife a conscious and willing participant.

In terms of the relationships between characterization and the use of obscenities, euphemisms, and figurative expressions, these stories allow us to set up some clear contrasts and correspondences. Trickster figures have a valid and immediate grasp of a concrete reality which their use of obscenities and figurative expressions permits them to report in a highly determinate and particularized way. Dupes employ euphemisms to render less immediate a reality their hyprocrisy will not allow them to admit, or they exhibit such confusion about the whole process of signification as to be blind to the actual referents in figurative expressions that make some arbitrary use of verbal signifiers.

The correspondence between plot and the use of obscenities or euphemisms is complicated, in a way that the correspondence with characterization is not, by the authors' own penchant for obscenities throughout their works. In a sufficient number of cases to make the point, however, careful authors can be shown to be using the contrast between euphemisms and obscenities to articulate stages in the development of the plot. Recognition that this is occurring in some stories may discriminate between obscenities used merely for shock value and obscenities that have thematic import in others. In order to make such a correlation, we need some description of what the typical stages in the development of a fabliau plot might be. Unfortunately there survive no medieval discussions of fabliau structure sufficiently detailed to assist us in this aspect of our investigation. However, one author of a rhetorical handbook, John of Garland in his *De arte prosayca metrica et rithmica,*[10] illustrates comedy with a story that would be classified as a fabliau had it existed in a contemporary French verse form. Briefly, it tells the story of a peasant who challenges a soothsayer, by name Ginnechochet, to say how many children he has. When the soothsayer says two, the peasant trium-

10. Giovanni Mari, "Poetria magistri Johannis anglici de arte prosayca metrica et rithmica," *Romanische Forschungen,* 13 (1902), 916–18.

phantly counters that he has four. He is abashed, however, when Ginnechochet tells him that two of the children he had assumed were his are in reality the priest's. The story has a double significance for our purposes; it neatly exemplifies certain classical theories about the structure of comedy, and it illustrates the medieval confusion of comedy with comic tales in predominantly dramatic mode, a confusion that helps justify applying those theories to the fabliaux.

Even by appropriating classical discussion of comedy, we are not furnished any extensive analyses of comic plots, since there is still very little material. The key principle I wish to apply is the suggestion from the unfortunately obscure and fragmentary *Tractatus Coislinianus* that comedy moves from *pistis* (opinion or illusion) to *gnosis* (fact or reality). This suggestion may be supplemented by extrapolating from Aristotle's scattered comments on comedy the idea that the moment of shift from *pistis* to *gnosis* constitutes the comic equivalent of *peripety* (reversal) and is accompanied by *anagnorisis* (recognition), terms he used in the *Poetics* in his analysis of the structure of tragedy.[11] These concepts are clearly applicable to the moment when the peasant in *Ginnechochet* learns the truth about his children. It is interesting to note that John of Garland's trivial comedy shares an oracle in a key role and startling revelations about parenthood with *Oedipus Rex*, the tragedy most frequently referred to by Aristotle in discussing his theories.

For the fabliaux, this rudimentary analysis at least serves to identify a climactic moment in the development of the plot and to connect that moment with the issues of illusion and reality that we have been dealing with in respect to fabliau diction. If our assumptions about the epistemological implica-

11. For a comprehensive examination of the significance of the *Tractatus Coislinianus* and its relationship to what can be gleaned of Aristotle's views on comedy, see Lane Cooper, *An Aristotelian Theory of Comedy* (New York: Harcourt Brace & Co., 1922).

tions of a choice between euphemisms and obscenities are correct, then we should expect this moment of transition in the development of the plot to be marked by some shift in the diction. This shift indeed happened in many fabliaux—at the moment of peripety, when the dupe suffers a reversal of fortune and when the illusions he has trusted are dispelled—in a sudden outburst of accumulated obscenities that are in contrast to earlier euphemisms.

Obscenities are carefully reserved for the moment of peripety in Jean Bodel's *Gombert et les deus clers*, the plot of which is familiar from Chaucer's use of it for *The Reeve's Tale*. The author, tongue-in-cheek as we suspect from the setting and as we realize from the later developments, sets the scene in the opening sequence on a note of courtly charm. This atmosphere is maintained throughout the rather sordid developments which follow by both the participants' and the author's employing a host of euphemisms: "gesir avec," "faire ses volentez," "consentir les bons de quelqu'un," "faire la folie," "faire ses buens," and "faire son delit." But when the clerk, who has been with the daughter, inadvertently reveals to the miller what has been happening, we get an agglomeration of obscenities and figurative expressions indicating that truth has finally emerged and serving to emphasize the force of revelation to the miller:

> A tant Sire Gombers s'esveille;
> Esraument s'est apercéuz
> Qu'il est trahis et déçeuz
> Par les clers et par lor engiens.
> "Or, me di," dist-il, "dont tu viens?"
> "D'ont?" dist-il, si noma tout outre,
> "Par le cul bieu, je vieng de foutre,
> Mès que ce fu la fille l'oste;
> Pris en ai devant et encoste;
> Aforé li ai son tonel. . . ." (*MR*, I, 243)

(Therewith Dan Gombert woke up. Straightway he perceived that he had been betrayed and deceived by the

> clerks and their machinations. "Now tell me," he said, "where have you been?" "Where?" said the other, spilling the whole story, "by God's backside, I've been fucking, with who else but the host's daughter; I had her frontwards and sideways; I broached her barrel for her. . . .")

A similar though slightly more complex example occurs in *Le Prestre et le chevalier*, in which the plot turns on an agreement made between guest and initially reluctant host that the knight will pay five sous for each item served him, and the priest will serve the knight anything he requests that is within the priest's power to bestow. Thinking he has tricked the knight into an agreement that he can exploit, the priest charges five sous for each item—the straw for the horses, the napkins, the pepper, and so forth—to run the account up to a staggering ten pounds. He retires, smugly satisfied with his intrigue; the knight's squire, thinking they will have to sell their horses to meet the bill and proceed on foot, is distraught; only the knight seems quite unperturbed. Indeed, subsequent events prove that he has the situation well in hand by virtue of his own stipulations in the agreement. Once in bed, he sends his squire for the priest's niece, telling the priest to put five more sous on his account or void their agreement and refusing a forty-sous remission. Then he sends for the priest's mistress, refusing a remission of seven pounds from his account. Finally, he sends for the priest himself and will not release him from his obligation under the agreement until he has remitted the whole account and consented to give the knight ten pounds in addition at his departure.

Throughout the negotiations that lead to the knight's bedding the two women of the priest's household, a quite courtly tone is preserved by the use of such euphemisms as "faire son bon," "faire son delit," "faire son plaisir," "gesir avec quelqu'un," "faire ses talens," "faire aise," and "faire deduit." Only when the knight sends for the priest does his absolute control of the situation begin to emerge, and the gradual dawning of this fact on each of the participants is signaled by their use of an obscenity in place of the initial euphemisms. The knight, who of course has had this possibility in mind as a trump card from the time the agreement was drawn up, is the first to resort to an earthily obscene expression of his plans in an exchange with his squire:

> "Mon délit
> Di au Prestre qu'il veigne faire,
> Sans atargier et sans atraire."
> "Vo délit, biaus sire, de quoi?"
> "De che que gésir viegne o moi
> Si le [foutrai] .iii. fois u .iiii. (*MR*, II, 81. The verb has been erased in the ms.)

> ("Tell the priest he is to come and do my pleasure, without hesitation or delay." "Your pleasure, good sir, in what way?" "In that he shall come and lie with me, and I shall fuck him three or four times.")

The squire uses the same words in reporting his master's demands to the priest, whose recognition of his own wretched situation is expressed with the same obscenity:

> "Amis," fait-il, "onc je n'iroie,
> Qui me donroit Pieronne ou Roie,
> Nevers, ne La Karitet toute,
> Par ensi soit que il me foute." (*MR*, II, 84)

> ("Friend," he said, "I would not go, even if I were given Pieronne or Roie, Nevers, or the whole of La Karitet, if the price were that he should fuck me.")

Finally the *prestresse*, delighted to discover that the priest has been trapped by the avarice to which he has already sacrificed his niece and herself, upbraids him in equally forthright terms, appending a wish of her own to add to his misery:

> "Ce soit à boine destinée,
> Sire, que vous foutus serés;
> Si Diu plaist, vous engroisserés,"
> Fait cele; "s'en gerrés en mai." (*MR*, II, 85–86)

("I hope your getting yourself fucked has a fortunate outcome, sir; God willing, you will swell up," she said, "and be delivered in May.")

A last example is taken from *Le Bouchier d'Abeville.* The pattern of euphemisms and obscenities is similar to that in the fabliau just quoted, but it merits inclusion because of its explicit recognition of the correlation between use of obscenities and a gradual dawning in the dupe's mind of the deception that has been practiced on him and of the extent of his misfortunes. *Le Bouchier d'Abeville* has been generally admired for the tightness of its plot and for some excellent character portrayal, enhanced by lively dialogue. The author's choice of words, as we might expect from so polished an artist as Eustace d'Amiens, is careful and exact. The butcher of the title, like the knight in *Le Prestre et le chevalier,* seeks lodging at the house of an avaricious priest, who refuses him until bribed with a sheep which the butcher has actually stolen from the priest's own flock. Having feasted on the sheep, the butcher then seduces the priest's maid and his mistress by promising each of them the sheepskin, which he later sells to the priest.

In the early part of the story the question of love naturally comes up several times. It is always referred to in the most courtly terms, the butcher, a *vilain,* the maid, and the author using between them the following euphemisms: "faire son plesir," "faire son bon," "faire son desir," "faire sa volenté," "gesir avec quelqu'une," and "se metre en la merci de quelqu'un." Not until the priest discovers that the butcher has been in bed with the maid do we get the first indelicate expression, and then it is fairly innocuous, used this time by the author:

Li doiens ot et aperçoit
Aus paroles qu'ele disoit,
L'avoit ses ostes culonée. (*MR*, III, 240)

> (From what she said the priest realized that his guest had balled her.)

The first obscenity accompanies the priest's discovery that what was true for the maid was also true for her mistress: "Je sais de voir qu'il ta foutue" ("I know for a fact that he fucked you"). The only other obscenity occurs in the priest's speech when he realizes that the sheepskin which caused all the trouble was from his own flock:

> Bien m'a engingnié et deçut
> Qui ma mesnie m'a foutue;
> Ma pel meïsme m'a vendue;
> *De ma mance m'a ters mon nés;*
> En mal eure fuisse jou nés
> Quant je ne m'en seuch garde prendre!
> On peut cascun jor mout aprendre. (*MR*, III, 245)

> (Certainly he worked a neat trick on me and deceived me when he fucked my whole household for me; he sold me my own sheepskin; *he wiped my nose on my own sleeve*. I must have been born yesterday not to have known how to guard against such treatment. One can learn something new every day.)

The idea of the discovery of truth—and consequently of misfortune for the dupe—accompanies each use of an obscenity. Furthermore, the type of discovery is carefully graded, and the degree of offensiveness varies accordingly. With the first mildly offensive word we have the verb *apercevoir*, indicating the first realization of misfortune which, since it is the maid who is involved, is not very serious. Then comes the verb *savoir*, indicating full knowledge of the treachery of his mistress, and this provokes the starkest obscenity. Finally, the summary of what the priest has learned—what has become assimilated as part of his experience—is subsumed under the verb *apprendre*, and there is a tendency to modulate the obscenity with the more abstract and euphemistic *mesnie*. The whole unhappy experience is expressed with a proverb that testifies to a recognition on the priest's part that he is one sufferer among many.

The structural function of figurative expressions is less easy to demonstrate in relationship to a comic peripety because they figure prominently in stories in which no such shift from illusion to reality is achieved or in which the formula has to be modified in a way that limits its usefulness for our purposes. In seduction stories such as *La Damoiselle qui ne pouvait ouir parler de foutre* the lovers mutually devise an obscene allegory capable of circumventing a prudishness that is not offended by the fact of seduction but balks at the appearance of any vulgarisms in its attainment. In stories such as *La Saineresse*, narration of the obscene allegory itself constitutes the trick, since the dupe fails to understand the implications of the account—which are understood by the trickster-narrator and the audience—so the dupe remains befuddled and no point of peripety and anagnorisis is reached. One story, however, *La Dame qui aveine demandoit pour Morel sa provende avoir*, begins similarly to *La Damoiselle qui ne pouvait ouir parler de foutre* but then develops in such a way as to generate a very clear reversal and recognition scene. The story is especially interesting, since it begins with a sensitive depiction of the relationship between the young husband and wife and of the physical and psychological stresses of marriage and concludes with one of the ugliest scenes in the fabliaux. It also provides some evidence that the authors of obscene allegory were consciously parodying conventional allegory, and its examination will be useful in establishing the fundamental differences between these two allegorical modes.

La Dame qui aveine demandoit pour Morel sa provende avoir begins with a description of the marriage couched in highly idealistic terms and employing the appropriate courtly euphemisms:

> Tristans, tant com fu en cest monde,
> N'anma autant Ysoue la blonde
> Cum si. .ii. amans s'entr'emmerent

Et foy et honnor se porterent.
Moult bel menoient lor deduit
Privéement et jor et nuit,
Et, quant venoit à cel solas
Qu'i se tenoient, bras à bras,
Où lit où estoient couchié
Et l'un près de l'autre aprouchié,
Adonc menoient lor revel. (*MR*, I, 319)

(Tristan, when he was alive, did not love Isolde the Fair as much as these two lovers loved one another, and they kept a mutual faith and honor. Sweetly they savored the secret joys of love day and night, and, when that blissful time arrived for them to lie in their bed, wrapped in each other's arms and drawn close together, then they feasted at love's banquet.)

After a while, however, it becomes clear that the sexual appetites of the wife considerably exceed those of her husband, and although he strives to participate in the sex act more than he would by natural inclination in order to protect the harmony of their relationship, he is eventually forced to devise a scheme that he hopes will moderate the demands made upon him. He proposes to shift responsibility for initiating love-making to his wife by insisting that she approach him with the formula, "Faites Moriax ait de l'avainne." He promises that he will always respond favorably to such a request but hopes that natural modesty will restrain her from soliciting oats for Dobbin too often.[12] Indeed, the wife receives his suggestion with shocked disbelief: "Tu ies tous sos,/Qui veus que die tel outrage" ("You must be crazy to expect me to say

12. The husband's thinking is quite in accordance with that of the social commentators of his time. Thomas Aquinas, in a discussison of the marriage debt, says that the husband is obliged to pay the debt at any sign from his wife, modesty prohibiting her from asking explicitly: "Quando scilicet vir percipit per aliqua signa quod uxor vellet sibi debitum reddi, sed propter verecundiam tacet. Et ita, etiam si non expresse verbis debitum petat, tamen vir tenetur reddere quando expressa signa in uxure apparent voluntatis reddendi debiti." S. Thomas Aquinatis, *Summa Theologiae,* ed. Petri Caramello (Marietti, 1956), III, 216.

anything so stupid"). Nevertheless, as the author tells us, no sense of shame will inhibit her desires, and before long the husband finds himself trapped by his own rash promise in a sex life of mounting rather than abating frenzy. Predictably, his health and vigor soon show signs of strain, and finally, in despair for his life if he cannot extricate himself from what has now become an intolerable situation, he answers his wife's latest request "por avoir Morel sa provende" with an act that respects the letter of their agreement but brutally shatters the tone of genteel harmony preserved with so much effort on the husband's part up to that point:

> D'estre mal haitiez samblant fist;
> Son cul torna en son giron,
> Et li chia tout environ
> Que bran, que merde, qu'autre choze,
> Et se li dist à la parclose:
> "Seur dès or mais te tien au bran,
> Et ainsis com tu veus s'en pran;
> Bien saches l'aveinne est fallie;
> Fait t'en ai trop grant departie;
> A noiant est mais li greniers
> Dont Moriax a esté rantiers." (*MR*, I, 328)

> (He made pretence that he was ill; he stuck his backside in her lap and defecated all over her—nothing but bran, shit, or whatever. And then finally he said to her: "Dear, from now on you will have to make do with bran [shit], and help yourself to as much of that as you want; rest assured that the oats are finished. I have made too prodigal a distribution of them. The granary from which Dobbin was provisioned has been stripped bare.")

Although the arbitrary substitutions in the figurative expression "faites Moriax ait de l'avainne" are clear, and the referents for *Moriax* and *avainne* quite specific, up to this point in the story the lovers have used the mutually acceptable formula almost as though it were a courtly euphemism, as a means, that is to say, of distancing the discussion of their sexual relationship from its true nature. Not until the husband defecates in the bed and confronts his wife with a repulsive and all-too-material reality does he extend the implications of the figurative expression to remind her forcefully that the *avainne* comes from a *greniers* which unbridled demand has depleted to total exhaustion. It would be hard to imagine a more startling example of illusion being dispelled and reality being reasserted. The peripety is achieved by the husband's insistence on breaking through the opacity of the verbal signifiers to a clear vision of the reality they signify.

The use in obscene allegory of some expression related to the feeding of an animal as an arbitrary equivalent for sexual intercourse seems to have been conventional. It occurs in *La Damoiselle qui ne pouvait ouir parler de foutre, Esquiriel,* and *Porcelet,* as well. If the author of *La Dame qui aveine demandoit pour Morel sa provende avoir* is merely following convention, it may be overly ingenious to see in his story a reflection on the allegorical habit of mind of his time. His use of the contrast between *avainne* and *bran* is, however, unique to the fabliau in which it figures so prominently. As is clear from the literary allusions, the abundance and variety of rhetorical figures, and the general polish of the whole work, the author was certainly a learned man. He would have been aware that the terms he introduces into his story are the key terms in the standard metaphor applied to conventional allegorical interpretation to distinguish between the spiritual meaning that is to be sought and the literal meaning that is to be transcended. The best-known example in English literature is probably in the conclusion of Chaucer's *Nun's Priest's Tale* where the narrator urges his audience:

> Taketh the moralite, goode men.
> For seint Paul seith that al that writen is,
> To oure doctrine it is ywrite, ywis;
> Taketh the fruyt, and lat the chaf be still.

The image appears frequently among Latin writers. The proemium to a commentary on the *Canticle of Canticles* attributed to Pope Gregory the Great states that "the letter covers the spirit as the chaff covers the grain."[13] In French, Jehan Bruyant in *Le Chemin de Povreté et de Richesse* exhorts his readers to "laisses le bren et pren la fleur."[14] Clearly in comparison with these commentators, the fabliau author reverses the direction of allegory, which moves away from the *phantasmata* of disparate material phenomena toward a spiritual sense of their mystical union as predicates of one essential, transcendental 'being' that is God, the kernel of wheat that exegesis teaches us to thresh from the husk of the sensible, and instead concludes resoundingly in favor of the concrete and particular, the *bren* as the ultimately real.[15]

This conflict between spiritual allegory and the kind of allegory found in the fabliaux is discussed by Christine de Pisan, herself a practitioner of the former mode,[16] in her discussion of Jean de Meun's conclusion to *Le Roman de la Rose*. She compares such writing with the books of the alchemists:

> Les uns les lisent, et les entendent d'une maniere; les autres qui les lisent entendent tout au rebours. Et chascun cuide trop bien entendre; et sur ce ilz oeuurent et aprestent fourniaulx, alembis, et croisiaulx, et entremeslent diuers metaulx et matieres et soufflent fort, et pour un petit de sublimacion ou congiel qui leur appert merueillable, ilz cuident ataindre

13. Quoted by Robertson, *A Preface to Chaucer*, p. 58.

14. In *Le Mesnagier de Paris*, ed. J. Pichon, *Société des Bibliothèques françaises* (Paris, 1847), II, 4.

15. With the fabliau view that, even in allegorical expressions, words necessarily signify concrete reality may be contrasted Saint Augustine's warning in the *De Doctrina Christiana*, III, 5: "He who follows the letter takes the figurative expressions as though they were literal and does not refer the things to anything else. . . . There is a miserable servitude of the spirit in this habit of taking signs for things, so that one is not able to raise the eye of the mind above things that are corporal." Quoted from *On Christian Doctrine*, ed. D. W. Robertson, Jr., Library of Liberal Arts (Indianapolis: The Bobbs-Merrill Co., Inc., 1958), p. 84.

16. *The Epistle of Othea*, trans. Stephen Scrope, ed. Curt F. Bühler (London: Oxford University Press, 1970).

a merueilles. Et puis quant ils ont fait et fait et gasté leur temps, ilz y sceuent autant comme deuant . . . car la matiere est tres deshonneste, ainsi comme aucuns arquemistes qui cuident faire de fiens.[17]

(Some people read them, and understand them one way; others read them and understand them in the opposite way. And each thinks he has understood perfectly; and with this knowledge they work away and prepare kilns, alembics, and crucibles, and they mix up different metals and other material, and huff and puff, and because of a little distillate or precipitate that strikes them as miraculous they suppose themselves to have performed miracles. And finally, when they have labored and labored and wasted their time, they know about as much as they did when they started . . . because what they are working with is worthless, so they are in the same boat as those alchemists who think they can do wonders with a dunghill.)

Clearly, what renders such writing particularly vicious from Christine's point of view is that, while the form invites us to seek the "gold" of a spiritual meaning, the matter returns us inevitably to the "dross" of the unsublimated physical. Now, whether Jean de Meun's decision to end a work as complex as *Le Roman de la Rose* on such a note reflects his essential sympathy with the philosophical attitudes of the authors of fabliaux, or whether it constitutes a deliberately ironic and distorted narrowing of the full scope of his investigation of love, is a moot point and not immediately germane to our interests.[18] However, when fabliau authors write obscene allegory, any failure to apprehend that the *significans*, although used in an arbitrarily unconventional way, has as its *significatum* a particularized, concrete reality, constitutes a profound failure of understanding, a state of illusion apparent to the audience, for whom a rude awakening may be expected.

17. Ward, pp. 91–92.

18. The question is discussed by Rosemond Tuve, *Allegorical Imagery: Some Medieval Books and Their Posterity* (Princeton: Princeton University Press, 1966), p. 262.

While I wholeheartedly endorse Nykrog's conclusions that the fabliaux comprise a courtly genre in the sense that they were intended for a sophisticated, courtly audience, he seems to me to have been in error in supposing that, from his necessary involvement with the social aspects of these stories, he could devise a satisfactory explanation of their humor as "un genre courtois burlesque." There is some social satire in the fabliaux, certainly, and some humor at the expense of the lowly parish priest and his lowlier parishioners, but this humor is peripheral to the central comic concern of the genre, which lies elsewhere, as this study is intended to show. Instead of a conflict between social classes and their constituent mores and rituals, there emerges from the fabliaux a more profound opposition between an attitude of mind that is essentially speculative, synoptic, and idealistic, and one that is materialistic, analytical, and existential. People with the former attitude are language oriented in the sense that they show a willingness to assume an absolute and faithful correspondence between objects and their verbal signifiers and to trust the efficacy and validity of deductive reasoning to organize experience toward meaning. Their verbal habits are characterized by a preference for the kind of abstractions that synoptically subsume disparate phenomena into an essential unity; their vision of the world finds its most natural expression in the allegorical mode that posits a mystical correspondence between all parts of a diverse creation through reference to a single divine creator. People with the latter attitude are object oriented in the sense that they find words a fallible and untrustworthy representation of reality, lack confidence in the relevance and reliability of deductive reasoning, and exploit for their personal benefit the ambiguities of verbal signifiers and the inadequacies of demonstrative logic. Their verbal habits are characterized by a preference for concrete terms conjoined with particularizing modifiers, so that their statements insist on the discretely pluralistic nature of the reality signified. Their vision of the world finds its most natural expression in literal narrative, and if they have recourse to allegory it is allegory in the classical rhetorical sense, one thing substituted for another.[19] Such allegory is read, not by recognizing the unifying principle that links its equivalences, but by identifying the *sensibilia* indicated by signifiers with conventionally different referents.

The function of obscene diction in the fabliaux is consistent with a fabliau espousal of the attitudes of this latter group. If an understanding of the philosophical conflict underlying fabliau humor cannot be satisfactorily extrapolated from an investigation necessarily confined to the one aspect of obscene diction, such an understanding is nevertheless essential to making sense of the authors' practices. Familiarity with the genre will eventually bring to mind evidence of other respects in which this same conflict manifests itself. The fabliau, that is to say, establishes its own ethos, and it has a firm and defensible philosophical basis. All the schoolmen would undoubtedly have disclaimed any community of interest with the attitudes expressed in the fabliaux, but in some respects the fabliaux do make a partisan comment on some of the central philosophical questions of the time; the genre was formed from the same cultural matrix as the philosophical debates. The attitudes expressed in the fabliaux are clearly closer to the nominalist position in the nominalist–realist controversy. Ockham's scrupulous separation of physics from metaphysics establishes philosophically the position on which the fabliaux have already taken their stand, and while Ock-

19. Quintilian, in *The Institutio Oratoria of Quintilian,* trans. H. E. Butler, Loeb Classical Library (London: William Heinemann, Ltd., 1921), III, 326–27, defines allegory as follows: "Allegory, which is translated in Latin by *inversio* . . . presents one thing in words and another in meaning. . . . [It] is generally produced by a series of metaphors." See also the definition given in the pseudo-Ciceronian *Rhetorica ad Herennium,* trans. Harry Caplan, Loeb Classical Library (London: William Heinemann, Ltd., 1954), p. 345.

ham would not have endorsed the fabliau's disdain for metaphysics, he may well have felt sympathetic toward the fabliau's skeptical insistence on particularized and concrete physical reality as the safest ground of certitude on which to order existence in the workaday world.

BIBLIOGRAPHY

The most complete bibliography for the fabliaux is in Per Nykrog's *Les Fabliaux* (1957). The following list is an attempt to bring that bibliography up to date, but it does not include works in the bibliographies to the individual essays in this collection which are not directly concerned with the fabliaux. We have included some important reprints and review articles.

Books

Alter, Jean V. *Les origines de la satire anti-bourgeoise en France*. Geneva: Droz, 1966.

Auerbach, Erich. *Mimesis: The Representation of Reality in Western Literature*. Translated by Willard R. Trask. Princeton: Princeton University Press, 1953. Chapter 9.

Baum, Richard. *Recherches sur les oeuvres attribuées à Marie de France*. Heidelberg: C. Winter, 1968. Pages 15–29.

Beach, Charles Ray. *Treatment of Ecclesiastics in the French Fabliaux of the Middle Ages*. Lexington: University of Kentucky Press, 1960.

Bédier, Joseph. *Les Fabliaux*. 6th ed. Paris: Champion, 1964.

Benson, Larry D., and Theodore M. Andersson, eds. *The Literary Context of Chaucer's Fabliaux*. Indianapolis and New York: The Bobbs-Merrill Co., Inc., 1971. (Texts of analogues to Chaucer's fabliaux.)

Beyer, Jürgen. *Schwank und Moral. Untersuchungen zum altfranzösischen Fabliau und verwandten Formen*. Heidelberg: C. Winter, 1969. Reviews: P. Nykrog in *Zeitschrift für Romanische Philologie*, 87 (1971), 426–28; B. Sowinski in *Archiv für Kulturgeschichte*, 53 (1971), 179–81; Erich Welslau in *Kritikon Litterarum*, 1 (1972), 109.

Bodel, Jean. *Fabliaux*. Edited by Pierre Nardin. Paris: A. G. Nizet, 1965.

———. *L'Oeuvre de Jean Bodel*. Edited by C. L. Foulon. Paris: Presses Universitaires de France, 1958.

Brians, Paul, ed. and trans. *Bawdy Tales from the Courts of Medieval France*. New York: Harper & Row, Publishers, 1972.

Christmann, H. H. *Zwei altfranzösische Fablels*. Tübingen: Niemeyer, 1963.

Diekmann, Erwin. *Die Substantivbildung mit Suffixen in den Fabliaux*. Tübingen: Niemeyer, 1969.

Douin de Lavesne. *Trubert: Fabliau du XIIIe siècle*. Edited by Guy Raynaud de Lage. Textes Littéraires Français 210. Geneva: Droz, 1974.

Dubuis, Roger. *Les Cent Nouvelles Nouvelles et la tradition de la nouvelle en France au moyen âge*. Grenoble: Presses Universitaires de Grenoble, 1973.

Les Fabliaux. Edited by Maurice Teissier and Henry Nicholas. Paris: Fernand Lanore, 1958. (Modern French translations.)

Fabliaux, contes, et miracles du moyen âge. Edited by Roger Henri Guerrand. Paris: Livre club du librarie, 1964. (Modern French translations.)

Fabliaux du moyen âge. Edited by Louis Fernand Flutre. Lyon: Editions de fleuve, 1958. (Modern French translations.)

Fabliaux et contes. Edited by Robert Guiette. Paris: Le Club du meilleur livre, 1960. (Modern French verse translations.)

Fabliaux et contes du moyen âge. Edited by Nelly Caullot. Paris: Hatier, 1957. (Modern French translations.)

Fabliaux et contes du moyen âge. Les Classiques Illustrés Hatier. Paris: Hatier, 1967. (Modern French translations.)

Frosch-Freiburg, Frauke. *Schwankmären und Fabliaux. Ein stoff- und Motivvergleich*. Göppinger Arbeiten zur Germanistik, 49. Göppingen: Kümmerle, 1971.

Greimas, A. J. *Dictionnaire de l'ancien français: jusqu'au milieu du XIVe siècle*. Paris: Larousse, 1968. (The most recent one-volume dictionary covering the period of the fabliaux.)

Harrison, Robert. *Gallic Salt*. Berkeley: University of California Press, 1974. (An anthology of eighteen Old French fabliaux texts, with lively English verse translations on facing pages. His bibliography contains several pre-1957 titles not listed by Nykrog.)

Hellman, Robert, and Richard O'Gorman, eds. and trans. *Fabliaux: Ribald Tales from the Old French*. New York: Thomas Y. Crowell & Company, 1965.

Johnston, Ronald C., and D. D. R. Owen, eds. *Fabliaux*. Oxford: Blackwell, 1957; rpt. with minor changes, 1965.

Le Grand d'Aussy, S.J., Pierre Jean Baptiste. *Fabliaux ou contes du XIIe et du XIIIe siècle traduits ou extraits d'après divers manuscrits du tems*. Paris: E. Onfroy, 1779; rpt. Geneva: Slatkine, 1973.

Medieval Comic Tales. Edited by Peter Rickard *et al.* Cambridge: D. S. Brewer, Ltd., 1973.

Ménard, Philippe. *Le Rire et le sourire dans le roman courtois en France au moyen âge (1150–1250)*. Publications romanes et françaises 105. Geneva: Droz, 1969.

Merl, Hans-Dieter. *Untersuchungen zur Struktur, Stilistik und Syntax in den Fabliaux Jean Bodels*. Europäische Hochschulschriften 13; Französische Sprache und Literatur 16. Bern: Herbert Lang, 1972.

Montaiglon, Anatole de, and Gaston Raynaud, eds. *Recueil général et complet des fabliaux des XIIIe et XIVe siècles*. 6 vols. Paris: Librairie des Bibliophiles, 1872–1890; rpt. New York: Burt Franklin, n.d.; also rpt. Geneva: Slatkine, 1973.

Muscatine, Charles. *Chaucer and the French Tradition*. Berkeley: University of California Press, 1957.

Nykrog, Per. *Les Fabliaux: Etude d'histoire littéraire et de stylistique médiévale*. Copenhagen: Ejnar Munksgaard, 1957; rpt. with Postscript, Geneva: Droz, 1973. Reviews:

M. Delbouille in *Le Moyen Age,* 65 (1959), 368–71; L.-F. Flutre in *Studia Neophilologica,* 29 (1957), 262–70; R. Glasser in *Zeitschrift für Romanische Philologie,* 75 (1959), 146–51; R. Guiette in *Revue belge de philologie et d'histoire,* 38 (1960), 452–55; Kr. Kasprzyk in *Kwartalnik Neofilologiczny,* 6 (1959), 60–64; H. Lausberg in *Archiv für das Studium der Neueren Sprachen,* 194 (1958), 310–16; J. Rychner in *Romance Philology,* 12 (1959), 336–39; A. Taylor in *Modern Language Notes,* 73 (1958), 373–75; K. Togeby in *Orbis Litterarum,* 12 (1957), 89–98.

Paris. Bibliothèque nationale. Mss. (Fr. 837). *Fabliaux, dits et contes en vers français du XIIIe siècle; facsimile du manuscrit français 837 de la Bibliothèque nationale, publié sous les auspices de l'Institut de France (Fondation Debrousse).* Edited by Henri Omont. Paris: E. Leroux, 1932; rpt. Geneva: Slatkine, 1973.

Regalado, Nancy Freeman. *Poetic Patterns in Rutebeuf: A Study in Noncourtly Poetic Modes of the Thirteenth Century.* New Haven: Yale University Press, 1970. Pages 244–49.

Reid, T. B. W. *Twelve Fabliaux.* Manchester: Manchester University Press, 1958; rpt. with minor changes, 1968.

Rutebeuf. *Oeuvres Completes. . . .* Edited by Edmond Faral and Julia Bastin. 2 vols. Paris: A. and J. Picard, 1959–1960.

Rychner, Jean. *Contribution à l'étude des fabliaux: Variantes, remaniements, dégradations.* 2 vols. Geneva: Droz; Paris: Minard, 1960. Reviews: R. Bossuat in *Bibliothèque de l'Ecole de Chartres,* 118 (1960), 245–50; H. H. Christmann in *Zeitschrift für Französische Sprache und Literatur,* 72 (1962), 212–15; P. B. Fay in *Romance Philology,* 15 (1961–1962), 378–82; A. Henry in *Revue belge de philologie et d'histoire,* 39 (1961), 867–69; O. Jodogne in *Les Lettres Romanes,* 17 (1963), 173–75; P. Nykrog in *Studia Neophilologica,* 32 (1960), 371–76; D. D. R. Owen in *Cahiers de civilization médiévale,* 4 (1961), 205–8; G. Raynaud de

Lage in *Le Moyen Age,* 68 (1962), 219–21; A. Varvaro in *Studi Francesi,* 5 (1961), 110–14; P. Zumthor in *Vox Romanica,* 23 (1964), 146–49.

Schlauch, Margaret. *Antecedents of the English Novel: 1400–1600.* London: Oxford University Press, 1963. Pages 40–46.

Tiemann, Hermann. *Die Entstehung der mittelalterlichen Novelle in Frankreich.* Hamburg: Stiftung Europa-Kolleg, 1961.

Valentini, Giuseppe. *Les Fabliaux de l'Espace.* Naples: G. Scalabrini, 1965.

Walters-Gehrig, M., ed. *Trois Fabliaux.* Tübingen: Niemeyer, 1961. Reviewed by Per Nykrog in *Zeitschrift für Romanische Philologie,* 78 (1962), 390–91.

Articles

Ageno, Fr. "A proposito di una fonte sacchettiana." *Giornale storico della letteratura italiana,* 137 (1960), 204–17.

Baird, Joseph L., and Lorrayne Y. Baird. "Fabliau Form and the Hegge *Joseph's Return.*" *Chaucer Review,* 8 (1973), 159–69.

Bausinger, Hermann. "Schwank und Witz." *Studium Generale,* 11 (1958), 699–710.

Bercescu, Sorina. "*Le vilain mire și Le Médecin malgré lui.*" *Analele Universității București. Literatură universală și comparată.* 21, no. 1 (1972), 87–95.

Brewer, D. S. "The Fabliaux." In *Companion to Chaucer Studies,* edited by Beryl Rowland. New York: Oxford University Press, 1968.

Burbridge, Roger T. "Chaucer's *Reeve's Tale* and the Fabliau *Le Meunier et les .II. clers.*" *Annuale Medievale,* 12 (1971), 30–36.

Cluzel, Irenée. "Le fabliau dans la littérature provençale du moyen âge." *Annales du Midi,* 66 (1954), 317–26.

Cooke, Thomas D. "Formulaic Diction and the Artistry of

Le Chevalier qui recovra l'Amor de sa Dame." *Romania,* 94 (1973), 232–40.

De Cesare, Raffaele. "Di nuovo sulla leggenda di Aristotele cavalcato." In *Miscellanea del Centro di Studi Medievali,* pp. 181–247. Universita Cattolica del Sacro Cuore. Milan: Vita e pensiero, 1956. (See *Romania,* 77 [1956], 409.)

Delbouille, Maurice. "Les Fabliaux et *Le Roman de Renart.*" In *Histoire illustrée des lettres françaises de Belgique,* edited by Gustave Charlier and Joseph Hanse. Pp. 45–51. Brussels: La Renaissance du Livre, 1958.

Di Stefano, Giuseppe. "Fabliaux." *Dizionario crìtico della letteratura francese,* edited by Franco Simone. Torino: Unione Tipografico, 1972. I, 419–23.

Dubuis, R. "La genèse de la nouvelle en France au moyen âge." *Cahiers de l'Association Internationale des Etudes Françaises,* 18 (1966), 9–19.

Flutre, L.-F. "Le Fabliau, genre courtois?" *Frankfurter Univ.-Reden,* 22 (1960), 70–84.

Follain, J. "Les Fabliaux." *Tableau de la littérature française,* edited by Arthur Adamov *et al.* 2 vols. Paris: Gallimard, 1962. I, 84–88.

Foulon, Charles. "Le Thème du berceau dans deux contes populaires du moyen âge." In *Littérature savante et littérature populaire,* pp. 183–87. Congrès National de Littérature Comparée. Paris: Didier, 1965.

Guiette, Robert. "Fabliaux: Divertissement sur le mot 'fabliau'. Notes conjointes. Note sur le fabliau du 'mari-confesseur'." *Romanica Gandensia,* 8 (1960), 61–86.

Holmes, Urban T. "Notes on the French Fabliaux." In *Middle Ages, Reformation, Volkskunde: Festschrift for John G. Kunstmann,* pp. 39–44. Chapel Hill: University of North Carolina Press, 1959.

Honeycutt, Benjamin L. "An Example of Comic Cliché in the Old French Fabliaux." *Romania,* forthcoming.

Jodogne, Omer. "Considérations sur le fabliau." *Mélanges offerts à René Crozet*, edited by Pierre Gallais and Yves-Jean Riou. 2 vols. Poitiers: Société d'Etudes Médiévales, 1966. II, 1043–55.

———. "Des fragments d'un nouveau manuscrit de *Constant du Hamel*, fabliau du XIIIe siècle." *Le Moyen Age*, 69 (1963), 401–15.

Kahane, Henry, and Renée Kahane. "Herzeloyde." In *Mélanges de linguistique romane et de philologie médiévale offerts à M. Maurice Delbouille*. 2 vols. Gembloux, Belgium: J. Duculot, 1964. II, 329–35.

Krömer, Wolfram. "Das Fabliau," in his *Kurzerzählungen und Novellen in den romanischen Landern bis 1700*. Grundlagen der Romanistik, 3. Berlin: Erich Schmidt Verlag, 1973. Pages 47–59.

Lecoy, Félix. "A propos du fabliau de Gautier Le Leu *De Dieu et dou pescour*." In *Mélanges de linguistique romane et de philologie médiévale offerts à M. Maurice Delbouille*. 2 vols. Gembloux: J. Duculot, 1964. II, 367–79.

———. "Note sur le fabliau de *Prêtre au Lardier*." *Romania*, 82 (1961), 524–35.

———. "Analyse thématique et critique littéraire. Le cas du *Fabliau*." Actes du 5éme Congrès des romanistes scandinaves. Turku (Åbo) du 6 au 10 aout 1972. Turku: Turun Yliopisto, 1973. Annales Universitatis Turkuensis, Ser. B, 127. Pages 17–31.

Legry-Rosier, Jeanne. "Manuscrits de contes et de fabliaux." *Bulletin d'information de l'Institut de recherche et d'histoire des textes*, 4 (1955), 37–47.

Lejeune, Rita. "Hagiographie et grivoiserie. A propos d'un dit de Gautier Le Leu." *Romance Philology*, 12 (1958–1959), 355–65.

Lian, A.P. "Aspects of Verbal Humour in the Old French Fabliaux." In *Australasian Universities Language and Lit-*

erature Association: Proceedings and Papers at the Twelfth Congress Held at the University of Western Australia, 5–11 February 1969, pp. 235–61. Sydney: AULLA, 1970.

Lindgren, Lauri. "Courtebarbe, auteur des *Trois Aveugles de Compiegne*, est-il aussi l'auteur du fabliau du *Chevalier à la robe vermeille*?" In *Mélanges de philologie et de linguistique offerts à Tauno Nurmela*, pp. 91–102. Turun Yliopiston Julkaisuja, Annales Universitatis Turkuensis, Ser. B, Tom. 103. Turku, Finland, 1967.

Lukasik, Stanislaw. "Fabliau." *Zagadnienia Rodzajów Literackich*, 4 (1961), 217–21.

McClintock, Michael W. "Games and the Players of Games: Old French Fabliaux and the *Shipman's Tale*." *Chaucer Review*, 5 (1970), 112–36.

Muscatine, Charles. "The Wife of Bath and Gautier's *La Veuve*." In *Romance Studies in Memory of Edward Billings Ham*, edited by Urban T. Holmes, pp. 109–14. Hayward, California: California State College, 1967.

Olevskaïa, V. "La nouvelle en France au XVe siecle et les fabliaux" (in Russian). *Annales scientifiques de l'Institut pédagogique Lénine à Moscou*, 324 (1969), 108–24.

Olson, Glending. "'The Reeve's Tale' and 'Gombert.'" *Modern Language Review*, 64 (1969), 721–25.

Otcherett, O. "Sur la définition du genre des fabliaux" (in Russian). *Annales scientifiques de l'Institut pédagogique Lénine à Moscou*, 382 (1970), 219–45.

Owen, D. D. R. "The Element of Parody in *Saint Pierre et le Jongleur*." *French Studies*, 9 (1955), 60–63.

Pearcy, Roy J. "A Classical Analogue to *Le Preudome qui rescolt son compere de noier*." *Romance Notes*, 12 (1971), 422–27.

———. "A Minor Analogue to the Branding in *The Miller's Tale*." *Notes and Queries*, 16 (1969), 333–35.

———. "An Instance of Heroic Parody in the Fabliaux." *Romania*, forthcoming.

———. "Chaucer's Franklin and the Literary Vavasour." *Chaucer Review,* 8 (1973), 33–59. (See especially pages 42–49.)

———. "*Le Prestre qui menga les meures* and Ovid's *Fasti,* III, 745–760." *Romance Notes,* 15 (1973), 159–63.

———. "Realism and Religious Parody in the Fabliaux: Watriquet de Couvin's *Les Trois Dames de Paris.*" *Revue belge de philologie et d'histoire,* 50 (1972), 744–54.

———. "Relations between the D and A Versions of *Bérengier au long Cul.*" *Romance Notes,* 14 (1972), 1–6.

———. "Structural Models for the Fabliaux and the *Summoner's Tale*'s Analogues." *Fabula,* forthcoming.

Rauhut, Franz. "Sanson in der 'Richeut'—ein Don Juan des Mittelalters." *Archiv für das Studium der neueren Sprachen und Literaturen,* 207 (1970–1971), 161–84.

Rychner, Jean. "Les fabliaux: genre, styles, publics." In *La Littérature narrative d'imagination,* edited by Faculté des Lettres de l'Université de Strasbourg, pp. 41–54. Paris: Presses Universitaires de France, 1961.

Schaar, Claes. "*The Merchant's Tale, Amadas et Ydoine,* and *Guillaume au Faucon.*" *Bulletin de la Soc. Royale des Lettres de Lund,* 2 (1952–1953), 87–95.

Sinclair, K. V. "Anglo-Norman Studies: The Last Twenty Years." (See Section 8: "Fabliaux—Satirical and Humorous Pieces.") *Australian Journal of French Studies,* 2 (1965), 225–26.

Spencer, Richard. "The *Courtois-Vilain* Nexus in *La Male Honte.*" *Medium Ævum,* 37 (1968), 272–92.

———. "Who is the King of *La Male Honte?*" In *Gallica: Essays Presented to J. Heywood Thomas by Colleagues, Pupils and Friends,* pp. 41–51. Cardiff: University of Wales Press, 1969.

Storost, Joachim. "Femme chevalchat Aristotte." *Zeitschrift für Französische Sprache und Literatur,* 66 (1956), 186–201.

———. "Zur Aristoteles—Sage im Mittelalter. Geistesgeschichtliche, folkloristiche und literarische Grundlagen zu iher Erforschung." In *Monumentum Bambergense: Festgabe für Benedikt Kraft,* pp. 298–348. Munich: Kösel-Verlag, 1955.

Tiemann, Hermann. "Bemerkungen zur Entstehungsgeschichte der Fabliaux." *Romanische Forschungen,* 72 (1961), 406–22.

Vàrvaro, Alberto. "I fabliaux e la società." *Studi Mediolatini e Volgari,* 8 (1960), 275–99.

———. "Il *Segretain Moine* ed il realismo dei *Fabliaux.*" *Studi Mediolatini e Volgari,* 14 (1966), 195–213.

Wailes, Stephen L. "Fortuna and Social Anomaly: Principles of Medieval Humour in *Asinarius* and *Rapularius.*" *Seminar,* 9 (1973), 87–96.

———. "Role-Playing in Medieval *Comœdiae* and Fabliaux." *Neuphilologische Mitteilungen,* forthcoming.

———. "Students as Lovers in the German Fabliau." *Medium Ævum,* forthcoming.

———. "The Unity of the Fabliau *Un Chivalier et sa Dame et un Clerk.*" *Romance Notes,* 14 (1972), 593–96.

Dissertations

Cantera, Angelo. "A Critical Edition of the Fabliaux of Rutebeuf." University of Michigan, 1960.

Cooke, Thomas D. "The Comic Climax in the Old French and Chaucerian Fabliaux." University of Pittsburgh, 1970.

Honeycutt, Benjamin L. "The Role of the Knight in the Old French Fabliaux." Ohio State University, 1969.

Kirk, J. H. "Rutebeuf's Treatment of Medieval Genre: The Fabliau." University of Sheffield, 1965.

Lacy, Gregg Farnsworth. "The Aesthetic Context of the Fabliaux." University of Kansas, 1972.

Lacy, Norris J. " 'La Femme au tombeau': Anonymous Fabliau of the Thirteenth Century." Indiana University, 1967.

Laughlin, Virginia L. "The Fabliaux and the Naturalistic Tradition." University of Arizona, 1972.

Olson, Glending R. "The Cultural Context of Chaucer's Fabliaux." Stanford University, 1969.

Pearcy, Roy J. "Humor in the Fabliaux." Ohio State University, 1963.

Thompson, Norma Jean. "The Old French Fabliau. A Classification and Definition." University of Southern California, 1972.

Valette, Francis C. "La tradition antiféministe dans la littérature française du moyen âge et sa continuation dans les contes du seizième siècle." University of Illinois, 1967.

Wailes, Stephen L. "Courtly Diction in Middle High German *Maeren* in the Context of Latin and French Traditions." Harvard University, 1968.

Williams, Clem C. "The Genre and Art of the Old French Fabliaux: A Preface to the Study of Chaucer's Tales of the Fabliau Type." Yale University, 1961.

INDEX

Index

CONTRIBUTORS

JÜRGEN BEYER, Professor of Romance Languages at the University of Konstanz and author of a major study on the fabliaux (*Schwank und Moral*), has recently been teaching German language and literature in Mexico. He is currently preparing a study on the modern Latin–American novel.

THOMAS D. COOKE, Associate Professor of English at the University of Missouri–Columbia, has completed a book-length study of the comic climax of the fabliaux, entitled "Th'Ende Is Every Tales Strengthe." He is now at work on a study of comedy in middle English literature.

HOWARD HELSINGER, formerly a Fulbright Fellow at the University of Paris and Assistant Professor at Boston University, is at the present devoting all his time to completing a study of Saint Augustine's *Confessions*.

BENJAMIN L. HONEYCUTT, Associate Professor of French at the University of Missouri–Columbia, has prepared a computer-generated concordance to the Montaiglon–Raynaud edition of the fabliaux and is presently engaged in developing a similar concordance to the *Lais* of Marie de France, to be used in a comparative study of the two genres. He is also the author of articles treating both the lai and the fabliau.

NORRIS J. LACY, Associate Professor of French at the University of Kansas, has published numerous studies in medieval French literature and is now at work on a monograph on Chrétien de Troyes and on a critical edition of the first French translation of the *Decameron*.

Besides his seminal work, *Les Fabliaux*, PER NYKROG, Professor of Romance Philology at the University of Aarhus, has written extensively on medieval French literature and has also pub-